A COWBOY'S REUNION

CAROLYNE AARSEN

D1636824

Misty Ridge
PUBLISHING

CHAPTER 1

"*B*etter slow down, Son." Zach grabbed the dashboard as if to brace himself against his son's crazy driving. "You don't need to be going full tilt down these slushy roads."

"I should probably drive faster," Kane replied, leaning sideways to look past the cattle liner he'd been trying to pass for the last mile. "You know I need to get that electric fence up and running before Joe and I can move those bulls into the pasture."

Kane fought down the panic of too many jobs piling up. Fences to be fixed. Cows to calve. Barns to muck out and decades of machinery, parts, and tools, even old furniture to sort for the potential auction.

He and the hired hand only had a couple of months to do it all before Kane had to go back to his job in the oil field.

And then they would sell the ranch.

Those last words resounded in his head, off-key and dissonant.

"You're lucky most of the snow is melted," Zach said as he leaned back in the seat, grimacing. "Roads would be trickier to drive this fast otherwise."

"Got it, Dad," Kane acknowledged, giving him a tight smile while fighting down a beat of annoyance.

It seemed everything bothered him lately, and he didn't like that feeling. Sunday's sermon had been on seeing grace in the small moments; but the past few years it seemed grace had been elusive. Bitter memories, broken dreams, and lost chances haunted him, and he'd spent the past two years burying the pain beneath long hours at work.

The truck's wipers slapped back and forth, fending off the spray spitting up from the lumbering cattle liner's tires. Kane slowed in deference to his father's wishes, pulling back from it. They rounded a tight corner then, and just ahead of the semi he saw a woman standing on the side of the road, her arms crossed, a suitcase and something else lying on the shoulder beside her. Kane slowed down as the truck ahead of him swerved to avoid her. But, in the process, it hit a huge puddle, sending a spray of muddy water over the poor woman.

She threw her arms up to shield herself, but she still got drenched.

"Whoa. Stop," Kane's father said, but not before they went through the same puddle.

Kane eased onto the shoulder.

"You splashed her," his father said, his tone accusing.

"Yeah. Thanks, Dad. I know. I saw her too late." Kane already felt horrible. He didn't need his father adding to his guilt.

Kane piled out of the truck and approached the sopping girl, who was pushing her wet hair from her face. A cool spring breeze kicked up, whistling across the open field, and he saw her stiffen at the chill.

"I'm so sorry," Kane called out, hurrying toward her. "Are you okay?"

His steps faltered when she picked up the guitar case at her side, brushing water from it.

Memories assaulted his mind at the sight of her pale skin, dark hair, and slight figure. Though drenched and dirty, Faith Howard's stunning profile was unmistakable and sent his heart racing with old attraction and emotions. It had been two lonely years since she'd walked away, choosing his brother over him. She had broken their engagement and with it, Kane's heart.

What was she doing here now, on this stretch of road, he wondered, angry at his unwelcome reaction to her.

When she looked up at him her eyes widened, and one hand fluttered to her throat as if she was having as much trouble breathing as he was.

"Hello, Faith," was all he could manage.

Even through the mud streaking her face, he saw her cheeks flush and her eyes flash. As his father joined them, the blush crept down her neck as well. "Hello, Mr. Tye," she said, ignoring Kane, her voice quiet as she wiped off her face.

"My goodness, girl!" His father's voice mirrored Kane's shock. "What are you doing here? Coming to visit your grandfather?"

Faith gave one quick shake of her head and said, "Work. I'm headed to Calgary."

The highway leading to the city was at an intersection two miles ahead. Calgary lay north, but Kane and his father were headed south. Would she really pass this close to Rockyview and not even bother to visit her grandfather?

She shivered again, still clinging to the guitar case, still avoiding Kane's gaze.

"You're not stopping by Rockyview?" Zach pressed.

She shook her head again.

"Why don't you come back to the ranch with us?" Zach said. "You can't travel all wet and cold."

"No. I need to get to Calgary," she said, her tone emphatic.

Kane's father looked at him, expecting him to join in on insisting his ex-fiancée come back to the ranch with them. But Kane couldn't do it. He hadn't expected to ever see Faith again, and he hated the memories she stirred in him. It had taken him so long to get over her.

"We can give you a lift to the highway," Kane said, resisting the urge to ask about Elliot. He had more pride and self-respect than that.

"No. I'm okay," Faith said, raising her chin. "I can walk. It's not that far, and I'd get your truck wet."

Even after two years, Kane felt the sting of this new rejection like a slap in the face. So she'd rather hike down the road two miles dripping wet than get in a truck with him and his father?

"Okay. Suit yourself." Kane shrugged, eyeing her soaked canvas coat, dripping blue jeans, and mud-covered running shoes. "But you should probably get out of those wet clothes."

She gave him an arch smile and asked, "What? You don't like my highway traveler look?"

"That's not what I meant—" Kane sputtered, thrown completely off balance by her smile and banter.

"I know what you meant," she said, letting him off the hook. She shivered again. "I appreciate the advice, but I'm not sure where I'd change." She glanced up and down the highway. There wasn't a gas station or old barn in sight.

"You could change in the truck," his father suggested. "It's not ideal, but it's better than staying in those wet things."

Kane sensed she wasn't crazy about the idea but also knew she didn't have much choice. She was shivering, and it was getting colder outside the longer they stood there. If she stayed in her wet things much longer, she'd risk hypothermia.

"Okay," she said, her teeth chattering. "Thank you."

"We'll turn our backs and leave you to it." Kane's father stepped away from the truck and pulled Kane with him.

Kane gave her one last look as he turned away. Did he imagine the regret he saw flash across her face? It was probably just wishful thinking.

Though his father had never spoken out against Faith when she'd left that horrible night with Elliot, Kane knew Zach struggled with his feelings toward this girl who had hurt his son so badly.

He turned away and walked down the road to give her some privacy as from behind he heard the truck door open and shut. He tamped his impatience at how quickly his attraction to her flew back.

He clenched his fists, angry at the coincidence of seeing again the woman who had broken his heart. And even worse, discovering she still held a part of it.

"Are you doing okay?" his dad asked.

"Not talking about that," Kane said.

The truck door squealed open again, and then Kane heard a low moan. He whirled around to see Faith trying to climb from the cab while doubled over and clutching her stomach, her eyes clenched shut in pain.

"Hey, you okay?" his dad asked, rushing to her side.

She waved him off as her feet hit the ground. "Just ate something that's not agreeing with me. I'll be fine." But when she straightened up, Kane could tell she wasn't.

He hated that he knew that. Hated that her pain still bothered him as if it were his own.

"You sure you're all right?" He was unable to keep the concern out of his voice.

"Yes, I'm sure." Her dismissive tone erased any sympathy he'd been nursing.

"Good." He poked his thumb over his shoulder. "We'll give you some space then."

She nodded, then turned away from him and opened her guitar case, more concerned for it than herself. He found himself wondering if she still had the same guitar she'd bought with money saved up from summer work. The one she'd practiced on until her fingers bled. The very guitar that had started her on a journey away from him and the future he had so carefully planned for the two of them.

She had left him so easily, but he couldn't even bring himself to drive away from her. She looked forlorn, lost, and bedraggled.

It was taking every ounce of willpower he had not to rush to her side and sweep her into his arms.

In frustration, Kane turned his back on her once again, walking away to give her some privacy.

His dad limped along beside him, and Kane slowed his steps. Six months ago, his father had broken his leg while trying to break in one of the new ranch horses. Kane felt guilty he hadn't been around when it happened. But Zach had assured him he'd be fine, and Kane should go back to work in the oil fields. So, Kane had.

Now his father had decided to sell the ranch. He said he was tired and weary and worn out. So, Kane had taken time off to come help get the ranch ready to sell and all that entailed. It was taking so much longer than he'd anticipated. And it wasn't just the work. It was the guilt. Kane knew he should have stayed to help run the ranch, but after Faith had left, he just couldn't. Every corner, every tree and blade of grass reminded him of her.

"Kane, are you okay?" his father asked softly, breaking him from his pensive thoughts.

"Yeah. No. I don't know," Kane said.

"Why would she be headed to Calgary and not home?" Zach asked. "It doesn't make sense."

"Guess she doesn't see Rockyview as home," Kane said, unable to keep the bitterness from his voice.

"Well, her grandfather misses her. What am I supposed to tell him? That I saw her on the side of the road and just left her there?"

"It's not our business, Dad. Faith and Mick have to figure things out for themselves."

Kane wasn't the only person who'd been hurt when Faith left. Her grandfather had done so much for her—paid for her education, given her an opportunity to become part of his law firm. And she'd thrown it all away. Faith had been the only family Mick had after her mother had died. He'd taken her leaving hard.

"And what about you?" Zach asked. "When are you going to figure this out for yourself?"

"This is not a conversation I want to have on the side of the road," Kane snapped. It wasn't a conversation he wanted to have ever. Especially not after the shock of seeing Faith.

"Well, you have to forgive them sometime. It's been over two years—"

"I know how long it's been." He didn't need his father lecturing him about forgiveness and letting go of the past again. The thing with Faith had torn the family apart, but that wasn't Kane's fault or his responsibility. "Elliot knows where we live," he pointed out, preferring to talk about his estranged brother than the woman who broke his heart.

"Maybe he's waiting for you to reach out to him," Zach murmured, thankfully latching onto the switch. "Elliot has his own demons to wrestle."

"We all have demons, Dad," Kane argued. "I was a foster kid too." But Elliot had it rougher. There was no denying it. Kane had been rescued from a neglectful mother at the age of ten and handed over to the Tye family who adopted him a year later.

Elliot, on the other hand, had been shunted back and forth between the Tye family and his seriously messed-up biological father for far too many years.

Because of that, Zach always gave him a pass.

And Elliot knew exactly how to take advantage of that.

"Think she's done?" Zach asked.

Kane shot a glance over his shoulder but Faith was still in the truck.

"She's not looking that great," his dad continued, clearly not done talking about Kane's ex-fiancée. "She looks skinnier."

"She'll be fine," Kane said. "Besides, you heard her. She doesn't want our help."

God must be playing some cosmic joke on her, Faith thought as she struggled to get into the truck. Of all the people in the area, Kane Tye was the one to offer her help?

The thought made her ill, and she had to swallow down another wave of nausea.

The last she'd heard of Kane was that he'd moved away from Rockyview and went to work in the oil fields. It had been hard for her to believe at the time. Kane had loved, lived, and breathed that ranch.

She dismissed the thoughts. Not her problem. She had to get it together. Get in the truck and change out of her wet clothes.

But it wasn't as easy as it sounded. Her stomach had been bothering her since last night's poor choice of dinner. She'd known the half-eaten gas station sandwich she'd saved from the day before was a little off. But she'd been hungry and almost out of money. Now, riding out the spasms, hoping they would go away was the price she had to pay.

That and knowing Kane was the one to stop and help her out.

It shouldn't matter. He was just a blip on her way to Calgary and the job interviews her friend Stacy had scored for her there. And Faith badly needed a regular income. Every penny the band made touring had gone back into equipment, travel, or the next gig or tour they'd booked. And somehow her life had become an endless progression from bad to very bad to worse. And her bank account showed it.

What would Kane think if he knew how far she had fallen from the straight-laced, obedient girl she had once been? The girl who always did what she should.

Faith climbed into the blessed warmth of the cab and dragged her suitcase behind her, ignoring the pain it caused. Much as it bothered her, she had to leave her guitar outside. The guitar she'd saved so hard for. The guitar that she had, at one time, thought was her passport to a life that wasn't prescribed by her grandfather and his demands.

She looked out the window. Kane and his father were walking down the road with their backs turned like the gentlemen they were. Kane had one hand shoved in the pocket of his faded denim jacket, his black cowboy hat adding to his already impressive height. He towered over his father.

The sight of them together created a claw of regret in Faith's heart. She had loved being a part of the Tye household. Kane's mother, before she died, had always given Faith a hug and a gentle kiss of greeting. And that was a big deal to a girl whose own mother had abandoned her as a young child. Mrs. Tye had been the mother figure Faith had always wanted. When she'd died, Faith mourned her almost as deeply as her own children had.

And what would she think of you now? Faith struggled out of her wet clothes and into dry ones. *What would she say? Would she be as cool and aloof as Kane was?*

Faith had imagined his anger. She had expected him to yell or glare at her with hatred in his eyes. At least that would have meant that somehow, on some level, she still mattered. His casual attitude hurt more than she wanted to admit.

She rolled her wet pants and shirt up and shoved them in a plastic bag, which went back into her suitcase. She almost thought the stomach pain had passed, until she climbed out of the truck and it hit her full force again, bending her in half.

She couldn't afford to be sick. At all. On Wednesday, she needed to be in the city to get ready for her interviews on Thursday. Although, it was beginning to worry her that Stacy hadn't been answering her calls or replying to her texts.

Three years ago, she would have been praying hard in a situation like this.

But not anymore.

She had turned her back on God, and she doubted He would

have anything to do with someone like her, especially after the life she'd led the past couple of years.

She closed her eyes as the nausea and pain blended with stark grief.

Don't think about it. Don't remember. Keith is out of your life now.

Pulling in a wavering breath, she walked over to her guitar case to make sure it was okay.

When she stood up from bending over the guitar, a new wave of pain hit her, and the road and sky suddenly swapped places as a narrowing tunnel of darkness closed around her vision.

She heard Kane call out and the sound of his hurrying foot-steps, then, in spite of not knowing which way was north or south, up or down, she managed to lurch toward the ditch, and that was the end of her self-control.

CHAPTER 2

*K*ane ran to Faith's side and knelt beside her. His arm slipped around her as she clutched her abdomen, still retching into the ditch, though nothing was coming out now.

He pulled a hanky out of his pocket and gave it to her.

She took it, trying at the same time to push his supporting arm away. But she was as weak as a newborn colt so he didn't budge.

"We're taking you to the ranch. Kane looked up at his father, who nodded in agreement as they helped her to her feet.

"You're too ill to thumb it on the side of the road," Zach said. "Your grandfather would never forgive me if I left you out here like this."

"No. I have to get to Calgary," Faith muttered, even as she stumbled, clutching her stomach again and moaning involuntarily.

Ignoring further protests, Kane scooped his arm under her knees, his other behind her shoulders, and carried her towards the truck.

"Please. Let me go. I'm fine," Faith insisted again.

She'd left the truck door open, so it was easy for him to slide

11

her into the cab and set her on the back seat. She leaned her head against the headrest and finally seemed to give up.

"Give me a couple of minutes." Faith closed her eyes and pulled in a shuddering breath. "Or just drive me to the junction. I'll be better by then. It's just food poisoning."

Kane didn't reply as he pulled the seat belt free and strapped it around her slight frame, noting her grayish complexion and the rings under her eyes.

He ignored the mental list of chores that crowded his brain, demanding attention. Or the voice reminding him how hard it would be to have Faith in his truck again. How hard it would be to have Faith anywhere near him for any length of time.

She needed help, plain and simple. And the Tyes did not turn their backs on someone in need, even when it might hurt them. His adopted parents had taught him that when they'd filled their house with needy, scarred, difficult foster kids.

As if on cue, his dad brought Faith's suitcase and guitar case and set them on the seat next to her. Kane didn't miss the way she reached out and put her hand on the case, patting it for comfort.

He felt his heart lurch, and he fought against it, dredging up pain to remind him not to fall for her again.

What happened, Faith? What did you need that I couldn't give you? What did Elliot have that I didn't? After all we had together, how could you leave me like that?

The questions raged in his mind, and he looked away from her. The pain she created would be a like a barbed fence around his heart. A reminder of what she had done.

Kane and his father climbed into the truck, and they drove without saying a word for the next couple of miles. Kane reached up and angled his rearview mirror so he could see Faith's face. Her mouth was pulled into a tight line. She was still in pain and holding it in, but she definitely wasn't okay.

He slowed when they got to the highway junction, and she raised her head weakly, saying, "I can get out here."

Kane pulled to the side of the road, stopped the truck, and kneaded his neck in an attempt to erase the tension growing there. He couldn't force her to stay in the truck against her will. If she refused to come back to the ranch until she felt better, what could he do about it?

He glanced at his dad, who shook his head but said nothing. Great. Why was it his job to convince her to let them help her?

"Here's the thing," Kane said, eyeing Faith in the rearview. "I can't, in good conscience, let you hitchhike to Calgary after what just happened." He was surprised how reasonable that sounded considering how shaken he felt about the whole situation. "This isn't a busy highway. It could be hours before a car comes by and you get a ride."

"I'll be okay," Faith repeated.

"No. You won't," he returned, keeping his voice firm but calm. He could do stubborn too. "If you don't want to go back to our ranch, how about your granddad's place? We could take you there."

"Grampa doesn't want anything to do with me," she said, her voice tinged with anger.

Kane doubted that, but there was no use arguing with her.

"Okay, then how about someone in Calgary?" he asked. "We could have them come pick you up at Cordell Run twenty miles south of here. I can drive you down, and we can wait for them."

Faith tucked one corner of her lower lip between her teeth, considering that option. "That might work." She nodded, digging into her purse and pulling out her phone. "Except I have no service."

Kane grabbed his phone from the truck's console. "Use mine. I have two bars."

He had already handed it to her before he realized his mistake.

The wallpaper on his phone was a picture of Faith astride a horse. The two of them had been riding up on Snakeskin Ridge, checking cows. He had proposed to her that day, and they had made plans for a long and loving future together.

Four months later she and Elliot were gone.

Why had he kept that photo on his phone all this time? As soon as he got back to the ranch, he was deleting it.

Thankfully, she said nothing as she tapped the numbers on the keypad. Pulling in a shaky breath, she looked out the window as she listened, waiting for an answer. Then, she tapped the End Call button and tried another number.

Again, it seemed no one answered.

"I don't get it," she muttered, trying again. "Stacy promised she'd be around today." She frowned as she waited, finally leaving a message telling her friend that she was using someone else's phone and that she needed to get ahold of her. "Can I give her your number?" she asked Kane without really looking at him. "So she can call me back?"

"Of course." Kane nodded, and she finished the message.

His dad turned to Faith. "I'm sure she'll call back soon. In the meantime, why don't you come back to the ranch with us?"

She hesitated, seeming to consider it, but then the phone rang.

"Hey, Stacy, this is Faith" she blurted into it, relief flooding her face. "Oh—sorry. No, this is his phone," she faltered, handing the phone to Kane. "It's for you."

Kane took the phone.

"Where you at?" Frank, their neighbor, barked into his ear. "We got a problem here. Your cows busted through a fence and got into my hayfield."

Kane closed his eyes and sucked in a long breath. If they hadn't stopped to help Faith, they might have made it back before the cows got out. Now, it was going to be a full afternoon of catching cattle before they could even get to the fence, not to mention compensating Frank for any hay he'd lost. And of course, Joe, the hired hand, was off today, so it was just Kane and his dad to handle it all.

Kane felt as if things were snowballing out of control.

"Me and Sarah got them rounded up," Frank was saying, "but I don't think your corral will hold them long."

"Thank you, Frank. And I'm so sorry. We owe you one."

"No, you don't. You and your dad helped me plenty of times over the years."

"We'll be there as soon as we can." Kane said goodbye and ended the call.

"Cows got out again?" his dad guessed.

"Yeah," Kane nodded. "Frank put them in the corral. But that won't hold them for long. We have to head back. Now." He glanced back at Faith. "We're taking you to the ranch," he said. "You can wait for your friend to call, and we'll figure it out from there."

"I don't know," Faith protested, but Kane could see her heart wasn't in it.

"Well, I do," he said, checking the road before he pulled a U-turn and headed north.

꒰◯꒱

Every bump in the road, every corner and hill, made Faith more nauseous. Yet she couldn't stay alert, couldn't keep her eyes open.

As her body betrayed her, she felt more and more helpless, but there was an uneasy peace in that. She had been running and struggling and fighting for so long, she had forgotten what it felt like to just be still. Now, she had no choice, because moving brought a world of pain. And how ironic that all her misfortune had somehow brought her right back to the Tye ranch, of all places.

Maybe God was in charge after all? But if He was, He had a sick sense of humor.

The vibration of the truck's engine and the murmured conversation between Kane and his father eased the dull memories for now. Her thoughts grew fuzzy and vague, and slowly sleep caught her and pulled her down.

The next thing she knew, cool air washed over her as Kane pulled the truck door open.

"Faith, we're here," he said. She dragged her eyes open to see him hovering over her like a dream. Or maybe everything else had been a nightmare.

He looked as handsome as he ever had with his deep blue eyes, sculpted features, and stubbly jawline. Her heart hitched at the sight of him, and she almost reached out to touch his face, to connect with him like she had so many times before. But then her stomach twisted in agony and reality came crashing back.

She and Kane were not together. The years and bad decisions loomed between them, impossible to ignore or wipe away.

"Do you need help?" he asked, holding out a hand.

She shook her head and sat up, climbing gingerly out of the truck past him. When he'd carried her to the truck, that had almost been too much. His touch resurrected memories she didn't deserve to indulge in.

"Can you take her bag and guitar to the house?" Kane asked his father. "I need to check the cows."

Zach nodded and pulled her things from the truck, then offered her his arm for support as Kane headed around the house to the corral.

She took Mr. Tye's arm, and he led her toward the sprawling ranch house. The imposing veranda covered the double front doors and was supported with stone pillars and aged timber. Large pots, crowded around the entrance, held brown remnants of last year's plants. Shrubs of every kind spread out from there, softening the foundation and setting off the beauty of the old wood.

The pathway to the house was curved, pebbled, and edged with dirt and dying plants.

The house was a showpiece and impressed her as it always had, but she could clearly see it was falling into disrepair. When Kane's mother, Grace, had been alive, the flowerpots were full of bright pansies and draping greenery. The flower bed was a manicured river of color. Everywhere you turned there was life and lushness and beauty. She would have never let it get so overgrown and unkempt.

But they had all lost Grace two-and-a-half years ago, a mere six months before Faith had left Kane and the ranch. Yes, it had been horrible timing. But events had led her along a path that seemed so bright at the time. In retrospect, they had been horrible choices at a horrible time. And now she had to live with the consequences.

Zach didn't go through the front entrance of the house. Instead, he led her to the garden doors, which were hanging open, their gauzy curtains fluttering in the spring breeze.

In the distance, Faith heard the sound of cows bellowing and a horse neighing in response.

She was definitely back in ranching country.

"Why don't you sit down?" Zach said, indicating a small wooden table, four wooden chairs of various styles tucked around it. Though the abundance of plants that once filled the bay window were gone and the African violet on the table was missing, the room still exuded a sense of cozy welcome. For a moment, Faith had a sense of coming home, which was followed by a surge of sorrow. How often had she sat at that table drinking tea with Grace talking about whatever came to mind?

I missed this, she thought but then shook it off. She should have pressed Kane harder to drop her off at the junction. Coming here had been a bad idea. She wasn't sure she could face this. Everything she'd thrown away. It was too much.

"I have just the tea to soothe your stomach," Zach said, limping toward the stove.

"What happened to your leg?" Faith blurted as she sat down.

She'd been so busy with her own agony, she hadn't noticed the limp until now.

Zach glanced down, then grinned back up at her. "Me and an unbroken colt had a disagreement last fall. I wanted to go left, he wanted to go right, and we both ended up mashed against the fence. Though I have to say he got the better end of the deal. He got away with a few scrapes. I ended up in the hospital with a broken femur."

"That must have been painful."

"Well, the worst of it was Joe wasn't around that day, so I had to haul myself to the truck to get my phone."

"Where was Kane?"

"He was gone. Working in the oil patch."

"Why did he leave?" she asked. "He loves this ranch as much as you do. And he always swore he'd bag groceries at the Co-op before he'd work on the rigs." She couldn't imagine Kane working rigs. He had such a strong connection to animals and nature and the open range.

"Why did you leave?" Zach asked softly. There was no accusation in his voice, but he was making a point. She had left something she loved, and so had Kane.

"It's complicated," was all she could muster in response. She couldn't afford to look back. That way was madness. She had to put one foot in front of the other and move forward. The past was a bleak and dark wasteland of grief and pain. Though her future was vague and uncertain, at least it had an inkling of hope in it. Things might get better. It was possible.

While Zach got her tea, Faith glanced around the kitchen she knew so well.

The cabinets were a warm golden oak, burnished with age. A large island with a countertop stove filled the rest of the space. Two doors led off the little nook where Faith now sat, struggling to catch her breath. *Only for a moment*, she told herself. She would drink some tea and take her leave.

But how? Until Stacy called back, she wasn't even sure she had a place to go. Faith hugged herself as a wave of nausea coursed through her body, hoping Zach wouldn't notice. As the kettle boiled, he made a sandwich she knew she couldn't eat.

A few minutes later, he set a plate and a steaming cup of tea in front of her.

"Thank you." Faith forced herself to smile at him as she picked up the tea, cradling the warm mug between her fingers.

The garden doors behind them swung open, and Faith didn't need to turn to know that Kane was back.

"You build the new fence and move the cows already?" Zach teased.

"The cows are okay for now," Kane said. "Frank overreacted a bit so I thought I'd check in before I head out there again."

"I'll pull the truck around and start unloading the fencing supplies," Zach said. "You sit down and eat this sandwich." He pushed the plate toward Kane, and Faith breathed a sigh of relief that she wouldn't have to choke it down. But her relief was short-lived when she suddenly found herself alone in the Tye's kitchen with Kane.

He crossed to the sink to wash his hands. Then sat down beside her and picked up the sandwich.

She sipped at her tea, trying not to look at him. But just as she sucked the warm liquid down, a wave of pain twisted her gut, and her hand began to shake, sloshing tea all over the table.

Kane set his sandwich down, reached out his hands, and wrapped them around hers, holding the mug steady and helping her set it down. "You aren't okay," he said, pulling his hands away. "Do you need a doctor?"

"No." Faith shook her head adamantly. "It's just food poisoning, like I said. I just need to sleep it off in a good bed." She regretted the words as soon as she said them—wished she could swallow them back. She didn't want Kane to think she was inviting herself to stay here. Because that was the last thing she wanted.

"We have beds," Kane said gruffly, his chair scraping loudly on the floor as he stood up. He picked up her suitcase and guitar and held out his arm to her just like Zach had.

"I told you. I'll be okay."

"You might, but neither Dad nor I have time to take you anywhere right now. So you may as well stay the night. Get some sleep, and tomorrow we can talk."

Arguing would make her look insensitive and selfish, so she simply nodded. Besides, he was right. All she needed was a good night's sleep.

She got up, wobbled a little, but didn't take his arm. She just couldn't.

He held her gaze a moment, shrugged, and took off down the hallway with her stuff.

Faith followed him, struggling to keep up with his long-legged strides, keeping her balance by placing her hand on the wall. He opened a door halfway along the hall and stood aside to let her in.

"You can stay here," he said, setting her suitcase on the floor of a large bedroom. A king-size bed with a rough-log headboard dominated the clearly masculine room. A tall wooden dresser made of rough-hewn wood held an assortment of framed photos all jostling for space. As she paused just inside the doorway, looking at the photos, she realized where she was, and it almost knocked her to her knees.

This was Elliot's room.

"I thought you'd prefer a familiar room," Kane said, setting her stuff down.

She probably deserved that. Even if it wasn't true. She wanted to tell Kane it hadn't been like that, but she knew there was no point in trying to defend herself again. He hadn't been able to hear her the first time. He had even less reason to listen to her now.

The room began to spin, and she reached out for the post of the bed.

At the same time, Kane reached out, putting his large, warm hands on her waist to steady her.

He was too close. Too familiar.

For a treacherous moment, she yearned to lean against him like she used to and have him hold her close and tell her how much he cared.

Instead, she pulled away from his touch, settling on the edge of the soft bed, which felt amazingly comfortable. Her body just wanted to melt into it and sink away. She was so exhausted. "I'm really sorry about this." She sighed. "I know it's inconvenient for all of us. I'm sure I'll be better in the morning, and Stacy will call, and I can get out of your hair."

"It's fine," Kane said. "Me and Dad will be right outside working, if you need us. And I'll bring you a glass of water before I go out."

"Thank you." Faith used the last of her energy to slip off her shoes and swing her legs up on the bed, weariness pulling her eyes shut as she lay back against the pillows, exhaustion clawing at her. She didn't have the strength to pull the covers back.

But she did feel Kane pull an afghan over her that he'd retrieved from the closet.

And a few minutes later, when he brought the glass of water, she rolled toward the window so he would not see the tears in the corners of her eyes.

Don't, she told herself as he slipped from the room. *Don't give in. You can't be weak.*

Because it wasn't food poisoning or the sting of being put in Elliot's room that would kill her.

It was Kane's kindness that would do that.

She could not stay here. She promised herself that as sleep took her.

She could not be in Kane Tye's debt.

CHAPTER 3

*K*ane shot the last of the staples into the insulator holding the electric fence wire. He and his father had hustled all afternoon to get the fencing done. Good thing too, because the cows were lowing and beginning to push against the rickety corral. Thank goodness the majority of the herd were on the upper pasture already. Then again, those fences needed repairing as well.

Kane appreciated that his father had said nothing about Faith the entire time they'd worked. But it would come up eventually. There was no ignoring his ex-fiancée sleeping in his brother's room.

"You're sure the other fences are okay?" Kane asked.

"Joe said they were," Zach asserted.

"Joe is never here when we need him," Kane snapped. He knew it was hypocritical of him to say it. After all, Joe had been hired to take Kane's place helping his father with the ranch. Because Kane wasn't there when his father had needed him.

"Joe needed a job," Zach said, ignoring Kane's irritation. And he didn't have to say more than that. Zach and Grace had made it their life mission to help those in need, including Kane and two other foster kids, none of whom were here now to return the favor.

Tricia was gone who knows where, Lucas had enlisted and was serving his second tour in Afghanistan.

And then there was Elliot. None of them had seen him for over two years. Not since the horrible night Kane had caught Faith kissing Elliot at that stupid dance, resulting in a huge fight between the three of them. Late that night, Elliot and Faith had left town. Together.

Kane knew his father was heartbroken with their falling out and, for lack of a better word, Faith's faithlessness, but there wasn't much Kane could do about it. And just like that, his mind shifted to Faith asleep in the ranch house. In Elliot's old room.

She had looked so pale and helpless, it had been hard for him to resist the urge to touch and hold her, which had really unsettled him. He tried to chalk it up to basic loneliness. He didn't like to think Faith still had that effect on him.

"When does Joe get back?" Kane asked his dad, turning his thoughts to all the work on the ranch.

"Not sure," Zach answered. "He was kind of vague when I asked him."

"Of course he was," Kane said with a sigh. Was Joe putting them off and looking for another job? He knew they were selling the ranch soon, and his days here were numbered.

"So I guess we can turn the cows out," Zach said. "Calves should be coming in a week or so. A bit late, but that way, when we sell, the worst work will be done."

Kane looked around the pasture, feeling once again the heavy dread that came over him every time he realized what the sale meant. Someone else would own Tall Timber Ranch and the Tye house. And Grace's gardens and plants. He would not be able to come back here. To his home. Ever again.

Two and a half years ago, his father had offered to let him buy into the ranch. To slowly take it over. But Kane had walked away from that when Faith ditched him. The ranch had been the dream for his and Faith's future together, living there and loving one another all their lives just like Zach and Grace had. After Faith was gone, how could he stay and be reminded of what he'd lost every hour of every day?

He couldn't.

Kane picked up the fence tightener and the bucket of insulators.

Together, Kane and his father walked to the horses that were tied up to a fence post and grazing happily.

Kane loaded up the supplies, pretending not to see his father struggle to get his foot in the stirrup, or the way he grimaced in pain as he pushed himself up. Zach was getting old and couldn't run the ranch on his own. Selling was really the only option.

Kane got on his horse, and they headed toward the main yard where the cows were complaining more than ever.

"I wonder if the new buyer will stick with purebred or move to commercial," Zach pondered aloud.

"Guess that will be his call," Kane said. He was quiet a moment, his thoughts flipping between the reality of his father's situation and his old dreams. "You still okay with this?" he finally asked. "Walking away from it all?"

"Limping away more like." Zach shifted in the saddle again, clearly uncomfortable. The day had been too long for him. "It's time. Besides, neither you nor Elliot are interested."

Though his father hadn't come right out and said it, Kane knew where the conversation was heading. Zach hoped maybe Kane could convince Elliot to come back.

"You know I texted him about the sale," Kane said, trying to keep his voice calm. "And he didn't answer. But he knows what's happening. If he wanted the ranch, he'd come back."

And if he came back, he'd be a better rancher than his older brother. Because Elliot, despite being younger, was better at everything. When they had competed in local rodeos, Elliot always got the higher score. When they had roped together, Elliot never missed, but Kane ran about sixty/forty.

But none of that had really bothered Kane, because he'd gotten the girl. He'd fallen in love with Faith the first time he saw her. She was the only girl he'd ever been interested in. They had hung out when they were thirteen, sitting together in school, going riding after school. She was the first girl he ever kissed. The first girl he ever loved. She had made him believe he was a good man and life was worth living.

Over the years they were together, their plans grew. Faith would finish school and, like her grandfather wanted, go to law school and come back to work in her grandfather's law firm. But Faith had balked at her grandfather's plans. She'd had dreams of playing the guitar. Of becoming a singer.

And that's when Grace, the matriarch and anchor of the Tye family, suffered a massive heart attack while out riding. The family was thrown into a dark and drowning grief. Everyone coped in their own way, but nothing had been the same since her passing.

"You know, I thought I could hold you all together after my Grace died," Zach said sadly, as if reading Kane's mind. "But I was wrong. And everywhere I look on this ranch, all I see is the void she left behind."

Kane heard the weariness and disappointment in his father's voice, and he totally understood.

"Which makes me wish you and Elliot would make up," Zach added. "You're brothers."

Kane released a ragged breath. "Elliot knows my number." Why couldn't his father understand he'd tried as much as he could. He'd texted and left Elliot messages. And Elliot had never called back. "It's not my fault he's kept himself running like a fool, always looking to score the best, be the best."

"He didn't look happy the last time I saw him."

"That's 'cause he didn't get into the money."

"It's not that, you know. Maybe he's waiting for you to reach out to him." His father sounded so reasonable that for a moment Kane was tempted to give in, pull out his phone and call his brother. Leave another message. Again. Wait for Elliot to return his call. Again.

No thanks.

"He's obviously not with Faith anymore," Zach pressed.

"Dad, enough," Kane snapped. "She's leaving as soon as she's well. She made her choice two years ago."

When Kane could admit it, he knew it wasn't just Elliot that had taken Faith from him. It had been the music too. Of course, Elliot had egged her on, filling her head with dreams about being a star. Bragging about his contacts with that stupid band at the dance that night, so she'd run off with him to play with them. And now look at her. The girl who had graduated high school with honors, gotten a full academic scholarship to university, and been slated as a shoe-in for law school, was now a roadside vagabond.

Today, when he'd seen Faith on the side of the road, bent over her guitar case, it had all come rushing back.

Kane's birth mother had entertained the same kind of musical dreams. After his dad left them on their own she dragged Kane along to every audition and then dragged him through her disappointment afterwards. He spent too many nights afraid of her when she got turned down. She'd leave him alone in the apartment then come stumbling back a couple of days later.

One time he had called the police because he was afraid. They couldn't find his mother, and they'd called Social Services.

"You look lost in thought," his dad said.

"Just thinking back to the first time I ended up at the ranch here."

His father shook his head, chuckling. "You were such a tiny scrap of humanity. Took Grace weeks to feed you up properly.

26

You ate everything she made. Which was a treat for her, given how picky Tricia was with her food."

"I remember being surprised that anyone would turn down what Mom made."

"Well, your mother spoiled Tricia. At least I thought so." His father shot him a sideways glance. "You know, we never talked much about that time, but you need to know how we fought when your mother petitioned to get you back."

"I knew," Kane said, smiling at his dad.

"And then we couldn't contact you at all. That was hard too. We were so happy when you came back the second time."

"I'll always be grateful for what you did for me," Kane said as they rode along.

"Was all done for love," his dad said.

They rode the rest of the way to the ranch in silence. Back at the corral, they tied the horses up, then made quick work of releasing the bawling cows a few at a time so they wouldn't rush the gates.

Half an hour later, the cows were spread out on the fresh, green grass, quiet as they ate their fill.

Once inside the house, Kane hung his hat up, toed his boots off, and washed his hands in the kitchen sink while his father cleaned up in the bathroom just off the entrance. The house was quiet.

"I'll throw on some soup and grilled cheese," Zach said when he came into the kitchen. "Why don't you go check on Faith."

Kane hesitated, glancing down the hallway. Zach and Grace had added an entire wing to the house for all the bedrooms their foster kids had required. His own room was just past Elliot's. His dad had taken nothing down, and the old posters still hung on the walls. The old books still lay stacked on the shelves.

"Why don't *you* check on her?" Kane suggested.

"I'm making supper." His dad held up a can of soup he had dug from the cupboard.

"Fine," Kane glared back at his father's innocuous gaze, then headed down the hallway.

Despite everything that had happened, Kane couldn't deny the surge of expectation he felt as he walked toward sleeping Faith. Even after all she had put him through, the thought of her could still get his heart racing.

Fool me once, he reminded himself. *She only came here because she had no choice. Help me, Lord,* he prayed. *Help me to keep my heart secure.*

He paused at the door, as if to give the prayer time to sift up to heaven. He knocked, softly enough that if she was awake, she'd hear it, but not loudly enough to wake her if she was still sleeping.

"Come in," she called out.

Kane opened the door a crack and peeked his head in the room. Faith was still in the bed, but she seemed less pale, less drawn. More like the old Faith he had known.

And loved.

He reined in his thoughts, focusing on the now. The real.

"Dad's heating up some of his world-famous canned soup," he said with a forced smile, going for a casual, easygoing tone. "You interested?"

"No thanks. Still not hungry." She gave him a wan smile and sat up gently. "And thanks again for picking me up and letting me rest here. I know it isn't ideal for either of us."

"It's okay. I've dealt with worse." His gaze drifted to the ribbons, buckles, and trophies competing for space on the shelves with pictures of Elliot and his posse of friends. Always in a crowd. Always laughing. Elliot had been a world-class partier in his time. Probably still was.

Faith followed the direction of his gaze and then looked around the room, not meeting Kane's eyes. At least she was wise enough not to bring up Elliot with him. And Kane certainly wasn't going to ask her where his brother was or what he was doing. Or what had happened between the two of them. He wasn't going down that road with her.

"I just want you to know, I'll be on my way tomorrow," she finally said. "I'm already feeling better."

But she hadn't wanted to eat yet, and she still looked exhausted.

"Don't stress about it." He jerked his chin toward her cell phone on the bedside table. "Have you heard from your friend yet?"

He was pleased he could keep his tone light and casual. As if she were nothing more than an unexpected house guest. Not the girl who once held his heart.

Faith shook her head, clearly distressed. "No. I've sent her a couple of texts. But I did get ahold of one of her friends, and she said she would pass my message on if she could."

"Well, for now just focus on getting better."

"Thanks. I will," she said, settling back against the pillows.

He wondered what had happened to her that she'd had to hitchhike to Calgary. Where was the band she'd joined? What were her plans for the future? Did Elliot even know where she was? But he didn't ask any of that.

"We'll save you some soup in case you get hungry later," he said instead.

"Tell your dad thanks from me."

"Will do." He turned to leave.

"And, Kane…"

He turned back much too eagerly, his heart racing at the pensiveness in her voice.

"Thanks again for picking me up."

And his heart crashed back to earth. What had he been expecting, exactly? Declarations of regret from the girl who destroyed him? Apologies? Pleading to get back with him? Man, he was a fool.

"Sure. No problem." He hoped he sounded more collected than

he was. Before she could say anything more, he closed the door, shaking his head at how easily she got to him.

Having Faith here was dangerous. He had thought he'd finally gotten over her, but this was messing everything up. The sooner Faith was back out of his life, the better.

CHAPTER 4

*F*aith rolled over, blinking as she woke up, early dawn light streaming through the curtains.

Slowly she shed the remnants of her troubled dreams and realized where she was.

At the Tye ranch. In Elliot Tye's room.

She draped an arm over her forehead, struggling with the reality of her current situation. Seeing Kane yesterday had been a shock, but she'd also sensed it coming. When the trucker giving her a ride from Lethbridge had made a detour through the Porcupine Hills because of construction, she'd felt a shiver of premonition. She knew that road would bring her dangerously close to the Tye ranch and her grandfather's place.

What were the chances she'd get sick and Kane would drive by just at that moment? It had to be like a billion to one.

And yet, here she was, at the place she'd been running from since their breakup.

She pulled her knees up and wrapped her arms around them, feeling a clench of despair at how her life had turned out. She had been so full of plans and enthusiasm when she'd left Rockyview two years ago. She'd just needed so badly to be free of her grandfather's heavy expectations. Free to do what she wanted, not what everyone else wanted for her.

From the moment Faith's mother, Susan, had showed up at her estranged father's home, Mick Howard's home, carrying a baby and bringing the ragged remnants of her life with her, Mick Howard laid all his unmet dreams and hopes on Faith's shoulders. When Susan died, the burden only grew. Mick had grand plans for his granddaughter, and he made it clear he expected her to take her place alongside him in his law firm. At first she had agreed, knowing she had to be grateful to him for giving her a home. For paying for her education. For giving her a future. But as she got older, she realized gratitude wasn't enough to build a life on. She wanted to be happy in her own right. She wanted to do something she loved. And she loved her music.

But Mick would hear none of it, growing angry when she even mentioned her music, telling her how ungrateful she was. Reminding her about the future he had planned.

During that tumultuous time Kane had been her sanctuary. His home was a place she could relax and enjoy herself, where the love was unconditional and flowed freely. And she and Kane had fallen *in* love. When he'd proposed to her, she thought her life couldn't get any better. They made plans. She would finish her degree, and instead of becoming a lawyer she would be a teacher, pursuing her music on the side.

And then Grace died, and the whole Tye family came unglued. Zach fell into a deep depression. The Tye siblings scattered like seeds on the wind. Kane seemed lost and angry and started taking her grandfather's side, saying she should stick with the family plan and become a lawyer after all. She felt betrayed by them all, and she was grieving for Grace herself, the only woman who had ever truly mothered her.

With all that going on, her music had become her only refuge.

Faith closed her eyes, trying to erase from her memory the

look of disappointment Kane had given her on the side of the road yesterday.

She had run away from love to follow her passion and hadn't even gotten that right. No wonder he could barely look at her.

Faith pulled in a long, slow breath, centering herself.

One day at a time. Her stomach wasn't hurting at the moment, which was a good sign. She tossed the blankets aside and sat up. Spots danced before her eyes, and she waited until they cleared. She just needed something to eat to get her strength back. That's when she saw a cup of orange juice and a bowl of yogurt with a spoon sitting on the end table beside her bed.

She hoped it was Zach who had brought the food and not Kane. The thought that he might have stood over her while she slept brought with it a range of emotions she couldn't even process. Either way, she would eat the food.

Twenty minutes later, she was showered and changed into clean clothes. She still felt weak, but at least she was keeping the food down.

She walked through the silent house to the kitchen. Kane and Zach must be working outside. She stepped out onto the sun-warmed deck and immediately sat down on a nearby wicker chair as a wave of dizziness washed over her. Still woozy, but at least she didn't feel nauseated anymore.

Laying her head back, she closed her eyes, letting the heat of the sun wash over her, the peace of the moment sink in. The past few months had been a storm of emotions, conflict, and chaos. She shuddered as memories leapt up, and she shoved them right back down.

She was here, at Tall Timber. The one place she'd always felt safe, loved, and cared for.

The place she ran away from, burning bridges behind her in a blaze of glory.

Faith dragged her hands over her face, fighting pain and sorrow mingled with regret.

Stop. Move on. Next step.

The words resonated through her mind. Words that had gotten her through the past few months. She had to focus on what was ahead because looking behind was a one-way trip down to the depths of despair.

The sound of a vehicle approaching broke through her self-talk.

Faith opened her eyes to see a small, rusted-out sports car roaring down the treed driveway, spewing a cloud of dust as it headed toward the house. She got up and walked toward it, curious to see who it was.

The car stopped by Kane's truck. A young woman got out and stared at the house a moment, looking unsure. She obviously hadn't seen Faith yet. She turned away, opened the back door, bent over, and took out a little girl who looked to be about two years old. The girl wiped at her eyes, her hair a sticky mat of curls, her chubby cheeks bright red. She wore a grubby pink T-shirt and denim shorts and nothing on her feet.

The woman set the little girl down, then dove into the car again, reappearing with a car seat and a suitcase. She set these on the ground by the little girl and went around to the other side of the car and did it all over again. This time she set a young boy on the ground. He wavered, yawning, his hair the same mat of unkempt curls as the little girl's. They looked about the same age, so were probably twins. The boy wore sandals that were too large, a pair of baggy shorts, and a hoodie that took over his body. "Come over here and hold my hand, buddy," the woman said.

She wore tight blue jeans, a snug T-shirt, a leather jacket, and stiletto boots. She did not look like the mother of two young children. In fact, she had handled them more like luggage than anything else. The woman looked up as she tottered up the walk and then, finally, saw Faith.

"So, who are you?" the woman asked as she came closer. She had a deep voice, harsh, as if she was a smoker.

Faith was surprised at her bold question. She stammered, "I'm just—I'm visiting."

"This is the Tye ranch, right? I was a bit confused, because the gate said Tall Timber."

"That's the name of the ranch," Faith explained. "You're in the right place."

"I need to talk to Zach Tye. About these kids." She looked around impatiently as if Zach should magically appear because she demanded it.

"I think he's out working. I'm not sure. I just woke up," Faith admitted sheepishly. She had no idea what time it was, but from the position of the sun, probably very late morning.

The woman chewed one side of her lip, as if trying to decide what to do. The girl yawned, and the boy squatted down, tugging on the grass.

"You have any idea when he'll be back?" the woman asked, looking annoyed.

Faith was about to answer that she didn't know, when, much to her relief, she heard the rumbling of a vehicle coming from the fields behind the corrals. The woman turned toward the noise as well, exhaling her relief as an open Jeep came into sight.

Kane stopped the vehicle, got out, pulled off his gloves, and shoved them in his back pocket as he walked toward them, frowning. His father was slowly making his way out of the Jeep.

Despite the tension between them, Faith couldn't stop a leap of her heart at the sight of Kane's tall, commanding figure. He had the sleeves of his twill shirt rolled up his forearms, his cowboy hat pushed back on his head, and faint laugh lines radiated out from his eyes. Those same eyes flicked to her in surprise.

"You Zach Tye?" the woman asked.

"I'm Kane. His son." Kane's gaze slipped back to the little boy and girl. "What's this about?"

"It's about these kids. They're your sister Tricia's." The woman delivered the news in a matter-of-fact tone, as if Kane should know exactly what was going on.

Tricia had kids?

Faith sucked in a quick breath, trying to sort this shocking information out.

Her mind ticked back, remembering comments Tricia had made before she eloped with Drew. How she had withdrawn from everyone. Faith had thought it was because of Grace's death.

But now...

Tricia was probably pregnant, confused, and lost.

Faith glanced over at Kane, who was scratching his forehead with one finger, staring at the kids.

"Oh, Tricia," was all he said, shaking his head.

"You don't believe me?" the woman asked.

"No. I believe you." He stopped there, hands planted on his hips. "She told Dad about them. It's just...he's never..." His voice trailed off as Faith tried to take this all in. Clearly Kane and Zach knew about the children.

"Where is Tricia now?"

"She took off a week ago. She said she'd only be gone a couple of days, but she hasn't come back."

"And you haven't heard anything from her?"

"Nope. I'm Tricia's roommate, by the way. Name's Lucinda." She gave Kane a wide smile, her eyes slipping over him in appreciation.

Really? Flirting with Kane while she dropped this bombshell on them?

But Kane didn't catch it. He was too busy staring at the children, who now sat on the grass by the car seats and suitcase Lucinda had pulled out. Faith had the sudden urge to go over and wrap them in her arms. She had been a kid like this once, abandoned and alone. But she didn't want to scare them or make a scene, so she held back.

"What's going on?" Zach asked as he hobbled up to join them.

"Apparently these are Tricia's kids," Kane said.

Zach's puzzled frown faded away, replaced by a sorrow that hitched at Faith's heart as he too stared at the children.

"Hope and Cash." Lucinda said. "Those are their names."

Zach made his way over to the children and painfully knelt down in front of them.

"Hey, Cash," he said. His voice broke, and Faith couldn't imagine what he was dealing with right now. "Here you are. Finally."

His words puzzled her. Finally? What did he mean by that?

Zach reached out to Cash, but the little boy jerked back.

"But how? How did this happen?" Kane stammered, pulling Faith's attention back to him.

"The usual way, I suspect," Lucinda said dryly.

"Not that," Kane blurted. "How did you end up with them?"

"My mom often babysat them," Lucinda explained, pulling her phone out of her back pocket. "Tricia asked her to take them for two or three days while she was gone for some training for her job. But this time Tricia didn't come back, and my mom ended up in the hospital with kidney stones. She can't take care of them anymore, and neither can I. I have to work. So, here I am." She turned to Zach. "Tricia never mentioned any of her real family. Just you, her mom, and this ranch. And in case you're wondering if these are Tricia's kids, I've got photos to prove it." Lucinda swiped at the screen on her phone.

While she showed them the photos the little boy whimpered, and Faith could stand it no longer. Ignoring the adults, she walked over to Cash, crouching down to his level.

"Hey, kiddo," was all she said, smiling at him, hoping he wouldn't pull away.

To her surprise, the little boy threw his arms around her, his sticky hands clinging to her neck. Hope, however, kept her distance, watching through a fringe of unkempt blonde hair.

Lucinda turned her phone to Kane. "See. This is Tricia, and here are the kids with Tricia. Took this a couple weeks ago."

Still feeling weak, Faith leaned against the tree behind her, holding Cash close while the adults figured out what to do. Hope continued to keep her distance, her eyes downcast.

Zach stood beside Kane, his expression one of familiar resignation. Was that a glint of tears in his eyes? Faith knew Tricia had left Rockyview after the death of her husband in a car accident. But had she never been back to the ranch since? Had Zach never seen his grandchildren let alone heard of them?

"This nice man is your grandfather," Lucinda said to the kids. "I want you to be good for him."

"Wait. What? No. We can't— What about Tricia?" Kane was having a hard time formulating a coherent thought. Not that Faith blamed him. Having his estranged sister's children dropped off at his doorstep without any warning had to be a pretty big shock. Especially when it seemed he'd had no idea they even existed.

"Told you. Not a clue." Lucinda pulled out a piece of paper and handed it to Kane. "Here's her cell number. She hasn't been answering though. She told me she was going to a training seminar. That's all I know, and it may have been a lie." She turned to Faith. "Clothes for the kids are in the suitcase, and here are the car seats. They're really good kids, and though they're only two years old they're both toilet trained, so that's a plus."

Lucinda walked over and patted each child on the head, as if they were puppies. "See ya, munchkins."

And without another word Tricia's roommate strode back to her car.

"Wait," Faith called out. "Do they need a nap? What about food? What do they eat?"

But Lucinda clearly believed she had done her part. Ignoring Faith, she got into her car, reversed quickly, and roared off down the driveway.

Kane watched her leave, stunned and silent.

Zach was looking back at the children as if he had found a rare treasure. "Oh, my goodness. Tricia's kids." His voice broke on the last word.

"Did that just happen?" Kane asked, still clutching the scrap of paper Lucinda had given him.

"I'm afraid it did," Zach said, sounding a little less dazed than Kane. Then again, he'd had kids dropped on his doorstep before. Many times before.

"We have to call her," Kane said. "Let her know what's going on." He glanced at the paper again, then back at the kids.

"I think the first thing we should do is take these two into the house," Faith said, struggling to her feet. "I'm sure they're thirsty and probably hungry."

Cash looked up at her. "I want my mommy," he said in a plaintive voice.

He sounded so lost. Faith flashed back to a painful childhood memory of her mother kneeling beside her bed, telling Faith she had to leave but would come back as soon as she could, Faith's grandfather looming behind her, glaring.

But she never came back. Two days after she'd left she died of a brain aneurism.

And Faith had never stopped wanting her.

Cash leaned into her side, and Faith took his hand, thankful she felt stronger than she had yesterday. To her surprise Hope grabbed her other hand and together they walked into the house, Kane and Zach following behind.

CHAPTER 5

*F*aith opened the refrigerator and pulled out some juice for the kids. The only other items in the cavernous rectangle were half a stick of butter, a loaf of bread, four cheese slices, and an old pizza box.

Grace Tye would be appalled. When she'd been alive the refrigerator had been overflowing with fruit, vegetables, sandwich meat, more condiments than any household needed, leftovers, and every kind of salad dressing you could imagine. Her family had teased her about having to play Jenga just to get anything out of it.

This fridge almost echoed, it was so empty.

Faith poured juice in the smallest cups she could find and handed one to each child. They could barely look over the table, they were that small.

Zach and Kane said nothing. They just kept staring at one another and then back down at the kids.

"So, this is a shock," Faith said, trying to rouse them from their silence. "What do you think we should do next? About Tricia's kids?" she prompted.

"We should try to get ahold of Tricia," Zach said. "She may be in trouble and need our help."

"She left her kids," Kane blurted angrily. "What kind of mother does that?"

Faith understood his anguish, and while she echoed it, she also knew they had to be careful what they said in front of the children.

"I'm sure Tricia is fine," she said with more confidence than she felt. "She will come get Cash and Hope as soon as she can. In the meantime, we should try to make them feel comfortable and safe."

"I want my mommy," Hope cried, setting down her juice, large tears rolling down her pink cheeks.

"Of course you do," Kane said, patting her awkwardly on the back, as if he was burping her.

"Why don't we try to call Tricia now," Faith suggested.

Kane pulled out his cell phone and with it, the piece of paper Lucinda had given him. He dialed, his eyes on the children. But a few moments later he ended the call and put the phone down. "It didn't even go to voicemail," he said worriedly.

"Should we call the p-o-l-i-c-e?" Faith spelled the last word out.

"Not yet," Zach said adamantly. "Until we know where Tricia is, we've got the kids. I'm not running the risk of having them taken away. They're my grandchildren. Mine," he said, touching Cash on the head as if testing to see if he was real. His face eased into a melancholy smile, looking like a man who just found a new lease on life. "I have grandchildren," he said quietly, stroking Cash's head again. And this time, thankfully, Cash let him.

"Do you think they're Drew's?" Kane asked, voicing the question that had been on Faith's mind as well.

"They look about the right age," Zach said. "I know Tricia told me she was pregnant when she and Drew eloped. And then there was that accident—" He stopped, pain and grief flashing across his face.

Faith remembered that day all too well. Drew, Tricia, and Elliot had, reportedly, been on their way back from the brief ceremony. All they knew was that it was a single vehicle accident.

The next day Kane told Faith that though the details of the car accident were hazy, Drew was dead, and Elliot and Tricia were in the hospital.

When Tricia was released she'd left town.

"You haven't been in contact with her since the accident?" Faith asked Zach.

Zach shook his head but wouldn't look at her. What had happened between them to make Tricia that estranged?

Wasn't that an ironic question coming from her? Her grandfather was only a few miles away, but she wouldn't be contacting him. He had made it abundantly clear, when she'd visited him in the hospital, that he did not want to see her. Families fell apart. Apparently, even the Tyes.

"So, what do we do?" Kane asked, rubbing his forehead, looking exhausted. "About our situation," he said, glancing at the children.

Hope yawned and, to Faith's surprise, crawled onto her lap.

Faith instinctively held her close, as Hope tucked her face against her. In seconds she was asleep, as was Cash who had laid his head on the table.

"Nothing but enjoy it," Zach said, smiling down at his sleeping grandson, shifting him gently onto his lap. "This is the good part."

"Dad," Kane said sadly, "we can't keep them here."

"You want them to go to foster care?" Zach shot back.

"No, of course not," Kane protested.

"Then we're keeping them until Tricia comes back." Zach wasn't going to budge. "And I think that's exactly why Faith was sent to us yesterday," he added, looking up at her.

"What?" Faith blurted. Hope jerked in her sleep but didn't wake up.

"Has your friend called back yet?" Zach asked pointedly.

"No," Faith said, knowing full well where this was headed.

"And you're feeling better?" he continued.

"Sort of," Faith said, not sure she wanted to carry through with this conversation.

"So, you're waiting to hear from your friend, and we're waiting to hear from Tricia," Zach reasoned. "Why don't you just wait here and help us with the kids. Of course, we'd pay you. I mean, it almost seems like it is meant to be." Thankfully, Zach didn't play the "God's plan" card. That really would have turned Faith off. But the fact that he was asking her to stay—no, offering to pay her to stay—without even consulting Kane, meant he was really desperate.

"Dad, don't put Faith on the spot like this," Kane scolded. "She has her own plans, and this isn't her problem."As usual, Kane had to make it sound like he was coming to her defense when, in reality, he just wanted her out of his house as soon as possible.

"You have a better idea?" Zach countered. "Faith is here. It would take us days—maybe weeks—to find a nanny willing to come out to the ranch."

"Weeks?" Kane's voice broke on the word. "You think we'll have them for weeks?"

"Maybe," Zach said. "I don't know. At least Faith could stay while we look for someone else to step in."

"Hello," Faith said, waving at them. "I'm right here, you two. You can speak to me directly. And I'd be happy to watch Cash and Hope until I hear from my friend or you hear from Tricia. But if Stacy calls with stuff lined up for me in Calgary, I have to go, in which case you'll have to find someone else. So you might want to start looking."

Kane caught her gaze, and she held it. She could tell he wasn't pleased. But this wasn't about Kane Tye for a change. It was about the little girl in her lap and the little boy now snoring lightly. She knew how hard it was to lose a mother. These kids needed her.

And it was also for Zach. It had scared her to see him so despondent and depressed, as if he still hadn't recovered from his wife's death.

But once Stacy called or Tricia came back, she would leave and be out of Kane's hair for good.

Again.

"Okay." Kane nodded reluctantly. "But we're paying you the going rate for a live-in nanny. I'll look it up."

"Maybe you should add personal grocery shopper to my salary," Faith said. "These kids are going to need more than canned soup and sandwiches. The fridge is basically empty."

"Right. Food." Kane said.

"For now, maybe we should get them to bed."

Faith slowly stood, thankful she felt better as Kane gently picked Cash up. Cash curled his little body against his. Faith caught a melancholy smile drift across Kane's well-shaped mouth. Her heart hitched at the sight, and she quickly turned away.

"We'll put them on Elliot's bed for now and leave the door open a crack," she said. "But we're going to have to come up with better sleeping arrangements before tonight."

Faith carried Hope, and Kane followed her with Cash, tucking both children into Elliot's bed. They didn't even stir. Poor things must have been exhausted after the trip with Lucinda.

When they were back in the kitchen, Kane asked, "Should we go get groceries while they're asleep?"

"No." Faith shook her head. "I have no idea what they like to eat, or if they have allergies. We'll take them along when they wake up. At least that way they can point at things they want. Kids love to beg for their favorite foods at the grocery store."

"How long will they nap?" Kane asked, glancing at his phone for the umpteenth time. "I have to get more fencing supplies today before the hardware closes."

"We'll wake them up in a couple of hours. That should give us plenty of time," Faith said, hoping she was right.

"Don't forget to check in with the real estate agent," Zach reminded Kane.

"Real estate agent?" Faith asked, surprised. "Are you buying more land?"

"No," Kane said, his eyes going hard and distant. "We're selling the ranch."

CHAPTER 6

*C*onfusion battled with all the other emotions Faith was trying to process.

"You're selling the ranch?" Her eyes flicked from Kane to Zach. "Why?"

"I can't carry on this way." Zach seemed intent on digging some dirt out from under his fingernails. "You've seen me limp around here. I can barely mount a horse since my injury."

Faith looked at Kane, puzzled. "But I thought you were—"

"Taking over the ranch?" Kane released a harsh laugh. "That was the plan before you left. I work rigs now. I just came back to help Dad sell. That's all."

Really? He was putting this on her? His decision to leave the ranch and now sell it? No, that wasn't fair. Elliot had left too. He was supposed to work the ranch by Kane's side. She hadn't made Elliot leave. Her decisions were her own, but she wouldn't own the Tye boys' decisions as well. No, they were men, for goodness' sake. Grown men.

"But what will you do?" She turned to Zach. "Where will you live?"

"I'll retire," Zach said. "Buy a place in Rockyview and maybe do some of those hobbies I always talked about starting."

Faith couldn't imagine Zach living in town, puttering around doing hobbies.

He belonged on a horse, out in the pasture, working cows.

His sons beside him.

"It's what has to be done," Kane said, his voice gruff.

"I think I'll go lie down," Zach said, looking at Faith, "if that's all right with you. An afternoon nap sounds pretty good right about now."

"Yeah, of course," Faith said. "I've got the kids covered. It's my job, remember?"

Zach stood up, reached out, and gently took Faith's arm, giving it a squeeze. "Thank you," he said. "I'm not sure what we'd do without you."

"You're welcome," she replied. He let go of her arm, heading down the hall to his bedroom.

When she was sure he was out of earshot, she turned to Kane. "Is your dad okay?" she asked worriedly.

"His leg still hurts him quite a bit," Kane said, frowning. "Especially if he rides. But I think it's also the shock of the kids. I can't believe Tricia kept the kids away from him."

Faith could feel the anger radiating off him, like it had long ago towards her. Kane didn't get angry easily, but when he did it was like a tornado that sweeps away everything in its path. Even just the hint of it now brought bad memories rushing back to her.

"I'll get the kids' suitcase and bring it in," she said, giving herself an excuse to escape. "Hopefully there are some clean clothes in there."

"Okay." Kane nodded, heading toward the back door. "I'm going out to the shop to make sure I know what parts to get at the hardware. And then I'll check the cattle. If you need me, just text."

Once she had the suitcase in the kitchen, Faith unzipped it, clothes spilling out as she did. It looked like Lucinda had just bundled everything together and shoved the whole business inside.

Faith untangled leggings from blue jeans, scattering socks as she did. There wasn't much to choose from, but she managed to find clothing for each of the twins that was passably clean and not too worn. She thought of the stylish clothes Tricia had always loved to wear. She had to have the latest style, the best and the most expensive. And Zach and Grace had allowed it. Faith knew they didn't play favorites, but as the only biological child, Tricia did seem to, at times, get preferential treatment in the Tye family. She and Grace would go on shopping trips and come home with beautiful clothes and endless manicures. Tricia was encouraged to take up barrel racing, a pricey sport if there ever was one. She had three horses and a swanky horse trailer that she drove from rodeo to rodeo, often with Elliot and Kane.

Zach always passed their treatment of her off as the fact that Tricia was the only girl in the family. While that may have been a large part of it, Faith often sensed something else was going on.

But in spite of that, Faith wondered what had happened to Tricia for her to fall this far down?

And how could Kane and Zach sell the ranch? It was a part of them.

It was a part of her.

⌒◠◠

Two hours later, the twins were awake, faces washed, dressed in clean clothes, and nibbling on grilled cheese sandwiches at the table. In place of booster seats, Faith had stacked some of Zach's larger books on their chairs. And she'd made sandwiches for herself and the men too, though now they truly didn't have a crumb of food in the house. But at least they wouldn't go shopping on an empty stomach.

Kane had already come in and downed two sandwiches. Now

he was out putting the car seats in his truck. They'd decided to let Zach sleep, but Faith had left him a note on the counter that his sandwiches were in the fridge.

When the kids were done eating, she washed their hands with a washcloth, helped them down from their chairs, and said, "Shall we go find Uncle Kane?"

"I want Mommy," Cash said, his lower lip quivering.

"I know," Faith said, "but she's still on her vacation."

It was the best she could come up with to explain to them why their mother was gone.

"I want to go," Hope said, wrinkling her nose.

"Well, okay then," Faith said, smiling and holding out her hands to both of them. To her delight, they slipped their chubby hands in hers, warmth radiating into her palms from them. As the three of them walked together out of the kitchen, other memories assaulted Faith.

She used to pretend that she lived in this house, that Kane was her husband, and that someday they would have a dozen children running through this kitchen, filling the house with laughter and busyness.

But her grandfather had thought that would be a waste of a good mind. He had other plans for her.

Faith pushed the thoughts aside. There was no point in thinking about what could have been. She had to look forward, not back.

The sun shone down as she and the children stepped out of the house. Birds sang from the branches of trees surrounding the yard, their leaves still holding the soft green of spring. Faith let the peace of the country slip over her. She had missed this more than she realized.

Kane was fitting the second car seat into the back of his truck.

He turned toward her as she joined him by the driver's door. "Is your dad going to be okay?" she asked. "I feel like we should stay with him."

"This is a huge shock for him," Kane said with a harsh laugh. "Both of us, quite frankly. Might be good if we give him some time to absorb it." He shook his head as if trying to settle the events of the past three hours himself. "Anyway, we better deal with what's in front of us right now," he said. "I wasn't exactly sure how to put the car seats in, but I think I figured it out. If you want to look them over…"

"They look fine to me," Faith said, bending to pick up Cash.

Kane stopped her. "You better take it easy too, Fiddy," he said, reaching for the boy.

Her heart folded at his use of his nickname for her. It spoke of an older, easier relationship. An innocent time when they were younger and so in love. Old memories tangled with new as their eyes held.

"Sorry," he said, his tone abrupt. "Slipped out."

He put Cash in the car seat, but it took him a minute to figure out the harness. By that time. Faith had gotten Hope around to the other side. While he buckled her in, Faith opened the passenger door.

Climbing in, she misjudged the height of the truck's running board step, or maybe it was wet. Either way, she slipped and went sideways, careening into Kane.

His strong hands were instantly around her waist, supporting and holding her up. Her shoulder was pressed against his chest, and she caught a whiff of a woodsy scent that was so purely Kane it made her heart stutter. Memories flooded her mind, and she had to fight to suppress them. She had no right.

Thankfully, Kane said nothing as she sat in her seat, reaching for the seat belt.

Kane closed her door and walked around the front of the truck, tapping his fingers on the hood as he always did.

Faith clenched her fists, struggling to maintain her equilibrium. She didn't want to *still* be attracted to a man who thought so little of her that he believed she'd been unfaithful when she hadn't.

A man who had tried to manage her life and push her down a path she couldn't go.

Just like her grandfather.

She had to keep reminding herself that was who Kane had become. Not the imaginary perfect husband she'd imagined him to be. And to be fair, she had changed too. She had new plans and a new focus. She was becoming a different person as well.

She wouldn't let Kane define her as the girl he had said he loved but couldn't trust.

Kane kept his eyes on the road ahead as he drove, his mind a whirl of thoughts and confusion.

Once again he was headed down the road with too many things on his mind.

This time the main one was the woman beside him, his easy use of her nickname, and how he had caught her when she almost fell out of the truck. Both easily brought back memories he thought he had buried. He used to be really good at that. Compartmentalizing his life, curbing memories he preferred not to dwell on. But since he was taken in by the Tye family he had lost some of his self-preservation skills.

Now, all he could think of was how she'd felt in his arms. How she was thinner than before. How her hair still smelled like fresh spring rain. At one time, they'd made plans for their future and shared everything. Now, she was like a cool stranger he must keep his distance from. They had both changed so much. They were both older, and he was definitely wiser.

"I want my mommy," Cash whimpered from the back seat.

"I know, sweetheart," Faith said, patiently. "We want her back too."

"Do they need more clothes?" Kane asked, eyeing their shabby attire.

"Yes, if we have time," Faith said. "There wasn't much in the suitcase."

Kane glanced back at the stained and worn pink T-shirt Hope was wearing and her raggedy shorts. Cash didn't look much better. He fought down a surge of frustration with Tricia. How bad had her life gotten that she would abandon her kids? But behind that came a lingering worry. What if something really bad had happened to her? What if she was injured or, worse?

But what could he do about it? They didn't even know where she'd gone.

"We can leave the clothes for another time," Faith was saying.

"Why?" Kane shot her a puzzled look.

"Well, you look rather ticked."

"No. Sorry, I was just frustrated—" He caught himself. He wasn't about to disparage his sister in front of Faith. She wasn't part of the family anymore. "I was thinking about something else," he finished.

Then Hope started crying because her straps were too tight, and Faith had to turn around in her seat and try and fix it. She was really good with the kids. There was no denying that. But what in the world had possessed his father to ask her to stay and take care of them? Zach knew Kane's painful history with Faith better than anyone else. But the deed was done and, though he didn't like it, he had to be realistic. There was no way he and his dad could handle the kids *and* the ranch. That was why Zach and Grace had made such a great parenting team. Zach loved the ranch and teaching his children a work ethic and how to be resilient and skilled. Grace, on the other hand, showered them with gentle, patient love. He'd seen that same love in Faith today, and it pained him to admit it.

Faith pulled back into her seat, Hope's straps loosened.

Kane glanced at the kids' reflection in the rearview mirror. They were both quiet, just staring out the window, now subdued. He recognized the pulling away they were doing. He had deployed it every time a social worker had come to his home and taken him away from his mother.

The first time he'd been brought to a foster home, he had clung to his mother's promise that she would get better. He had sat on the steps of the house every day, waiting, hoping. A month later she returned. And the cycle started over again. The third time he ended up in the Tye household. His mother promised she would behave, and she was awarded custody. Again.

His mother had watched herself the first couple of months. She found an apartment in Rockyview but then started staying out again. Later and later each time.

She would head out of town, taking him along, playing for bands, auditioning for others. The rejections piled up. Then, one evening, in a small town in Saskatchewan, the band had told his mother to stop wasting her time. She was washed up. His mother had screamed at the band, thrown a glass of beer at the owner when he told her to leave. Then she'd grabbed her guitar case in one hand, clutched his arm in the other, hauling him out of the bar into the darkness. He was ten years old. Too young to protest, but old enough to talk back.

And he had. His mother, drunk and still furious, had slapped him. Hard. Then again. Then she walked away, leaving him on his own. He didn't know where he was. He waited for her, hoping she would come back. But she didn't. He'd wandered the streets for two days trying to find his mother, avoiding danger. He thought she was dead.

Finally the police had found him huddled near a Dumpster. He went back to the Tye home.

But by that time he learned to keep his emotions deeply buried. Hope was a fragile creation he didn't dare nourish. So, he'd initially held himself aloof from Zach and Grace and their daughter Tricia as well.

But slowly, with each month he stayed, hope grew despite his walls and fences. The day he was officially adopted, he felt as if he could finally breathe. Shortly after that, two more siblings were welcomed into the Tye home. Elliot and Lucas. It was a busy, noisy household, and it took Kane another two years to fully believe he wouldn't be taken from it.

He owed Zach and Grace so much. And now Grace was gone. How could he let Zach sell the one thing the family had left tying all of them together?

Once again he fought down his second thoughts about letting Zach sell the ranch. About finding a way to stick around. There had been many times he'd wondered if he could come back. If Zach would let him.

But he didn't dare think, after leaving his father in the lurch, that he could simply come waltzing back and ask to take over. Zach hadn't offered a second time, and Kane wasn't asking. He didn't feel he had the right.

CHAPTER 7

*K*ane parked in front of the grocery store and turned the truck off. "I'll come in with you," he told Faith, just in case she was going to argue with him. He knew how stubborn and proud she could be. Or used to be.

"I'll be okay," she said. "You have your own things to get done."

And there it was. Just as he predicted.

"Maybe, but the kids are feeling pretty disoriented. It would help if they each had an adult to take care of them."

Faith bit her lip but then nodded. "Of course. That makes sense."

He fought down his disappointment at her terse response.

He got out of the truck and then struggled with the buckles he had so easily clipped together on Cash's car seat.

Cash looked at him as if trying to figure out where to place him. Pretty sad that his own nephew didn't even know who he was.

Faith had gotten Hope out of the car seat quicker than he had accomplished the task so she was already heading toward the grocery store by the time he got the truck door closed.

But she wasn't carrying Hope, which showed him that she still wasn't feeling that great. He resisted the urge to rush over to help, knowing she wouldn't appreciate it.

The inside of the store was cool and, thankfully, quiet. Kane really didn't want to run into anyone he knew with his ex-fiancée and two mystery kids in tow. That would raise questions he did not want to answer. And the rumor mill in a small town like Rockyview ran hard and fast.

"Do you know if they have any allergies?" Faith asked as they started down the aisle.

"Not a clue."

"You really don't know these kids at all?" Faith asked, her tone incredulous.

"Today is the first time I've seen them." He hated how admitting that made him feel.

"That's sad. Elliot always talked about how close you guys were."

Kane fought down a beat of annoyance at the mention of his brother sharing family issues with Faith. "Elliot always did talk too much," was all he said.

The silence that followed made him regret his outburst.

Kane blamed his lashing out on the stress and exhaustion that had dogged him since coming back to the ranch. All the work that needed to be done. The fact that the ranch would be sold.

Thankfully, it didn't take long to fill the carts. Faith would offer the twins a choice, and they would pick. This cereal, not those cookies. Yes to chicken, no to pork chops.

He tried not to look at his watch, tried not to let himself worry about all the other tasks he still had to do.

"I think that's about it," Faith said. She looked a bit pale and was clutching the handle of the cart with white knuckles.

"Are you okay?" Kane asked, concerned.

"Just tired," she assured him. "But Cash is upset, poor thing."

Kane's heart twisted when he saw the silent tears streaking down the little boy's cheeks. He picked him up out of the cart and settled him on his hip, curving his arm around his small body. As he did, he felt another stab of anger with his sister for abandoning her children. To his surprise, Cash turned his face into Kane's shoulder, as if hiding from the world.

Faith led them all to the line for the cashier. They were almost done unloading groceries onto the conveyer belt when a jovial voice called out, "Hey, Kane!"

Kane's heart dropped, but he forced a smile as he turned to look at his good friend, Nathan Raphel.

"What are you doing in town?" Nathan asked, grinning broadly. "I mean, it's great to see you around again. You back for good?" Nathan was tall and lanky with a beaky nose, flashing gray eyes, long hair pulled back in a messy ponytail, and a thick, heavy beard that often hid a grin that made anyone who met him feel he was thrilled to meet them.

"No. Just here to help my dad," Kane said, forcing a smile.

"Right. I heard he's selling the ranch. Too bad." Nathan swung the bag of oranges he carried as his eyes flicked to Cash still hiding in Kane's shoulder. Then his glance went to Hope and finally landed on Faith, who had her back to them as she pulled the final items out of the cart. Nathan's grin tilted, and he gave Kane a look laden with questions.

"Tricia's kids, Hope and Cash," Kane said before the third degree started. Nathan was a good friend, but he was incorrigibly nosy and a persistent tease. And right now, Kane wasn't in the mood. "And you remember Faith?" He held Nathan's eyes for a beat, hoping the warning in his gaze was enough to deter his friend from pushing any further.

At the sound of her name, Faith turned. Then, to Kane's surprise, she flushed. "Hey, Nathan," she said, her voice soft but holding a warm undertone that gave Kane a flash of jealousy. Why couldn't she look at him that way?

What was he thinking? That was the last thing he wanted.

"Faith, honey," Nathan said, putting on his best Southern

drawl. "Haven't seen you around since—well, I don't know when. How's school? You a lawyer yet?"

"No, I'm—I didn't go to law school."

"What? Since when?" Then Nathan snapped his fingers. "Right. I forgot. You're in a band now, right?"

When he snapped his fingers, Hope spun around in her cart seat. She took one look at Nathan and let out a wail, grabbing onto Faith's shirt with her little fist and glaring at Nathan.

"Don't!" Hope cried, pointing her finger at Nathan, her voice loud and tinged with fear. "You go. No!"

"Hey, honey, I'm a good guy," Nathan said, moving toward her. "I got a little girl just like you."

"You a bad man," Hope insisted, her voice growing shriller. The cashier looked up from scanning groceries, and an older couple Kane vaguely recognized slowed their steps, watching with concern.

"Everything okay?" the portly older man asked.

"It's all good, Dietrich," Nathan said, backing away from Hope, who was crying now, but still waving her finger at him, her other hand clinging to Faith. "I don't think she likes my beard."

Dietrich Bogal glanced from Nathan to Hope, his thick glasses glinting in the bright overhead lights. "You got kids now, Kane?" he asked, frowning in confusion.

Kane groaned. This was getting worse and worse.

"No. These are Tricia's kids," he said, wishing they could get out of the store before half of Rockyview showed up to find out just exactly how messy things were for the Tye family this time around. "We're taking care of them for a while."

"Oh, my goodness, it's Faith Howard," Mrs. Bogal said, her hand pressed to her chest, her bright lips curved in sympathy. "How are you, my dear? Your grandfather must be so excited you're back in town. I know he's been terribly lonely since you left. He never really recuperated from his heart attack."

Faith lowered her eyes and muttered, "I just got in yesterday. I haven't seen him yet."

"Oh, I see. Where are you staying then?" nosy Mrs. Bogal pressed.

A beat of heavy silence dropped like a rock, and Kane felt a flicker of sympathy for Faith's predicament. Nothing like coming back to the old home town and having all your secrets hung out on the line for everyone to see.

"Faith is helping my dad with the kids," Kane put in, saving her from further interrogation.

"At the ranch?" Mrs. Bogal frowned disapprovingly.

"For now." Kane glanced at the cashier, who was scanning the last of the groceries while obviously enjoying the drama unfolding before her. "It was nice seeing you," he lied, stepping up to pay for the groceries as fast as he could. "Got to rush. The kids need their nap," he said to Nathan. Hope was still giving him the stink-eye. But Faith had given them each a sucker out of the grocery bag, so they were momentarily distracted.

"Kane," Mrs. Bogal called as he pushed them all toward the door. "If you need any help with those wee ones, just call. I'm sure we can get the Ladies' Society to pitch in with meals or childcare."

Kane almost burst out laughing at the offer. The last thing he wanted was more people coming by the ranch, trying to figure out what in the world was going on with Kane Tye and Faith Howard, the woman who had run off with his brother. Oh, and how about the mystery of why Zach was selling Tall Timber Ranch, and where Tricia was, for goodness' sake?

They made it out to the truck, and Kane started loading the groceries into the box of the truck like a madman. Faith was right on board, loading the sucker-sucking kiddos into their car seats.

But Nathan didn't give up that easily. Plus, he was parked right next to them.

"Whoa, that was close," Nathan said, sauntering up. "I thought

Melinda Bogal was going to rehash your history right there in the checkout line."

"Nathan." Kane growled a warning.

"Seriously, man, I just wanted to offer my non-town-gossip help. We have all kinds of kid stuff at our place. Maybe we could have a playdate with our little girl and these two."

Playdate? Really? Would it come to that?

"Sure. Thanks for the offer," Kane said, just to end the conversation so he could climb in the truck cab.

Nathan grinned, got in his car, and drove away.

"Well, that went well," Faith said, shaking her head as they pulled out of the parking lot.

"Yep," Kane said. "How long do you think it'll take the entire town to know you're staying at the ranch?"

"Fifteen minutes?" she ventured. "Sooner if Melinda Bogal has learned how to text."

CHAPTER 8

"I think that's it," Faith said, scanning the list on her phone one last time as Kane stood holding bags of kid's clothes. Between this, the groceries, and the stuff he still needed at the hardware, he was going to have a killer credit card bill.

Yep, they had everything on her list. Shoes, rubber boots, raincoats, light jackets, sweaters, pants, shirts, dresses, and some black shiny Mary Janes for Hope. For Sunday, Kane had told her, for church.

Did he just assume they were all going to church like some big, happy family? Because she didn't really have anything suitable for church. Besides, church meant facing her grandfather. So, no thanks.

"I firsty," Hope said, tugging on Faith's hand.

"Me too." Cash chimed in, crawling out from under the nearest clothing rack.

"We'll have some juice back at the ranch," Faith told them, leaning against the counter. She was so tired, and she knew Kane wanted to get going.

"I'll go check out, and we'll head home," Kane said, glancing at her. "I think everyone is tired."

"I'm fine." The words were automatic and she guessed, from his skeptical look, that he didn't believe her. "Besides, don't you need to talk to the real estate agent?"

Kane shrugged her question off. "I'll call him when I'm home. But I have to get the fencing materials. I called my order in, so it should just be a quick stop."

Faith nodded, Kane paid, and they headed out.

A few minutes later, they were all in the truck, bags piled around the kids in the back seat. Thankfully, both of them fell asleep on the way to the hardware store where Kane went inside, and Faith stayed behind, laying her head back against the seat and closing her eyes. She had been tired before. Now, she was bone-weary.

Her thoughts drifted to Melinda Bogal claiming Faith's grandfather was missing her. She might feel guilty about that if he hadn't sent her away after his heart attack with the command to never return.

Maybe she should she try again. But she couldn't face his disappointment and anger, especially when all his warnings about her choices had come true.

Stop. Shut the lid. Move on.

Faith opened her eyes and peered beyond the tree-lined streets of the town to the rolling hills, now green with new grass undulating toward the mountains. Their gray-blue peaks were still capped with snow, stark-white against a bluebird sky.

Her heart softened at the sight, and a melancholy smile curved her lips. This was home—would always be home. But she couldn't stay here.

Which reminded her...

She pulled out her phone and texted Stacy again. She waited a few more minutes, but still nothing. She dialed Stacy's number, but no answer either. So she left a message. But even if Stacy called back, could she really leave Kane and Zach high and dry with the kids? Hope and Cash had connected with her more than anyone so far.

But staying meant more time spent with Kane.

She slipped her phone into her pocket, dragging her hands over her face as she blew out a breath of frustration. It was harder being around him than she'd anticipated, especially with the kids added to the mix. Faith had not missed the look on Melinda Bogal's face when she'd seen her with Kane and the twins. The woman had been doing mental math, until Kane had corrected her unspoken assumption. But people would believe what they wanted. And, she realized with a jolt, the math sort of worked.

The door of the hardware shop opened, and Kane came out carrying what looked like a trailer axle. Behind him came Erik Peet, an old schoolmate of theirs, carrying a couple of plastic bags. His step faltered when he saw Faith, but he gave her a small wave. Obviously, he was wondering what she was doing back after being gone for two years. And, he worked for her grandfather occasionally, doing yard work and maintenance. Great. She knew she would bump up against her past here in Rockyview. Just the way Pete looked at her, Faith felt judged, as if he knew all the horrible details of her breakup with Kane and couldn't believe she'd had the gall to come back.

It shouldn't matter what people thought, she told herself, extinguishing another flicker of guilt.

Kane climbed into the truck, closing the door quietly so as not to wake the twins, and Pete went back into the store.

As they drove back to the ranch, Faith watched the too-familiar landscape slip by, thinking back to many other trips she and Kane had made when she was attending college in Calgary. He would come and pick her up every weekend and bring her back to Rockyview.

But the memories hurt, and the silence seemed oppressive. She suddenly wished she could bridge the gap between them, but what good would it do? They were headed different directions.

"Boy, Hope got fierce toward Nathan, didn't she?" Kane asked. "What do you think that was about?"

"I don't know," Faith said. "They both seem subdued for kids their age, even given the circumstances. And she was fierce, but she was obviously also terrified."

"Which makes me wonder what type of men Tricia has been hanging around with," Kane said.

Faith thought of Keith, wondering what Kane would think of him.

"You must be worried about her," Faith said, feeling a thrum of sympathy for him. "I know I am."

"I don't know what to think," Kane said. "But I hope she's okay, and I hope she comes back for the kids."

"When was the last time you heard from Tricia?" Faith dared to ask.

Kane shrugged. "When she left the hospital after the accident, I got a text from her saying she would be okay. And to leave her alone. But since that, nothing."

"That's a long time." Though Faith wasn't too surprised. Tricia and her were friends and they had talked about Kane. A lot. Tricia kept telling Faith she should date Kane. But Faith also knew that Kane and Tricia weren't terrible close. Kane had often accused Tricia of being a spoiled brat.

"I tried texting her back," Kane admitted, "but she didn't reply. Told her she could always come home." He released a heavy sigh.

Faith wished she could say something reassuring but felt at a loss. As an only child whose own mother had left her, she wasn't in any position to give him guidance on maintaining family relationships. Not when her own was in such shambles.

She looked out the window, watching the empty fields flash by. Soon tractors would be pulling implements over the stubble, planting again, the first steps of the cycle that went on every year.

As long as the earth endures, seedtime and harvest, cold and heat, summer and winter, day and night will never cease.

64

"While we're on the subject of family," Kane said, "what about you and your grandfather?"

Faith glared at him for asking the question but, to be fair, he'd answered her questions about Tricia.

"I don't know. It depends on him," she answered.

"What do you mean?"

"When he had his heart attack," Faith said, surprised at the sharp pain that rose up in her as she spoke, "I found out he was in the hospital through Facebook. An old friend posted it. So I made the trek to Calgary. But when I got to his room, he turned away and told me to leave." She kept her face averted, looking out the window, while she delivered this news. Watched the rolling landscape slip past, concentrated on the hum of the tires, the faint snoring coming from one of the twins in the back seat. Anything but the hurt of her grandfather's rejection. "I tried to stay, but the nurses came. He told them not to let me in again." She'd had to work up a lot of nerve to go see him in the first place. Had she really deserved to be cut off like that?

"I can't believe he did that," Kane said. "He cared so much for you."

"He cared that I do what he wanted," she said before she could stop herself.

"But he only wanted the best for you."

"Why do you always side with him?" Faith choked out. "And what about what I wanted?" She knew the conversation had gone too far now, delved too deep, and she was drowning in the need to finally make Kane understand her sorrow, anger, and frustration.

"When you left with Elliot, was that what you wanted?"

The question came out so casual, but when Faith looked over at him in surprise, she saw the clench of his jaw, the narrowing of his eyes.

She wasn't sure what to tell him.

"I wanted the freedom to make my own choices. Besides, Elliott didn't stay around very long," was all she managed.

"I guess I shouldn't be surprised." Kane sounded bitter, and Faith wished for the hundredth time that she could redo the moment he thought she'd betrayed him. Take back the words that spilled out of her dissatisfaction and shame. That horrible fight when he assumed that the kiss he saw meant more than it had. She knew she had used Elliot and her fight with Kane as a convenient out. It had been easier than trying, once again, to make Kane understand she needed more than her grandfather had planned for her. More than Kane had planned for her, even. She had been terrified that, if she stayed, the two of them would craft a life for her she couldn't maintain. Better to leave before she was in too deep and really disappointed them.

"You shouldn't blame Elliot," Faith said. "He's had his difficulties."

"You mean the accident?" Kane pulled in a heavy breath. "Tricia lost her husband that night, for goodness' sake. All Elliot lost was a year on the rodeo circuit."

"Drew was his friend," Faith shot back. "And you don't think his injuries and that loss made him face his own mortality?"

Kane just stared ahead, his jaw set in a hard, uncompromising line. What was he thinking? She could tell he wanted to say something, but he was holding it back. A muscle in his jaw jumped, and he finally opened his mouth. "Is he okay?"

"Who? Elliot?" She gave a bitter laugh. "I have no idea. I haven't seen him in almost a year."

"That's more recently than I have," Kane said.

"He never came home?" Faith asked, surprised. "You haven't talked to him since he left? But surely he's talked to Zach."

"Not a word." Kane's frown deepened, and he turned his attention back to the road.

"Kane, I'm sorry," Faith wanted to reach out and touch his arm, but she didn't. "I never expected my choices to break your family apart."

"Really?" He glanced at her, anger blazing in his eyes. "You kissed my brother and didn't expect it to impact my relationship with him?"

"I told you that night, and I'll tell you again," Faith said. "It wasn't that kind of kiss. I was just excited the band had invited me to play with them, and he was right there, excited for me. And it just happened. I thought of Elliot as a brother. That's all."

"Well, that's not how he thought of you," Kane said, his voice getting louder. "In fact, just before you both left, Elliott told me I didn't deserve you. He said he was leaving with you, and he was going to give you the life you deserved." Kane's eyes flashed with anger. He was practically yelling now. "So please, explain to me again how I got it all wrong?"

And that's when Hope woke up screaming and crying in her car seat. Which woke up Cash, and he joined in as well.

"You can't yell like that with kids around," Faith said to Kane. "Pull over so I can get in the back."

Kane pulled the truck to the side of the road, glancing at Faith sheepishly as she climbed into the back seat with the sobbing twins.

"I'm sorry I scared them," he said. "I shouldn't have raised my voice."

"No, you shouldn't have," Faith agreed, doing the best she could to soothe the twins with pats and handholds. Poor little mites. They were probably still confused about where they were and what was happening to them. "As for what Elliot said to you," Faith said, softly and calmly, "I can only speak for myself. I left with the band that night, Kane. Elliot chose to come along. I know how that looked to you after the kiss and our fight, but it wasn't that way between us from my end. Ever."

Kane stared at her, as if measuring the truth in her words. Then he simply nodded and pulled back onto the road.

CHAPTER 9

"*D*o you suppose Faith made supper for us?" Zach slid the barn door closed and arched his back, groaning.

"I don't know," Kane said. "She looked tired when we got back from town, and the kids were pretty upset. It may have taken a while to get them settled."

And then there was the fact that they'd fought in the truck, and he'd yelled at her. When they arrived back at the ranch, she'd been upset, and he didn't blame her. All the anger he'd stifled about her and Elliot had come rushing to the surface. But the tension between them had been driving him crazy. Not to mention the attraction that, despite everything, he still felt for her.

Could he believe what she'd said? Could it actually be true that she hadn't been with Elliot in a romantic way? That he'd just tagged along when she'd run away, and then left when the going got tough? That did sound like Elliot—all bluster and showmanship, and no real follow-through. Still, Elliot or not, Faith had left. They had been engaged, and she'd just left, pursuing another dream.

Yes, after you said some horrible things to her that might not have been true.

"Well," his father said, interrupting Kane's confused thoughts. "There is always my world-famous canned soup and grilled cheese."

"Seriously, Dad, you've got to come up with other menu options."

Zach glowered at him. "You want to cook?"

Kane held his gaze then shrugged his surrender. "Make sure you put mayonnaise on my sandwich," was all he said.

But when they entered the house, they caught the savory smell of food cooking, and the gurgle of the kettle boiling.

Zach shot Kane a hopeful look as he slipped his boots off. But the table wasn't set, and Faith and the twins were nowhere to be seen.

Zach lifted the lid off one pot, sniffing appreciatively. "Looks like chicken with some kind of sauce. And I think there's rice in the other pot. Smells amazing."

As they were washing their hands, Kane heard the faint strains of music drifting down the hall.

"Do you hear that?" Zach asked, limping toward it. Kane followed him to the half-open door of Elliot's room.

Faith was perched on the edge of the bed facing away from the door and strumming her guitar, her rich alto voice singing a lullaby to Hope and Cash, who were tucked under the covers and already nodding off. The most startling thing was Kane knew the song. Grace had sung it to him the first few months he'd been at the Tye ranch when he couldn't sleep, even though he'd insisted he was way too old to be sung to.

She would ignore him and sing anyway, perched on the edge of his bed. Then, once he relaxed, once he accepted he was staying, once he dared accept the love she was offering, he would let her stroke his head. Let her kiss him goodnight.

Faith's soulful voice singing that song, her fingers plucking out a harmony on the guitar, made something warm and painfully familiar rise deep from his soul. Yet again, he felt a sting of regret.

He had never asked Faith to play for him. Never wanted to acknowledge her passion. Would things have turned out differently if he had?

Words unspoken could haunt you as much as words spoken, he thought.

But now she was here, singing to a niece and nephew he barely knew. He might have another chance, if he was brave enough to take it.

Zach knocked lightly on the door, and Faith turned, her voice fading.

"I was hoping I could say goodnight to the kids," Zach whispered.

"Of course," Faith said, waving them both in. "They've already had dinner. They were so tired I just made them some macaroni and cheese."

Zach walked around the bed and brushed Hope's hair out of her eyes, smiling down at both children. "Goodnight. Sleep tight, you two" he said, and Kane saw a flash of pain and regret cross his face. What had happened between Zach and Tricia to warrant that reaction?

"I want my mommy," Cash said, blinking slowly as he fought sleep.

"She's coming," Zach said, a little too quickly.

He kissed them each on the forehead, then straightened with a groan.

"I'll go set the table," he said, giving Faith a gentle smile. "Since you made the dinner."

"Dinner has to cook for a few minutes yet," she said, her hands fiddling with the strings, playing a random tune. "But that would be nice."

Kane knew he should follow Zach out the room, but memories and the faint touch of Faith's hand on his arm a few moments ago made him stay. That and what she had told him about Elliot.

Like his father, he wished the twins a quiet goodnight. They were curled up together and wearing their new pajamas. Their hair was brushed, and their shiny cheeks were red. They looked neat and clean but exhausted.

"There are bunk beds in another room where they could have their own place to sleep," Kane said. "I meant to mention it earlier."

"They'll be fine here tonight," she said. "The bed is big enough, and if they wake up in the night scared, I'll be right here." Faith didn't look at him, her fingers dancing over the strings, the melody a haunting counterpoint to the emotions humming between them.

"Makes sense," he said. "But you need sleep as much as they do."

"I'm feeling better," she insisted.

He paused, listening to her play, the notes flowing in a rich melody. His heart contracted.

"I never knew you played so well," he said, his voice quiet.

"I know."

Only two short words, but they created an unexpected surge of guilt. He had known music was important to her when they'd been together, but he'd been gripped by an untamable fear that she was headed down the same path as his mother. Supposedly, love conquered all, but it hadn't been able to conquer that. Maybe he hadn't loved her enough. No, that wasn't fair either. He'd known her music dream would lead her away from him. She'd said as much the little they'd talked about it. Letting her pursue it would have had the same result.

"Was it everything you thought it would be?" he asked gently. "Playing music with that band?"

Faith's fingers froze, and the music stopped abruptly. The twins were both asleep beside her. She looked at them, not Kane, when she answered. "It was, at first." There was pain in her voice, and he'd caused it with his probing question. He'd stopped her playing again.

"Will you finish the song?" he asked. "Mom used to sing it to us. I haven't heard it in years."

Faith looked surprised, then flushed. "I guess. Sure."

He sat on the corner of the bed, giving both her and the kids room.

"How can there be a story that has no end?" Faith sang, transporting him to his childhood. *How can there be a baby with no cryin'?"* Her voice was truly amazing, and the rich notes of the guitar melded past and present.

As she sang and he looked over the sleeping children, an old dream drifted to the surface of his mind. He and Faith, living in this house, doing what she was doing now. Singing a beloved song to their own little ones.

He wanted to ask her how things could have gone so wrong for them, but with that question came a tangle of emotions. During that fight two years ago, she'd been adamant that he was sucking her dry. That he didn't understand her.

Trouble was, he understood her all too well. Too easily he could recall his mother's insistence on following her own musical dreams and what that had done to both her and his life.

"A story full of love, it has no end, a baby when she's sleeping, has no cryin.'" Faith finished the song, and Kane felt a bittersweet yearning at the words.

When she'd left him, he thought their story had truly ended. But now here she was, in his home.

But only for a while. Don't be a fool. She's gone as soon as she has another place to go.

Faith laid her guitar in its battered case, closed it, then stood.

He stood up too and stepped closer to her, reaching out and taking her arm. Their eyes locked, and he couldn't look away. His breath swept out of his body.

"Faith," he said. Her name lingered between them as the last two hard and difficult years faded away.

Then, to his surprise, she rested her hand on his shoulder. She sighed, and he wondered if she felt as confused as he did.

Her fingers curled into his shirt, and her eyes, so close to his, shimmered with unshed tears. The sight of them was like a blow to the gut.

"What's wrong?" he asked, stroking her cheek. She caught his hand, keeping it on her face, and closed her eyes.

"It doesn't matter," she whispered, a tear escaping.

"Tell me," he urged, her sorrow creating an answering pain inside him.

She swallowed and shook her head, then moved away saying, "Zach is probably waiting for us and nearly starving."

The moment was over. They both made their way to the kitchen.

Zach was at the stove, stirring the chicken. "I think it's done," he said when he saw Faith. "You want to check?"

"Looks good to me," she said.

"Oh, and before I forget, Kane," Zach said, setting the plates on the table as Faith put the chicken and rice into bowls. "Floyd from the real estate office called. He has someone who is very interested in the ranch. They want to come out in a week or so."

Kane looked at the food Faith was setting on the table, suddenly no longer hungry, a vise of panic clamping around his midsection. There was too much to do in not enough time. Cows would be calving, and now they had to get the ranch ready to show a prospective buyer. That meant more than fixing things. It meant making them look good. Simply fixing them was already proving a challenge. His father couldn't work the way he used to. Joe wasn't here. It was all on Kane, and he was feeling the pressure.

But it was more than that.

Someone was buying the ranch.

Faith brought a salad to the table and sat down to join them.

Zach held his hand out to Faith and then Kane. "Let's thank the Lord for this bounty," he said, smiling at Faith.

With a shy smile, she took his hand, and Zach cleared his throat. Stifling a sigh, Kane reached out to Faith. She blinked, her smile fading away. For an awkward moment he thought she wouldn't take his hand, but then she slipped hers into his. It felt cool and soft, and for a split second they were a few years younger, sitting here in this kitchen, blissfully in love. He swallowed down the memory, closing his hand around hers.

Zach gave them both a smile that seemed like a blessing, then he lowered his head. "Thank you, Lord, for the food you have blessed us with and the hands that have prepared it." He paused a moment, then continued, "Please be with Tricia wherever she is. Keep her safe. Watch over Elliot and Lucas as well. Keep us always mindful of the needs of others. Amen."

When the final syllable left Zach's lips, Faith tugged her hand loose. As if she couldn't remove the contact soon enough.

She handed the bowl of rice to Zach, avoiding Kane's eyes. Kane sent up a quick prayer for patience. And added one to his father's that Tricia would return soon.

"So the twins are sleeping now?" Zach asked.

"They're out for the night," Kane said, handing Faith the bowl of chicken and sauce. It smelled so good his mouth watered. He and Zach seldom made a fuss of supper, so it was a treat to have a home-cooked meal.

"This is amazing," Zach was saying, wiping his mouth on a napkin. "Better than anything Kane ever managed to rustle up."

"It helps to have the proper groceries to work with," Faith replied with a smile.

"Thanks for making it," Kane said, her smile tugging at old emotions.

"It's your mom's recipe," Faith replied. "One of the few things I can make by heart."

Kane flashed back to a memory of Faith, his mother, and Tricia in the kitchen, laughing as they worked together.

Now his mother was dead, Faith was passing through, and Tricia's children lay sleeping in his estranged brother's room.

Suddenly, a phone rang, and Kane reached for his pocket, but it wasn't his ringtone. Faith glanced over her shoulder, then quickly got up. "Sorry. That's my phone," she said. "Maybe it's Stacy about the job."

She snatched her ringing phone from the island. "Hey, there," said as she walked away. I've been trying to get ahold of you for days." Her voice was happy and animated as she moved into the living room to get some privacy, leaving Zach and Kane behind.

Zach heaved a heavy sigh. "If that's her friend, I imagine she'll be leaving soon."

"Yeah."

"Probably just as well." Kane knew his father was upset when Faith broke their engagement. He was too. But hearing his father's matter-of-fact statement bothered him. As if Zach had completely written Faith off.

Kane wasn't hungry anymore and sat back from the table. "At any rate she's making her own plans to leave. Soon, neither you nor I need to worry about her."

He should have felt relieved about the idea, but for some reason, it still bothered him.

And he didn't want to analyze why.

CHAPTER 10

"*S*orry about not calling sooner," Stacy was saying. "I took a quick holiday, and I didn't feel like answering my phone."

Faith choked down an angry reply to that. Stacy had promised to stay in touch with her, and the fact that she didn't see a problem with her actions was, well, a problem. But Faith needed Stacy right now. She needed her connections in Calgary.

"Okay, well, tell me you have good news," Faith said instead.

"Sort of," Stacy said. "I couldn't get you a full-time position where I work, but a friend of mine said she could get you a server position where she works. It's a pretty high-end restaurant, but it's only part-time. For now."

"How part-time?" Faith asked.

"Three days a week," Stacy said. "But the tips are phenomenal."

Faith rubbed her fingers across her forehead, mentally calculating. Working three days a week as a server would barely cover her expenses. Which meant there was no way she would be able to save up enough to pay her grandfather back. She needed another plan. But what?

Stacy had been her last-ditch effort. Faith had exhausted all her other contacts outside of Rockyview, and she needed to make money right away.

Oh, how the mighty fall. Once she was on track to becoming a lawyer, now she would be working as a waitress.

"So, when would I start?" Faith asked, bowing to the inevitable.

"Not until the fourth."

That was ten days away. Could she stay at the ranch that long?

"So, when can I move in?" she asked Stacy.

"My roommate is leaving in a couple of days. You can come any time after that."

If she did that it would give her some time to settle in, but it would be at least three weeks before she got her first paycheck. Three weeks in the city with no income, which was going to be rough.

"Um, okay," Faith said. "I won't be able to chip in on rent until after my first paycheck, though. Hope that's all right."

"You don't have any money?" Stacy's angry surprise only underlined her own shame. "I was counting on your rent upfront, you know."

"I'm sorry," Faith said, though she really wasn't. "I spent everything I had just trying to get to Calgary."

"Okay, whatever." Stacy said. "Call me when you can move in." And she hung up.

Faith stared down at her phone, then slipped it back in her pocket. Stacy was a piece of work. Faith knew living with her would be a challenge, but what choice did she have?

She looked around the Tye living room, remembering Sunday afternoons there. Grace would be doing a crossword or reading. Zach napping. Elliot and Lucas would be playing some game. She and Kane would be cuddling on the couch, reading while Tricia paged through some gossip magazine.

Now the murmuring conversation from the kitchen sliced through her memories. Zach and Kane were probably deciding what needed to be done before the buyer came. She fought down a surprising and unwelcome bout of sorrow. It shouldn't matter to her if they sold the ranch.

But if they did, where would she envision Kane in her mind when she thought of him? This ranch was where he belonged.

You could always stop thinking about him.

But she'd tried that, hadn't she? If she hadn't stopped thinking about Kane Tye in two years, when would it happen?

At the front of the house, a door slammed, and a male voice boomed out, "Honey, I'm home!"

Curious, she walked into the kitchen just as a large bearded man burst in from the porch. His reddish hair was pulled into a messy ponytail under a battered cowboy hat. He wore a heavy plaid coat over a stained shirt tucked into worn blue jeans.

"So, you finally decided to show up," Zach said, leaning back in his chair.

The man shrugged off his coat and tossed it onto the floor behind him. The cowboy hat followed. "Better late than never," he said.

Faith had no idea who this guy was.

"It's about time," Kane said dryly, getting up and grabbing an extra plate from the cupboard. "But now that you're here you may as well join us for supper."

"So, who's the blonde babe scoping us out?" the guy asked, his gray eyes flicking over to Faith as he settled himself at the table.

Kane glanced over his shoulder at her.

"The woman you're talking about is named Faith Howard," Kane said, sounding a little touchy. "Faith, this is Joe. Dad's hired hand. When he remembers, that is."

Joe pushed his chair back with a screech and pulled out the empty one beside him. "Please, madame, sit down," he said with a flourish.

Faith smiled in spite of herself and shook her head. "I should go check on the children," she said. "Make sure they didn't wake up through all this."

Joe frowned, pulling his bushy eyebrows together. "Children?"

"You shouldn't stay away so long," Zach said, sounding touchy. "Things happen while you're gone."

Joe's puzzlement grew. "I'll say."

"How did your phone call with Stacy go?" Kane asked Faith, ignoring Joe's bewilderment.

"It was...fine." She was hesitant to talk about her plans, especially in front of a stranger.

"So, you'll be leaving soon?" he asked, his eyes boring into her.

"Leave the poor girl alone," Zach said.

"Joe, help yourself," Kane said curtly, standing up. "There's plenty. I'm going out to check on the cows."

"Any of them calving yet?" Joe asked.

"Come see for yourself when you're done," Kane said, brushing past Faith without even a glance in her direction.

Was he mad she hadn't said anything about the call with Stacy, or was it something else?

Faith made her way to Elliot's room, feeling more confused than ever. Thankfully, the kids were still sleeping peacefully. She fussed with the blankets, pulling them up around their shoulders. She let her hands rest on their heads a moment as if giving them a silent blessing, wondering what would happen to them when she was gone.

She wished she could simply dismiss her concerns. Wished she just walk away.

Joe was gone to see the cows, but Zach was still in the kitchen looking at his phone. "Have you heard anything from Tricia?" she asked hopefully.

"No," Zach said sadly, tucking it away in his pocket. "But I talked to my friend at the police station. He's putting out a low-key bulletin and checking some of his sources."

"Oh, Zach." She sat down beside him. "I'm so sorry. You must be worried sick about her."

"I am." Zach pinched the bridge of his nose with his thumb and forefinger. "I sometimes can't help but wonder where me and Grace went wrong. We gave these kids our best."

"I have a feeling that all the things you've done for your kids will return to you one way or the other," Faith said. "It just might take time."

Zach gave her a careful smile. "We don't always do the right thing for our children, but I believe we did our best. I sure know Grace did." He rested his forearms on the table, leaning forward. His eyes held hers, as if looking deep into her soul. "I think your grandfather did the best he could with you after your mother left. I know he struggled a lot with the decisions she made—"

"She made one mistake," Faith interrupted. "She was only human."

"Yes, she was only human." Zach nodded, looking like he wanted to say more.

"But…" Faith stared at him, the plate in her hands forgotten.

Zach slowly shook his head as if he wasn't sure he should speak.

"Please, tell me," Faith prompted.

"It's not really my story to tell. Your grandfather should."

Faith released a harsh laugh. "That's where things fall apart. When I visited him in the hospital, he sent me away and told me not to come back."

Zach looked at her, shocked. "I knew Mick was harboring some bitterness," he finally said. "But I didn't know it had gotten this bad."

"Yeah," Faith said. "It's bad."

Zach looked pensive, fiddling with the fringe of the place mat Faith had put on the table.

"Your grandfather is a stubborn and proud man," he said after a long pause. "And I know he had high expectations for you, and that he pushed you hard. I know he pinned a lot on your shoulders. More than you think he should have. He may have overcompensated for your mother's faults, but he did have your best interests at heart. He knew he wasn't a healthy man, and I think he wanted to make sure that you could take care of yourself when he wasn't around. He didn't want you to end up like—"

"Like my mother?" Faith said with a resigned sigh, finishing his sentence. "Maybe she wasn't educated, but she loved me."

"She did," Zach agreed. "The best she could. But I know from experience, believe me, that a parent's best is sometimes not good enough. It just isn't."

"What are you talking about?" Faith asked, a coldness seeping into her chest.

"Did she ever tell you why she moved back to Rockyview?"

"No. Just that we were going. And we were only here six months before she left again. Why?"

For a long moment, Zach said nothing, biting his lip.

"You know something. Just tell me," Faith pressed.

Another sigh, and then he leaned forward, holding her gaze. "You said your mother managed to take good care of you, and I'm sure she did, but the only reason she was able to do it was because your grandfather sent her money every month."

Faith drew back, frowning. "My mother never said anything about that."

"Probably too proud. A trait she and Mick share, sorry to say," Zach said with a faint smile. "And he never told me outright. It was something that slipped out one time when we were having coffee together."

Faith couldn't seem to wrap her head around that fact. "Are you sure?"

"I don't think that's something a father would want to admit to very quickly," Zach said, giving her a gentle smile. "And knowing how proud your grandfather is, yes, I'm quite sure. After you were born, her finances were in shambles. It was thanks to him that she was able to even get by. I know it's wrong to speak ill of the dead, and I know you have your own opinion of your mother, but I just wanted to give you a little more information to use when you think about her and when you think about your grandfather."

Faith felt as if the ground beneath her feet had shifted. All this was new to her, and for a moment she wanted to refute it. But short recollections returned as Zach spoke, as his words shifted her perceptions. She remembered vague moments: her mother on the phone with someone, asking where the money was. Her mother leaving to get groceries, she would say, but not coming back for a few hours. Once she needed new shoes, but her mother told her they couldn't afford it.

Then they moved in with Faith's grandfather, and suddenly Faith got new clothes and new shoes, and her mother stayed home more often, at least the first couple of months.

"I know this is a lot to take in," Zach said. "But I think you need to know one more thing." He took a deep breath, holding her gaze, as if trying to gauge her reaction. "When Kane came into our home, his biological mother fought tooth and nail to get him back even while her own life was falling apart. She wanted him to be happy, but she couldn't stand the fact that someone else could do that for him. Your grandfather knew all this. When your mother was around, she and Kane's mother would go out drinking together. He knew how bad the partying got. Because of Mick's intervention, Kane was taken away from her and put in our home. Kane knew that, and I believe he felt like he owed your grandfather a favor. He saw your grandfather as someone who had rescued him from his haphazard life with his mother."

Tears prickled Faith's eyes as what Zach told her melded with her memories. Her mother? Drinking? Partying?

It was as if a window was opened in her mind and light from another angle shone on her preconceived and long-held beliefs.

Had her grandfather been afraid she would end up like her mother? Was that why he pushed her so hard?

And why hadn't Kane told her about his connection to her

grandfather? But would it have made a difference in the outcome? Would she have been able to hear it back then?

"I know this is a lot to take in," Zach continued, his voice holding an edge of sorrow. "And I'm sorry if I dumped all this on you, but I couldn't keep it to myself anymore. I know you feel betrayed by your grandfather and that you didn't think Kane supported you, but maybe now you've heard a bit more behind what they were doing and why."

"I guess there's always more to the story," she said, her voice quiet.

"Every story has two sides, cliché as that might sound."

She wrapped her arms around her midsection, her brain swirling in circles. "It's a lot to process," she admitted. "But thank you for telling me."

"You're welcome," Zach said. "Perhaps God brought you to us again for this very conversation. And for Cash and Hope, of course."

And that reminded Faith about the phone call with Stacy. "Zach," she said, dreading what she was going to say, "my friend in Calgary has a job and a place lined up for me."

"I see," he said. "Well, we knew this was coming."

"It's what I need to do." Now more than ever. She had to prove to her grandfather that she was not her mother, running home for financial support because of the bad choices she'd made. She was going to pay back what he'd sunk into her all those years.

"So, when do you leave?" Zach asked.

"Day after tomorrow," Faith said. "But I feel terrible leaving you in the position of having to find someone else for the kids so soon."

"You've helped us more than you can imagine," Zach said. "We've already asked too much of you."

"No. Not too much. I was glad to help out."

"You always were a generous person," Zach said, his gentle smile creating both warmth and a tiny internal quake of sorrow.

Right now she didn't feel generous at all. She felt selfish and small, torn between needing to leave to take care of herself and wanting to be with Kane.

Especially after hearing what Zach had to say about his reasons for him taking her grandfather's side.

He's not your problem.

Trouble was, she didn't see him as a problem. Right now, despite everything she knew she should do, she saw him as a taste of sanctuary.

She shook the thought off. She'd had her chance with Kane and she'd blown it. She had no right to expect anything from him.

"I should clean up," she said, pushing her chair away from the table.

Zach got up as well and headed into the living room.

Faith watched him go, then turned back to the dishes, Zach's words echoing through her mind, melding with her own memories of her mother and her grandfather.

Had he really been protecting her? And what about what he had done for Kane? Did that change her perception of him?

Faith wished she could dismiss it all.

And, once again, she wished she could go back. Change what had happened.

Done is done, she told herself with a shake of her head as she rinsed and piled dishes in the dishwasher. She had to look ahead. Not behind. Focus on the future.

But did the future have to seem so bleak?

CHAPTER 11

*K*ane shoved his hands in his pockets as he strode across the yard toward the cows. The sun was sinking toward the horizon, but it was still light enough to see.

Why hadn't Faith wanted to tell him what her friend had said on the phone?

Because she's leaving.

Kane clambered over the fence and slowed his steps as he walked toward the gathered cows. Many of them were lying down, a few standing up, watching him with their large dark eyes.

One of the cows was off on her own, tail swishing. She tossed her head when he came near.

"You having a calf soon?" Kane asked, keeping his voice low. She lay down, groaning as she did. Guess so.

He should get her inside where they could watch her more closely. He went into the barn and dragged a straw bale into an empty pen. He yanked on one of the strings with a jerk and half the bale burst open. Slipping the other strings off, he spread the straw around. The light work and the sound of the swishing straw eased the tension that had been gripping him all evening.

Faith was just as amazing as she'd always been, and in new

ways he'd never let himself see before. Her music. The way she mothered those kids like she'd been doing it for years.

Don't go down that road. It's madness. She's leaving.

He blamed his lapse on the tears she had shed. Faith wasn't a crier. And seeing sorrow shimmer in her eyes had created a feeling of helpless weakness.

Shaking off the memory, Kane strode out of the barn just in time to see Joe clambering over the fence.

"Thought I'd join you," he said. "See if you needed any help. Zach doesn't seem too impressed with me." He grinned at Kane.

"If you would stick around a little more, he wouldn't get so ticked at you."

Joe shrugged, his shoulders hunched. "Yeah, sorry about that. I didn't think I'd be gone so long. But I ran into some trouble at home. A friend of mine got into a fight, and I had to help him out."

"That fight better not follow you here," Kane said.

"It won't." Joe shook his head. "And I promise I'll stick around."

"Good," Kane said. "Because the cows are getting ready to calve, and we'll need your help to get things ready for the sale." Kane leveled a serious look at him. "I know the ranch is getting sold, but we still need to be able to depend on you."

"Got it. I'll stay until it's all done."

"Help me move that cow into the barn," Kane directed. "Looks like she's our first mamma."

Joe moved through the herd, gently and without spooking them. He got the cow, who was already in labor, into the barn with ease. And that was exactly why Zach had hired him. The guy was great with animals. He had a quiet, but steady air and didn't get angry or flustered.

But what would he do once the ranch was sold? Would anyone else put up with his erratic behavior? Any other employer would have fired him by now.

Not your problem.

As Kane closed the door on the stall, he rested his hands on the top rail, watching as the cow circled the pen, then lay down with another groan.

"So, this Faith in the house," Joe said. "She's the one you used to be engaged to?"

"That would be her," Kane said, trying to keep his voice even. Joe had moved into the community six months after Faith and Elliot had left. No doubt he'd heard about it all via the Rockyview rumor mill. Kane certainly hadn't told him.

"What's she doing back? You two together again?"

"Not a chance." The words came out harsher than Kane intended.

"So, the kids aren't yours then?"

"No," Kane blurted. "They're my sister Tricia's. Faith was just nice enough to stick around and help us with them."

"Where's Tricia?"

"She's—on a holiday," Kane said. He didn't know Joe well enough to trust him with the details of the family drama. Kane pushed away from the gate, and he and Joe did a final walk-through of the cows to see if any more were calving yet, but they saw no signs.

"So, what time do you want me tomorrow?" Joe asked, heading to his little cabin on the back meadow. His battered pickup was parked beside it, and the light was on inside. He must have stopped in before coming to the house.

"Six would be good," Kane said.

"Okay. I'll see you then. Should I come to the house?"

"Yeah. I'll make breakfast. Nothing fancy, but thanks to Faith we got groceries. So, if you're lucky, I'll fry you an egg."

"I'll take anything I don't have to make myself." Joe tugged on the brim of his hat, a self-conscious gesture. "I won't buzz off again. I promise you."

Kane didn't trust Joe's promises, but he didn't have the time or energy to reprimand him or, conversely, to find a new hired hand to replace him. Not when everything was headed to the auction mart anyway. "Please don't promise. Just do." And with that, he returned to the house.

The kitchen was all cleaned up. The food put away. Faith nowhere to be seen. He heard a rustling sound, then followed it to his father's office, just off the living room.

Zach sat at his desk, phone to his ear. He put it down as Kane entered the room.

"I've called everyone I can think of about Tricia," he said, worry in his eyes. "I think tomorrow I should file a missing person's report."

Kane nodded. He didn't know what to say. Things weren't looking good.

Please, Lord. Let Tricia be okay. Watch over her wherever she is.

His prayer was automatic. A reaching out for strength when he and his father had none left.

"Did Faith go to bed for the night?" Kane asked.

"Yeah. Said she was tired. You want some tea?"

"Sure." Kane waited while his father walked past him and followed him into the kitchen. "We got a cow that might be calving tonight or tomorrow morning. I'll get up and check later."

"And so, it starts," Zach said, pouring out two glasses of tea and handing one of them to Kane. "At least this will be the last time I do all this."

Regret clawed at Kane at the melancholy note in his father's voice.

Zach drew in a deep breath and then glanced over at Kane. "You're a good son, you know," he said.

"I don't feel like I am," Kane said, looking away from his father. "I've disappointed you more than once."

"You've never disappointed me," Zach said, his voice quiet.

"I walked away from you. From this ranch."

"Understandable. Your heart was broken. You needed to leave to get some perspective."

But his father's easy forgiveness only served to pile on more guilt. "I was selfish when I left," Kane said. "I was only thinking of what I needed to get away from. I wasn't thinking about you. You had just lost Mom—" Kane's voice broke on that last word and he clenched his fists, struggling to keep his emotions in check.

His father laid his hand on Kane's arm. "I had a community to help me through."

"But you didn't have your kids beside you. Tricia left. Elliot took off. And so did I. At least Lucas had a good reason."

"I wish you'd stop making it sound like you all abandoned me," Zach said. "Kids grow up. That's what they do. And I fully understood why you didn't want to be here. This isn't all on you. I lost a lot of interest in the ranch after Grace died. It will be good to be done with it. To move on."

Kane's heart sank at the finality of his father's words.

"Moving on is good," Kane said, but it didn't feel good.

"Speaking of that," Zach said, "How are you doing with Faith here?"

"It's fine." Kane brushed off the question.

His dad raised a skeptical eyebrow. Zach was the one person who knew how hard Kane had taken his breakup with Faith. Kane had tried to stay at the ranch after it happened, and it was the worst month of his life. Then he ran off to the oil rigs where he could forget, distracted by the backbreaking work. But at least the money was good. In fact, he had lived on the cheap the last two years and had a decent amount stashed away.

But for what?

It wasn't enough to buy his father out. Kane knew exactly what the ranch was worth. He and Zach had discussed the value when Kane and Elliot were considering taking it over together. Of course, their father had been willing to give them a deal, slowly working them into the ranch without them paying as much as anyone buying it outright. But Kane had blown that chance when he'd left. Plus, there was no Elliot to go in with him or work beside him. And Kane knew how much his father would need to buy a house in town. He needed to be able to live off the proceeds of the sale. Kane didn't have enough money to compete with real buyers.

"You don't seem fine," Zach pressed.

"Yeah, well, there's a lot to do, plus the Tricia thing. You don't seem fine either."

"Good point," Zach said. "You should know that Faith's friend has a job lined up for her in Calgary. She's leaving the day after tomorrow."

"That's good then." Kane forced a smile. He'd known this was coming.

"But," Zach went on, "she's finding it hard to leave the kids behind. She seemed very torn about heading to Calgary."

"Really?" Kane asked, trying to keep the hope out of his voice.

"Kane," Zach said, staring at him.

"What?"

"Don't forget the state you were in last time she left."

"I haven't forgotten," Kane said, unclenching his jaw so he could toss back the rest of his tea. "I should get to bed. I'll try not to wake you when I get up to check on that cow."

His father got up as well, smiling at him. "You always were a good cowman," he said. "It's in your blood. Like father, like son."

"Thanks, Dad," was all he could manage as Zach limped toward his bedroom.

Kane brought his glass to the sink, rinsed it, and set it aside, looking out the window to the barn. How often had he seen his father stand by the window, doing exactly what he was doing? Wondering about the animals outside. Hoping they would be okay.

Like father, like son.

Kane shook his head as if to dislodge the direction of his thoughts. And they went straight to Faith, who was leaving.

Kane walked toward his bedroom, but his steps slowed as he passed the door to Elliot's room.

He paused a moment, listening.

Silence.

He placed his hand on the door, as if to connect to the woman inside, tatters of old dreams tangling his brain. And he prayed a silent prayer.

Help me, Lord. Help me do what is right for both of us.

CHAPTER 12

She wouldn't catch her on time.

Hope was just out of her reach, running away, crying as she headed down the driveway. Faith pushed herself harder, tried to run faster. A car was coming. It was going to hit Hope. She had to catch her.But the car came closer, and Hope kept running. The car sped up, and Faith watched in horror as—

She jolted awake, heart pounding and palms sweating.Slowly, reality set in as Faith looked around the bedroom. She was still in bed, and the morning sun streamed through the window.Hope lay curled up on her side, sleeping soundly next to Cash on the other half of the bed. Sort of. Her little bare feet were kicking Faith in the ribs.

*Just a dream. It was just a dream.*Faith sucked in a slow breath, giving herself a moment for her heart rate to slow.

Maybe it had only been a dream, but the panic and desperation she'd felt had been so real they threatened to overwhelm her, even now. Swallowing again and again, Faith clenched her fists and pushed it down. She knew where that terror came from, and she'd tried to leave it behind, but here it still was, haunting her.

Hope shifted her little feet, moaning as she curled herself up tighter, pulling her hands over her face. Cash didn't move at all, but Faith could see his little chest rising and falling gently.

They would probably sleep a bit longer, so Faith slipped into the ensuite of the bedroom and had a quick shower. As she stood under the warm water, she wished she could wash away the harsh pain and regret that had dogged her for the past year.

She made quick work of her hair, pulling it back into a ponytail. She then dug up a clean pair of blue jeans and T-shirt and quickly put them on, forcing herself to focus on the here and now.

The kids needed her. She could comfort them, even if she couldn't comfort herself.

She sat down beside them, catching Hope's soft hand in hers and stroking her chubby knuckles.

Kane was so good with them. He would make a great father someday. Of course, she had always known that, but she'd expected the kids to be hers, not someone else's.

Kane with someone else.

When she thought of that, it invoked the same feeling as the nightmare she'd just had—panic, desperation, impending doom. It wasn't the first time she'd imagined that scenario or felt that way about it. In fact, she'd fully expected Kane to be with someone else by now.

But he wasn't, and she didn't get the impression he had much time for a girlfriend while he was working the oil patch.

Good.

No. Kane wasn't for her.

Was something happening between them? A renewal of old feelings? But it couldn't. She'd messed up too badly to redeem herself. She could never tell Kane about Keith and what he'd done to her.

Zach had basically said last night it was best for her to leave. And he was right.

There was movement on the bed, and she smiled as Cash sat

up, stretching his hands over his head. He rubbed his eyes, then turned to her and gave her a quick smile.

"I hungwee," he said.

Hope rolled over, opening her eyes, then jerked upright. Her head swiveled, her eyes flicking back and forth, her arms wrapped around herself in a defensive posture. Exactly like Faith had done when she'd woken up from her bad dream.

"It's okay, sweetie," she said, pulling the little girl into her arms. "You're at the ranch. You're safe here."

Hope was rigid in her arms, but as Faith stroked her head, rocking her, she slowly relaxed against her.

Would some random nanny do this? Would she have the patience and understanding Hope and Cash needed so much right now?

Hope pulled back and gave Faith a lopsided smile. "I yike you," she said.

Then, to Faith's surprise, the little girl sat up and plopped a damp kiss on her cheek.

"Well, I yike you too," she said, giving Hope a quick hug then helping her off the bed.

"Now, why don't we get dressed, and then we'll get some breakfast."

A few minutes later, Faith had them in some of their new clothes with their hair brushed. "You two look great," she said.

Hope smoothed her hands over the flowered top she wore. "I so pretty."

"Yes, you are."

Faith caught a glimpse of Tricia in the little girl's smile, the tilt of her chin.

Where, oh where, was their mother?

"Okay, let's go get some breakfast," she said.

They slipped their hands into hers, and together they walked down the hall.

Faith entered the kitchen, and her heart flew into her throat as soon as she saw Kane.

Like a silly schoolgirl. What is wrong with me?

He sat at the table, laptop open, with a pad of paper and a pencil beside him. She had thought he might be working outside already. He had so much to get done on the ranch. But there he was, and he looked up with a gentle smile that had her heart fluttering even more.

"How'd you sleep?" he asked, leaning back in his chair, his eyes holding hers.

"Not bad," she said, trying not to think of the nightmare that drove her awake. And the hard memories that kept her tossing and turning with regret.

Kane got up, and for another heart-stopping moment she thought he would pull her close. Kiss her. Create even more confusion in her very scattered life.

Instead he bent down on one knee in front of the kids, his hand resting lightly on Hope's head. "How are you, little girl? Did you have a good sleep?"

Hope nodded, then to Faith's surprise, she let go of her hand and grabbed his. "Unker Kane," she announced, sounding pretty pleased with herself.

Kane gently tucked a curl of hair behind her ear with his other hand. Faith knew she shouldn't be jealous of the bright smile he gave the little girl, but she was. "You're right. You're a smart munchkin."

"I smart munchkin too," Cash put in.

"Of course you are," Kane said reaching out for him as well. He stood then, towering over them all. His eyes caught and held hers, and for a moment it was as if time stood still. "Good morning to you," he said quietly, gently touching her shoulder.

Not fair. So not fair. She wasn't in any mental space to resist him now.

95

With each glance, each touch, she felt herself going back to the place she thought she'd run from for the last time.

Guilt nudged her with an accusing elbow. *You're not the same person.*

"What do you want?" she asked, the question slipping out of her, then regretting the edge in her voice, and yet, needing to hold her ground.

But he didn't respond with anger like he would have two years ago. Instead, he bit his lip, holding her gaze, his sky-blue eyes steady on hers.

"I don't know." His honest answer was almost more devastating than anything else he could have said.

Because she felt the same.

"Hungwy. I—I—I'se hungwey." Cash's quiet stutter brushed the connection aside, and Faith blinked, as if coming back to the present.

Her dream surged back, and with it came the jagged reminder of what she had become.

She pulled herself from the edge of the cliff she had been so ready to jump off.

"Okay, Cash. Let's make some pancakes."

"I wike pancakes," Hope said, reaching out and tugging on Kane's hand. "You wike pancakes, Unker Kane?"

"Yes, I do," he said, turning toward the fridge. "And you're in luck. I actually know how to make them."

"Don't you need to go out and check the cows?" Faith asked.

"You trying to get rid of me?" Kane turned, raising an eyebrow at her.

"No. No." She blushed as she protested. "I just thought—you said there was a lot to do on the ranch."

"There is. But I was out until two this morning with a cow. Joe is out there now taking the next shift. I'll be heading back out as soon as I've had a second breakfast."

"Then at least let me make the pancakes," Faith said, stepping up to the refrigerator next to him. "You were up half the night."

He held her gaze another long moment, then nodded. He went back to the table and the kids followed him.

"What to see some pictures?" he asked, settling them on either side of him.

While Faith mixed pancake batter, she found herself far too aware of the man behind her, clicking keys and murmuring to the children, his voice low.

"Horse. Horse," Hope shouted, obviously more comfortable with him now.

"Yes, that's a horse. Maybe I can give you a ride on one sometime," Kane said.

"Horse. Ride horse," Hope called out again, her excitement catching.

"I wike horse," Cash put in.

Faith shot a quick look over her shoulder. Kane now had both kids on his lap as they looked at pictures. He looked so natural with them, it hooked her heart.

With a shake of her head to dislodge the fantasy, she shifted her attention back to her work. She slipped the final pancakes onto a plate and carried them to the table. She quickly got plates and utensils, syrup and butter, all the while feeling Kane's gaze graze over her from time to time like a palpable touch.

Finally, everything was ready. Kane put away his laptop, and they all sat down for breakfast. Faith sat beside Hope and put a pancake on her plate.

"We should pray," Kane said quietly.

Faith swallowed, feeling suddenly foolish. After sharing supper with them last night, she should know this. It was just that she had gotten out of the habit of talking to God.

But she took Hope's hand and bowed her head.

"Thank you, Lord, for today," Kane's voice rumbled. "For food and the hands that prepared it. Thank you for family and friends. Please be with Tricia." He paused there a moment as if adding his own silent prayer for his sister. "Could you bring her back here safely? Amen."

Faith kept her head down a few seconds more as she let the prayer settle into her. Kane hadn't always been a devoted Christian. In fact, she remembered how he would behave at a youth group meetings. He would lob angry questions at the leader and make everyone uncomfortable. But slowly, as he spent more time with the Tye family, he grew more receptive at church and at meetings. Faith suspected it had much to do with the love he'd experienced at Grace and Zach's home.

How strange that their lives had flipped, Faith pondered, as she spread butter on Hope's pancake then drizzled syrup over it. Once, she had been the solid and faithful Christian, and Kane had been the rebel. Now, she was the one who couldn't face the Lord or believe He had a place for her. Not after the choices she'd made.

Faith blinked back unexpected tears, fighting down feelings of regret warped with shame.

"You okay?" Kane asked, his voice quiet.

"Just feeling tired, that's all," she replied, keeping her attention on Hope, who was struggling to fork a piece of pancake. "Here, honey, let me help you," she said, thankful for the distraction.

But the entire time she helped Hope, she was far too aware of Kane sitting on the other side of the table, watching her.

Then his phone buzzed, and he pulled it out of his pocket. "Sorry. That's Joe. I've gotta go."

Faith glanced up at him.

"See you later?" he asked.

"Sure." She nodded as he left, relief and grief washing over her as he shut the back door. How did he recognize so many confusing emotions in her? Emotions she didn't have the strength or time to process.

Once the children were done with breakfast, Faith set out the container of toys Zach had found in the back of a closet last night. Thankfully, they seemed to be able to entertain themselves, which gave Faith a chance to make her bed and catch up on some laundry.

She took the children outside so she could hang the clothes on the line, smiling as they discovered the old play center that still took up one corner of the lawn. They seemed content to lie on their stomachs on the swings, pushing with their feet. She couldn't get over how good they were. How easy to have around. In spite of Tricia's seeming irresponsibility, she must have done something right with them.

Just as Faith was finished pegging up the last towel, the phone rang inside the house. Shooting a quick look over at the kids, who were still playing, she hurried inside to grab the handset. "Hello," she said, breathless as she rushed outside again.

The kids hadn't moved, thank goodness.

"Is this the Tye place?" a woman asked. "I'm trying to reach Zach." Her tone was abrupt. As if she didn't have time for anyone else.

"Sorry, he's out. Can I take a message?"

This was followed by a dramatic sigh. "I guess. This is Irma Tunney. He called me last night. Tell him I can take that nanny job. I can start tomorrow at noon, but I'll need to have the kids at my apartment here in town. And I can't pick them up. He'll have to bring them here. I have my puppies and flowers to tend to."

Nanny job. The words reverberated through Faith's mind like a clanging bell. So, Zach had already found someone to take over for her. It certainly hadn't taken him long.

The kids were now giggling, chasing each other around the swing set, wrestling when they caught one another.

"Excuse me, did you say apartment?" Faith asked. She didn't remember an Irma Tunney from her days living in Rockyview. Maybe she'd moved to town since then.

"Yes. I'm a widow," Irma explained, sounding annoyed. "I live in a small apartment in town with my three little dogs and my collection of rare orchids. Zach already knows that."

Faith bit her lip, struggling with her own plans and the reality of what would happen to the children if she left. She knew she shouldn't judge but, based on this woman's tone, Faith wasn't so sure she liked Irma Tunney.

"Okay. I'll pass the message on," she said as she walked toward the children.

"Oh, and tell him I'll need a little more than he was offering. I didn't realize the children were so young until Melinda Bogal told me. They'll be a handful, I'm guessing."

"They're good children," Faith protested, tucking the phone between her chin and shoulder as she helped Hope onto a swing. "They're not much work."

This was greeted by a moment of silence, then, "Is this Mick Howard's girl I'm talking to?" It sounded like an accusation.

"Yes. This is Faith Howard."

"I see."

Those two words brought Faith's hackles up. Hard. Who did this woman think she was? But Faith held her tongue. "I'll pass the message on to Zach," was all she said.

"And make sure you tell him about the money."

"Yep. Got it." Faith made a face at the handset and hung up.

Cash and Hope were laughing and giggling, the sun glinting off their hair. It was a beautiful day, and Faith was glad the children could play outside instead of being trapped in a tiny apartment with crabby Irma and her three dogs amidst a jungle of rare orchids.

Of course, Hope and Cash would behave for that woman, and she would probably take care of them. But Faith wanted them to be more than be cared for. She wanted them to be happy. To be loved.

My, how quickly and easily they'd worked their way into her heart. How could Tricia have left them like this? Faith wasn't even their mother, had known them only a few days, and she couldn't bear the thought of leaving them.

Neither Zach nor Kane came in for lunch. She fed the kids and waited an hour, but still nothing. The men would be hungry.

She packed up a lunch and put it in her backpack, throwing in a few cold bottles of water as well.

"Shall we go find Grandpa and Uncle Kane?" she said to the kids.

They nodded, not quite sure what she was getting at. But they took her hands, and together they walked out of the house. It was slow going. The kids jumped and played on the way. Faith wasn't sure exactly where Kane and Zach were working, but at least it was an adventurous outing for the kids. And it would tire them out, so putting them down for an afternoon nap would be easier.

As they walked along the fence line toward the corrals, Faith heard voices and the pounding of hammers. She followed the sounds to the large hip roof barn.

Joe, Zach, and Kane were rebuilding the corrals, nailing boards to posts outside the barn.

Kane straightened as she came closer, dropping his hammer in the tool belt hanging low on his hips.

"Is everything okay?" he asked, worry in his voice. "Did Tricia call?"

"No, nothing like that. I just thought you guys might be hungry, so I brought lunch."

Joe immediately dropped his hammer at that. "You're an angel. I'm starving."

Zach looked over as well, a curious expression on his face. "Why don't we go sit in the barn where it's cooler," was all he said.

Kane walked over and opened the gate for her.

"Hi, Unker Kane, we have food." Cash pulled free of Faith's hand and ran toward his uncle.

Kane grabbed the boy, threw him up in the air to peals of laughter, then caught him easily and slung him over his shoulder.

"Thanks for bringing me this sack of potatoes, Faith," he said. "I think I'll go feed it to the cows."

"Nooo," Cash cried, wiggling and giggling. "I's not tatoes."

"What?" Kane said, swinging around with Cash still slung over his shoulder. "Did someone say something? I couldn't hear you. This sack of potatoes is being too noisy."

"I's. Not. Tatoes," Cash insisted. "I's a boy."

"What? Oh, there you are, Cash," Kane said, setting him down. "But now what am I going to feed the cows?"

"Pancakes," Cash said, grinning. "They wike pancakes."

Joe grabbed the handle of the sliding door into the barn and pushed it open, the rollers screeching a protest.

It was darker and cooler inside. Joe picked up a couple of straw bales and set them on the floor with a thump. "We even have chairs," he said.

"We already ate," Faith said. "I should get the kids back to the house."

"They seem fine," Zach said.

"Yeah, stay a bit," Kane said, smiling at her.

Faith hesitated, but then Hope ran over to her grandfather, who was already easing himself down on a straw bale, and clambered onto his lap. And Cash was climbing onto the bale to sit next to his new favorite person, Unker Kane. So Faith set down her backpack and unzipped it, handing out sandwiches and water bottles.

"This is awesome," Joe mumbled around a bite of sandwich. "All Zach knows how to make is grilled cheese."

"What's wrong with that?" Zach protested.

"Too much of a good thing isn't always a good thing," Joe said sagely, taking another big bite, then a swig of water.

"Have a seat," Kane said to Faith, gesturing at the empty bale next to him.

Faith sat down and turned to Zach. "I have a phone message for you. Irma Tunney called. She said she could start tomorrow."

Faith didn't want to say too much in front of the kids. If she was going to turn them over to Irma, she wanted a chance to explain it to them first.

"Tomorrow? The children?" Kane sounded puzzled. Had Zach not spoken to him about this?

"We need a nanny," Zach said matter-of-factly. He wiped his mouth with a napkin, then lifted his shoulder in a careful shrug. "Faith is leaving, and Tricia's not back yet." His voice broke on those last few words, and once again Faith felt as if she was abandoning them in their time of need.

Kane didn't say anything to that, nor, thankfully, did he look at Faith.

"So when did she say she could start?" Zach asked.

"She said you could bring the kids to her apartment tomorrow."

Zach nodded his head slowly. "I'm glad to hear that."

"But she said she'd have to do it at her apartment in town," Faith added.

"Apartment?" Kane blurted out. He turned to his father. "If she's going to be a nanny shouldn't she come here?"

"I thought that's what she said," Zach said, looking puzzled.

"Sorry," Faith said, glancing over at the kids to see if they understood anything they were talking about. "And she wants more money than you offered. She wanted to make very sure I mentioned that part."

"That sounds like Irma Tunney," Joe said, rolling his eyes.

"You know her?" Zach asked.

Joe nodded slowly as if trying to figure out what to tell them. "Everyone knows about Irma Tunney. She's a little bit crazy and has three yappy dogs she treats like her children. She dresses them up in little outfits for the different seasons."

"Oh boy," Faith said, glancing at Hope and Cash.

"That's…worrisome," Kane said, leaning back against a barn post and taking another bite of his sandwich, one arm curled gently around Cash. Kane's eyes slowly drifted to Faith. He was trying to act casual, but she could tell he was tense.

Hope eased herself off Zach's lap and headed towards the ladder leading to the loft. Cash was right behind her.

"Up?" she asked, pointing at the ladder. "Go up?"

"No, honey. You better stay down here," Kane said, getting up and bringing them both back to the straw-bale picnic.

"I should take them back to the house," Faith said, getting up. "They need a nap."

"Horse. A horse." Hope pointed out the door and then, before anyone could stop her, scooted out the door.

Kane jumped up and ran after her.

Faith grabbed Cash and followed Kane out the door, Zach and Joe right behind her.

Kane had managed to hook his arm around Hope's waist, catching her before she climbed up the corral fence where the horses were standing.

"Ride horse," she said pointing to them. "I ride horse."

"No, honey," Faith said as she came up beside Kane. "Uncle Kane and Grandpa are too busy. And it's nap time."

Hope twisted away from Faith, reaching toward the horses. "Ride horse," she called out.

"It's fine," Kane said. "I did promise her, after all."

"I'll get a halter," Zach said, walking toward the tack shed.

"I thought we had to finish the corrals today," Joe muttered.

"We will," Kane said. "We'll work tonight until they're done."

Joe mumbled something under his breath, but Kane ignored him.

In a matter of minutes, Zach had caught one of the horses and slipped a halter on him. He led it out of the corral, Joe closing the gate behind him.

"Are you sure you want to put that little thing on that horse?" Joe asked.

"This is Cusco," Kane said. "He's bombproof. I'd trust him with anyone."

Faith smiled at the term, the ultimate compliment for any horse. And she knew firsthand how bombproof Cusco was. Once, she and Kane had been riding and the horses scared up a deer. It had bounded right in front of them on the trail.

Kane was riding another horse, which had jumped back, reared, and almost unseated him.

But Cusco simply stood, watching, almost bemused.

"I wanna ride," Cash called out once he realized what was going on.

"You'll get your turn," Kane said, setting Hope carefully on the horse. "Grab here," he told her, lifting up a hunk of Cusco's mane. "That's your handle."

Hope looked tiny on the horse, but Faith pressed down her concern. Kane knew what he was doing. She believed that. Yet it still felt scary, seeing Hope atop such a large horse.

She was completely unfazed, however, rocking a little as if to get the horse moving.

"Look at her," Zach said, a note of pride in his voice. "She already knows what to do. Just like her mother."

"Tricia was fearless on a horse, that's for sure," Kane said. "Didn't surprise anyone when she was crowned Rodeo Queen."

Kane led the horse around the yard, keeping an eye on Hope, ready to catch her if she fell. Hope's smile almost split her face, she was so happy. Zach had lifted Cash to the top of the rail fence, so he could see. Faith stood back, watching the little tableau.

The kids seemed happy in spite of not having their mother around. It probably helped that they now had four adults around them, spending time with them.

Last night Hope had been crying again, and Faith had slipped between the two children, wrapping her arms around them, holding them close. What would happen when she left? Would someone cuddle them if they woke up in the night?

"Me ride," Cash called out, wriggling out of Zach's protective grasp. Zach caught him before he fell, and Joe reached up to support him as well.

Kane brought the horse back to the fence, lifted a protesting Hope off the horse, and put Cash on. Hope yawned and rubbed her eyes as Zach set her on the fence.

"Just a short ride," Faith called out as Kane led the horse away from them. "They're both tired."

Kane nodded his acknowledgement as he walked away.

Even though his twill shirt was sprinkled with sawdust, his blue jeans dusty and torn, his cowboy hat battered and worn, he exuded a familiar appeal that created a lightness in her heart. A sense of coming home.

She closed her eyes a moment, as if blocking him from her vision would erase the feeling.

It didn't work.

She opened her eyes and saw him leading the horse her way. His eyes found and held hers, and their deep blueness nearly stripped away the fragile defenses she was struggling to maintain. Her breath, once again, caught in her throat as memories of them together became so real she had to put her hand on her chest to hold them in.

Thankfully, Cash was ready to get off the horse, and with a quick farewell, Faith settled Hope on her hip and took Cash's hand.

Back at the house, the twins were asleep in minutes. Faith got up, sliding her hands down her thighs as she glanced out the window. She couldn't see the corrals from here, but she could hear the faint ringing of the hammers through the open window.

Her guitar was propped in the corner and she grabbed it, sitting down on the floor. She played softly at first, watching the twins to make sure it didn't wake them. But they were dead to the world.

She played a few bars of a song, then fooled around with the tune, then segued into something she'd composed herself. Gavin, the leader of the Prairie Wanderers, had caught her before a rehearsal once, playing a song she had written. She'd felt completely self-conscious, but he had encouraged her to keep at it —to let her creativity flow. Keith, the bass player, wasn't quite as encouraging. As an award-winning musician, he'd felt he had the authority to criticize what she was doing.

Not for the first time, Faith wondered why she had let him put her down like that.

Gavin had asked her the same question numerous times.

That was before things had gotten really bad.

Faith's fingers hit a wrong note, and she stopped, gripping the guitar neck. Keith had been a mistake—one of her bad choices. After Elliot had bailed on her, she'd gotten so lonely, and Keith had initially been understanding and supportive of her music and talent. So, in her loneliness and, if she were being honest, rebellion against Kane and her grandfather, she'd hooked up with him. It hadn't taken her long to realize Keith wasn't good for her. He was just one more bad choice in a line of them. But, by that time, she needed desperately to prove she hadn't thrown everything with Kane away for nothing.

No, for less than nothing.

So she'd stuck it out until she couldn't, which was way too long. Then she got a ride out of town, which took an unexpected detour and landed her right back where she'd started. Apparently, you couldn't run from your past. Or hitchhike from it.

You have a plan, she reminded herself as she picked out another tune. A step toward a different life and better choices.

The notes wove through her soul, nourishing a deep and empty part of her. This was who she was. Her identity.

Her heart folded at the thought that she wouldn't have a reason to play her guitar anymore when she moved to Calgary. She had been down that road, and sadly enough, it hadn't yielded the results she had hoped it would. All it had done was place more guilt and a constant heavy regret on her shoulders.

And now, she felt as if leaving was letting these children down.

Faith didn't know why she felt so depressed. This was exactly what she wanted. Zach had found a nanny, which meant she was free to go.

Then why wasn't she more excited about the idea?

Excitement was overrated, she reminded herself. Life just happens, and you need to roll with it. She played a few more songs, then put her guitar away and walked out of the room, leaving the children still sleeping.

Thankfully, the rest of the day slipped by quickly. She did some housework, played with the kids after they woke up, and prepped and put dinner on the stove.

She thought maybe she should text Kane, but thought better of it. Kingdoms might rise and fall, horses might be calling, cows might be calving, but when Grace cooked supper, everyone showed up at the dot of six. She always said she didn't need a bell. You either showed up on time or you missed dinner.

For her, however, suppertime came and went, and they never came. Perhaps the cows had started calving in earnest and the men couldn't get away, but when they did come in, they'd be starving. So she and the kids ate, but she set aside three plates of food, covered them, and put them in the refrigerator.

After dinner, Faith took the children through their usual bedtime routine, singing them a silly song she'd made up while they were in the bath. Already they were used to her, comfortable around her, and now she was going to disrupt all that.

You can't stay here. You're getting too close to Kane. It won't work. It can't work.

He deserves better.

And it was that final thought that set Faith's confusion to rest. She had to leave.

CHAPTER 13

"Okay, thanks very much. We'll be waiting." Zach hung up the phone and sat at the table, his brow furrowed in concern.

"Who was that?" Kane said. "Is it news about Tricia?"

Zack shook his head. "No, that was Floyd, the real estate agent. He wants to bring the buyer by next week sometime instead of on Monday."

It was early Thursday morning, and he and Zach had already had breakfast. Just toast and coffee, but it would be enough. They'd been up late with all the calving last night, but, thankfully, Faith had set aside dinner.

"Sounds like he's seriously interested," Kane said. His father was asking a hefty price for the Tall Timber Ranch. If someone was coming all the way out for that price tag, they were interested. "That's sooner than we thought. So, what is the priority before he comes?"

Zack stroked his chin looking thoughtful. "We could put some new paint on the barn, and the machine shed is a mess. It's where I put all the odds and ends I don't know what to do with."

Kane caught movement out of the corner of his eye and turned to see Faith standing in the doorway.

"You have a buyer already?" she asked.

It wasn't hard to hear the disappointment in her voice. Kane felt the urge rise up in him to do something to comfort her. But it wasn't his place. This was his father's decision. He had no say in the matter.

"Potential buyer," Zach corrected. "Coming next week to have a look."

Faith gestured toward the bedroom. "The kids are still sleeping. I think the horse rides yesterday tired them out."

Kane hated the idea of sending Hope and Cash to this Irma Tunney lady, but with the need to get the ranch ready to show, it was more necessary than ever.

And there was still no word from Tricia. He was really beginning to worry for her safety.

"When did you want to leave to take them to Irma?" Faith asked Zach.

"Oh, I'm taking you," Kane said. "We'll drop the kids off, and then I'll drive you to Calgary. I have some errands to run in the city anyway. So, I was thinking we leave around noon. That way, we could give the kids an early lunch, and they won't be so cranky when we arrive at Irma's."

"That sounds good," Faith said, but her face said otherwise. Something was bothering her. Maybe it was dropping off the kids. Maybe it was him driving her to Calgary. Whatever it was, Kane didn't have time to navigate it. He just wanted this day to be over.

"I better move then," he said, pushing back from the table. "I have a list of things to get done before we leave."

Out at the corrals, Joe was already waiting for him. "You look grumpy," the ranch hand said. "I don't suppose that has anything to do with your girlfriend leaving."

"She's not my girlfriend," Kane snapped.

Joe released a disbelieving laugh. "I've seen how you two look at each other. You can't tell me there's nothing happening. I'm not blind."

"Nothing to see, nothing to hear, nothing to talk about." Kane slashed the air with his hand as if cutting off the conversation.

"Sure. You keep saying that," Joe said with a shrug, shoving his hands in the pockets of his oversized pants. Kane brushed past him and Joe followed behind, unfazed by Kane's angry outburst. "But I'm not blind." Joe kept pushing. "I can't believe you're letting her walk out of your life again."

"Not a lot I can do about it," Kane said, "even if I wanted to, which I don't." He needed to change the subject. Joe was as persistent as a badger. Once he got his teeth into something, he wouldn't let go until he had worked it to death. "We've got to go through the machine shed today. Floyd is bringing a potential buyer next week."

"Buyer? Since when?"

Kane figured dangling that tidbit in front of Joe would distract him from the Faith track.

"Since the real estate agent called this morning."

Kane ignored Joe's surprise, marching to the machine shed. When he opened it, he let out a low whistle and shook his head in dismay. Zach hadn't been lying when he'd said it was a mess. It was beyond that. It looked like someone had picked up a used vehicle lot and dumped it right into the small building. He and Joe were staring at days, maybe weeks, of work.

He could just leave it for the new owner to deal with. But that might impact the price his dad got for the ranch. He owed it to Zach to help him get the best deal possible.

"Fire up the tractor and let's get started," he told Joe, thankful he had something to keep himself busy—something to distract him from the fact that Faith was leaving today, and he would be the one driving her away. Again.

He was pouring sweat by the time they came to a stopping

point. The sun was beating down, and he had taken his shirt off and hung it on a nearby post. Joe had done the same.

Kane wiped his face with his handkerchief, shoved it in his pocket, and positioned his cowboy hat back on his head as he surveyed what they had accomplished.

"Not bad," Joe said. "And you can sell all this scrap metal."

Kane glanced at the pile Joe was referring to. It wouldn't make much, but it might cover the cost of hauling all the other stuff.

"Kane?" Faith's voice spun him around and made his stupid heart beat faster. "Will you be ready to go soon?"

She stood in front of him, her dark hair shining and curled, flowing over her shoulders. She wore a white dress, her arms bare. She looked amazing.

Joe's quick intake of breath told Kane he wasn't the only one who appreciated the affect.

"We were just finishing up here," Kane said, grabbing his shirt and slipping it on as he gave her a quick smile. "Then I was hoping for a quick shower before we leave. Do I still have time?"

All she did was give a tight nod, then she whirled around and strode away. Was she angry with him? He glanced at his watch. They were supposed to leave at noon, and it was only eleven-thirty. Kane gave Joe a puzzled glance, then followed her to the house.

The twins sat at the table with Zach, munching on some carrot sticks. He muttered a quick hello, then strode down the hall to his bedroom.

Ten minutes later, he wore clean clothes and his hair was brushed but still damp.

Faith was waiting in the kitchen, wiping the kids' faces.

"We're bringing you to a lady who is taking care of you this afternoon," Faith said. Her voice sounded strained, and Kane guessed this wasn't easy for her.

"No lady," Hope said dropping her chin on her chest with a pout. "Wanna ride horse."

"You'll only be there for a little while," Zach assured her. "And when you get back, you can have another horse ride."

That seemed to mollify her, but Kane could tell she was still leery about going to Irma's.

"I packed a bag for them," Faith was saying, "and the car seats are already in the truck."

"And your stuff?"

"It's out there too."

"Guess we're all ready then," he said with a forced smile.

She said nothing to that as she lifted Hope off the chair.

The kids were all cleaned up, their hair brushed, and their clothes all neat and tidy.

"Goodbye, my dear," Zach said, getting up. "Thanks so much for all your help. We couldn't have done this without you."

Faith gave him a tight smile, then moved in for a hug.

Zach held her close but looked at Kane over her shoulder, a sad look on his face. Hey, it wasn't his fault she was leaving. Not this time.

Kane shrugged at his father, then picked up Cash, and walked to the porch. He grabbed a clean cowboy hat, opened the door, and stepped out. He didn't even bother to see if Faith was behind him. He wanted to get this done.

They got the kids buckled in, working as a team. Then Kane lifted Faith's suitcase and dropped it in the back. Her guitar was inside the truck already, parked between the kids' car seats. Precious cargo, he thought, as he got into the driver's seat.

The trip to town was quiet, the kids content to look out the window. Kane thought of the last time he and Faith had driven to town with the kids. It seemed like ages ago, instead of only a few days.

Kane turned the radio on to fill the silence. A twangy country tune came on, and he saw Faith tapping her fingers on her knee in time to the music. She was quietly singing along.

He forced his attention back to the road, his hands gripping the steering wheel. It was going to be a long drive.

When they arrived at Irma Tunney's, she was waiting at the door of her tiny first-floor apartment, three dogs yapping at her heels.

Faith, Kane, the kids, and all their stuff managed to squeeze in without letting the dogs out, but it was a challenge.

"They don't have any food allergies that I know of," Faith said as she handed Irma their bag. "They've already had lunch, but they could use a nap."

Irma nodded, glancing down at the children. She was a heavyset woman, her graying hair chopped short. She wore yoga pants with hopeful optimism, and a T-shirt that proclaimed that she had been to the Grand Canyon. A pair of Crocs finished the look.

All that would have been fine with Faith. She wasn't one to judge by appearances. But it was the permanent frown on the woman's face that gave her misgivings. That and the fact that the three dogs hadn't stopped barking since they'd arrived.

"Do they mind sharing a bed for their nap?" Irma asked, her arms still folded over her ample chest.

"No, they've been sharing a bed at the ranch too."

"We sleep with Faith," Hope offered.

Irma's frown deepened at that. "I hope they don't expect me to do that?"

"No, no," Faith assured her. "It was only a temporary thing, until they got settled." She didn't know why she felt she had to justify herself to this woman. She just seemed so disapproving.

"Well then, let's get them in bed, so they can have their nap," Irma said. She reached out for their hands, but Hope clung to Faith's hand and Cash to Kane's. They didn't seem willing to let go.

"I don't wike dogs," Hope said with an emphatic note in her voice.

Irma crouched down, her dogs milling around her. "These are

friendly dogs," she said, giving Hope a genuine smile. She stroked one dog and lifted it up to show the little girl. "This dog's name is Alfie. He likes little children a lot."

As if to prove this, Alfie leaned in and licked Hope's face. The girl giggled, and Faith felt the tension ease from her shoulders. This would be okay. The kids would be okay.

Hope released her death grip on Faith's hand and reached out to stroke Alfie. Cash, encouraged by her actions, did the same.

"This might be a good time to leave," Irma said to Faith without looking at her.

Faith bit her lip, looking down at the children. Her heart trembled, overcome with another wave of regret. She felt like she was abandoning these children. Bending down, she brushed a quick kiss over Hope's soft cheek. Then did the same with Cash.

"You be good for Mrs. Irma," she said, not knowing what else to say.

Goodbye? Have a good life? Hope your mom is okay?

Faith quickly pushed herself to her feet. Then, before she changed her mind about everything, she spun around and strode out the apartment door.

When she got to the truck, the tears came. Drawing in a shuddering breath, she dug in her backpack for a tissue and dabbed at her eyes. She hadn't spent twenty minutes putting on makeup only to have it smeared. Nor did she want Kane to see her crying.

Thankfully, he was still inside, and by the time he made it to the truck, she'd pulled herself together.

But when Kane climbed in and looked at her, she saw in his eyes the pain she felt. "I think they'll be okay," she said. "Did they cry when you left?"

He shook his head. "Thank goodness, no. And Irma, she seems all right." But Faith heard a note of reservation in his voice. "Though she asked me to pay her for today in advance. And speaking of that…" He reached in his back pocket and pulled out his wallet. "I looked at the going rate for live-in nannies, and here's what we owe you." He reached out and handed her a large wad of bills.

"Oh, no." She shook her head and tried to hand it back. "This is too much."

"How do you know?" he asked. "You haven't even counted it."

"Because it wasn't hard work. I loved caring for them. I would have done it for free."

"Yeah, well, you earned that," Kane insisted, ignoring her outstretched hand as he started up the truck. "We're not taking it back."

Faith looked down at the money in her hands. She didn't want to count it in front of Kane. That felt greedy or rude. But she certainly could use the cash for when she got to Calgary. Stacy might front her the rent, but Faith still had to eat. She slipped the bills in her pocket. She'd count it later. It felt weird for Kane to pay her, though. Like she was just another employee, like Joe the ranch hand.

He closed the door, and as he walked around the front of the truck, Faith's eyes followed him. Imprinted on her brain was the picture of him this morning—no shirt, a faint sheen of sweat glistening on the muscles of his chest and arms. He'd always been well-built, but the last couple of years working on the oil rigs had really filled him out.

Faith clasped her hands tightly together, looking down at them and trying to think of anything but Kane without his shirt. She was moving on. He was not for her.

Kane had started the truck, but they were still sitting in the parking lot of Irma's apartment complex. His eyes drifted to her door. "Where will they play?" he asked forlornly.

"There's a park down the road," Faith said, trying to sound hopeful. "Maybe she'll take them there."

Kane nodded, but Faith could see he didn't quite believe her. Still, he put the truck in gear and pulled away. They sat in silence for a few miles and then he said, "I'm worried about Tricia. She wouldn't just leave her kids. I mean, I know things got rough after the accident, but people don't change that much, do they?"

"Trauma does weird things to people," Faith said, speaking for more than Tricia.

"And Elliot? You think it messed him up bad too?"

Faith was surprised he'd asked. Elliot was such a touchy subject between them.

"He didn't talk much about it," Faith admitted. "And then he left. But, yeah, I think he was struggling."

"And you and he—you never…?"

"No," Faith shook her head. "I know what he told you that night, but we were never like that."

"So what happened after you left?"

Faith was surprised that he asked. But part of her wanted to clarify the events of that evening. "That night we drove to a motel. I stayed with Clarise, one of the backup singers, and he bunked with Frank. He was lead guitar. Not that you'd remember."

"No. I wouldn't remember. They weren't on my radar that night."

Faith knew what he meant. Her, kissing Elliott, was exactly what was on his mind.

"I hope you believe me when I tell you, there was nothing between me and Elliott. He came with me because he wanted to make sure I would be okay."

"I believe you." Kane gave her a gentle smile. "I was a bit blinded by what I'd seen that night—so when he defended you and what you wanted to do, I just assumed you knew, and that it was mutual."

Faith nodded. It wasn't an apology, but it was as close as he'd ever come.

Kane turned his attention back to the road, slowing down as he came to the intersection that led to the highway. As they drove up the hill leading out of town, Faith turned back, looking at Rockyview one last time.

"Imprinting it on your memory?" Kane asked.

"Something like that," Faith said. In reality, she'd been thinking about her grandfather and how she was leaving so much unresolved with him. The things Zach had told her had explained a lot, but she still wasn't sure how to span the chasm that lay between her and Mick Howard.

Kane tapped his fingers on the steering wheel, then glanced at the guitar tucked behind her seat. "You really are a talented musician," he said. "I'm sorry I didn't understand that before, when we were together."

And there was the apology she'd been waiting on for two years, dropped like a bomb in the middle of the truck cab.

Faith didn't know what to do. Or how to react. What did it even mean that he was apologizing now when they were on their way to drop her off in Calgary? It was easy to apologize when you were about to say goodbye to someone for good. Because he wouldn't have to follow that apology up with any real action, would he? He wouldn't have to live a life that supported her music or confront his fears of her becoming like his mother. He could just say sorry and goodbye.

"Faith," he said, reaching out and taking her hand in his, "I know that apology is way too late. I should have been a better man for you. That is something I will always regret."

Faith felt a ball of tears rise and choke her. She couldn't cry right now, or she would never stop crying. So, instead, she undid her seat belt, moved closer to Kane, and pressed a soft kiss to his stubbly cheek.

He gave a swift intake of breath. Then he squeezed her hand, lifted it to his lips, and gently kissed the back of her fingers.

For a moment, time stood still, her fingers to his lips, their pain and history wiped clean.

But only for a moment.

Then he let her hand go, Faith moved back to her seat, and they drove in silence toward Calgary.

CHAPTER 14

So that wasn't the smartest thing to do.

Kane looked over at Faith, but she glanced away, peering out the window. The silence was heavy with tension and unspoken feelings. Why had she kissed him like that? Last time they had parted, it had been amidst anger and yelling. Maybe this time they just both wanted it to be different. Better.

But as soon as his lips had touched her hand, he'd wanted more. He wanted to kiss her on the lips, harder, more urgently. He knew they were shifting back to their old roles, giving in to the old attraction, and he didn't care. That's what his body was saying. But his heart and mind knew that things had changed. They weren't who they had been, to themselves or each other. What could he offer her now that he wouldn't have the ranch? Long sweaty days of him off in the oil patch. What kind of life was that? Besides, he sensed a deep sorrow in Faith, hidden away. Something she was guarding very carefully that she might never trust him with.

The muted ringing of his cell from its dash holder broke into his thoughts, and he tapped it, answering on speaker phone.

"Hey, Dad. What's up?"

For a moment Zach said nothing, and Kane's heartbeat jumped a notch. "Dad, what's wrong?"

"They found Tricia," Zach said, his voice choked. "She's in a hospital in Okotoks."

Hospital. The word echoed through his brain, sinister and frightening. Kane glanced at Faith. She was as fixed on the phone call as he was, leaning forward and hanging on every word.

"Is she okay?" Kane could barely get the words out.

"She got beat up and has been unconscious for days," Zach explained. "Some kind of head trauma, but they think she'll make a full recovery. The nurse only told me that much because Constable Siler called ahead and explained who I was." His voice faltered again. "Apparently, they can release her today, but she'll need help for a while."

Kane's emotions veered from thankfulness to anxiety to fury. Who had beat up his sister? How had this happened? Where had they found her?"

His hands tightened on the steering wheel as he fought with his anger. Anger that had no target. At least not yet.

"I'm about twenty minutes out from Okotoks," Kane said, "I can pick her up, but I have to get Faith to Calgary first."

"No," Faith said, shaking her head. "Tricia is your priority. You need to at least stop in and see her before you take me. She must be terrified."

"Are you sure?" Kane asked.

"Of course."

"Thanks for that," Kane said, giving her a careful smile.

"I wish I could be there," Zach continued. "But give my daughter my love. And Kane, bring her back to the ranch when they release her. I want her safe at home. Whoever did this will have to go through both of us to ever touch her again."

"Exactly," Kane snapped. "And she'll come once she knows Cash and Hope are with us."

"Let me know as soon as you see her," Zach said. "Give me a call."

"We'll stay in touch," Kane said, then touched the screen to end the call, his fingers shaking.

They found her. But she'd been beaten to unconsciousness. Talk about good news, bad news.

"Poor Tricia," Faith said, her hands pressed against her cheeks. "What happened to her?"

"Guess we'll find out." Kane shot Faith another glance. "You're sure you're okay with stopping in?"

"Yes. She was my friend, remember?"

"How could I forget?" he said with a melancholy smile. "She was the one who got us together, if I'm not mistaken. We were all on that hayride at Slaters' ranch for youth group." Tricia had been pushing him steadily toward Faith, but Kane didn't think the granddaughter of the town's lawyer would be the least bit interested in him, a cowboy with a ragged family history.

"I remember wondering what took you so long," Faith said with a light laugh.

Kane wasn't sure why she was taking this trip backwards. Maybe she too wanted to acknowledge their shared past before they moved on.

"Well, your grandfather intimidated me," Kane admitted. "I never thought I could measure up to his expectations."

"Oh, you didn't," she teased. "No one can. But he liked you more than he liked most people."

"Maybe, but he knew who I was and where I'd come from." He didn't tell her that Mick had made that quite clear when Kane had asked for his blessing on their engagement. Mick knew all about his mother and told Kane that he would be watching him. Making sure he did right by Faith.

"Kane," Faith said, a catch in her voice. "Your father told me what my grandfather did for you. I never realized."

"I owe him a lot."

Faith swept her hair away from her face as she turned to him again. "Do you?"

Kane tapped his fingers on his leg as he sorted out his thoughts. They only had this time together and then they would each be on their way. Why not lay some old ghosts to rest? Let each of them move onto their life with some peace between them?

"I told you what my life with my mother was like," he said. "But I only told you the parts I wasn't too ashamed of. I didn't tell you about the many times I was so hungry I would have eaten her guitar if I only had gravy to go with it. Or the times I lay awake all night, hiding under the blankets because I was afraid, waiting for her to come home. She was often gone to either a gig or a concert or a date after a gig or a concert. We moved constantly, and each time I had to start another school I had to catch up and ignore the teasing."

"Were you teased when you started school in Rockyview?" Faith's question held a note of concern.

"Not by you," he said, giving her a quick smile.

"I knew things had been bad for you, before, with your mom, but I never knew how bad," she said, wringing her hands.

"It's no exaggeration to say that being placed back in the Tye household was the best thing that ever happened to me. It was the first time I ever had any schedule and routine in my life. I didn't like it at first. I fought a lot and, to be honest, resented Tricia's easy life with all she had. I used to think she was spoiled."

"Maybe she was, in a way. She was an only child for a while, after all."

"So was I," Kane said with a note of irony.

"Do you know where your mother is now?" Faith asked.

Kane shook his head. "No. She hasn't tried to contact me in ages."

"That must be hard."

"It's for the best," he said. "Her music was always more important to her than I was."

Faith turned her head away, and Kane realized too late how that basically described their situation too. But he couldn't take it back. Besides, wasn't it true?

The rest of the trip was quiet, each of them caught up in their own thoughts.

As they got closer to Okotoks Hospital, Kane grew more agitated. What should he say to a sister he hadn't seen in years? A sister who had just left her children with her roommate's mother.

They pulled into the parking lot and he and Faith climbed out and silently walked into the hospital. Kane gave his name, Tricia's name, and their relationship to the receptionist at front desk and was told which unit she was in.

A young, attractive nurse, her blonde hair pulled up in a loose topknot, looked up when they arrived at the nurses' desk on the proper floor. She gave Kane a wide smile. "Hello, can I help you?"

"I'm looking for Tricia Tye. Sorry, Tricia Bouche. I was told she was here. I'm her brother."

The nurse frowned. "We don't have a Tricia Bouche, but we do have a Tricia Tye."

So, his sister was going by her maiden name.

"Yeah, I'm her brother, Kane Tye."

"Follow me," the nurse said, leading them down the hall. "Your sister has been here for a while," she commented, a faint tone of condemnation in her voice.

"We just found out," Kane explained. "We've been looking for her." Why did he have to explain himself to this nurse? Because he wanted people to know Tricia had a family that cared for her. And he was a part of that family.

"Sorry," the nurse said, looking sheepish. "I just started my shift. I should have looked at this morning's notes." She stopped outside Room 107. "This is her room. But only one visitor at a time," she said, looking pointedly at Faith. "We don't want to overwhelm her."

"Sure, I'll stay out here," Faith said, touching Kane's arm.

"Yeah, okay," he said, pushing the door open as Faith leaned against the wall, and the nurse turned to go back to her station. As he entered, he took a deep breath and let out a quick prayer. *Please Lord, let her be okay. Please, help me say the right thing.* He knew he needed divine intervention right now.

The first thing he saw was a blue curtain pulled halfway around the bed, the light from the large window silhouetting a figure sitting there. He took a few steps and peeked around the curtain.

It was Tricia all right.

She sat on the bed, her hands folded in her lap, her long blonde hair curling halfway down the back of her hospital gown. Her hollow cheeks were colored with purple and blue bruises. The same bruises Kane could see on her arm held up in a sling.

All his anger at her fled at the sight of her injuries.

"Hey, Trish," he said, keeping his voice quiet, the way he would talk to a spooked horse.

Her head turned, blue eyes wide, and then her face seemed to cave in as her lips trembled and her hand flew to cover her mouth.

But not before Kane saw the stitches on her lips.

"Oh, baby girl. What's happened to you?"

She got up slowly, obviously still in pain. He closed the distance between them in two steps and carefully pulled her into his arms.

She huddled against him, her shoulders shaking with silent tears. Then, "I'm so sorry. I made such a mistake." The sorrow and brokenness in her voice gripped his heart and twisted it hard.

"Haven't we all," he murmured, holding her close, but not too close. He still wasn't sure what was hurting and what had happened to her.

She drew back, wiping her eyes, her grief replaced by fear. She grabbed his shoulders. "Kane, where are my kids? Where are Cash and Hope? You have to find them."

"It's okay. They're at the ranch," he said. Well, technically they were at Irma Tunney's, but he wasn't about to explain that right now. "They're both fine."

Tricia sank down on the bed, her hand on her heart. "Thank the Lord for that. I was so worried when I woke up. No one could tell me anything."

"Dad got a call from Constable Siler. Said that you asked the nurse to call him?"

"I was too scared to call myself," she said in answer to his unspoken question. "Too ashamed."

"Well, they said you could be discharged today."

Trish nodded, looking down at her hospital gown. "My clothes are in pretty bad shape," she said, pointing to a clear plastic bag tucked under the bed full of bloody torn clothing. "I don't have anything to wear."

"I can get something new for you in Calgary. I have some errands in the city today, and I can pick you up on my way back. Is that okay?" He didn't mention Faith. It was just too complicated to explain right now.

"Of course. Sure." She gave him a cautious smile, and Kane's heart twisted once again at the sight of her torn lip. He so badly wanted to know more, but now was not the time.

He gently stroked her hair back from her face. "You're coming back with me to the ranch, you know," he said.

"No." She shook her head. "You can take me back to my place."

"You're still recovering," Kane said, firmly. "Your roommate brought the kids to us because she couldn't care for them. Do you really think she's going to take time off to look after you? Besides, Cash and Hope are at the ranch. They need you there." Maybe it was a low blow, but he'd use whatever he could to get Tricia home. He wasn't entirely sure how he and Zach would manage this. Tricia and the twins and all the work they had to do yet to get the ranch ready to sell, but right now it didn't matter. Tricia needed them, and that was more important than anything else.

For now, however, he had to take Faith away and then move on. Again.

CHAPTER 15

Faith leaned awkwardly against the wall outside Tricia's room as nurses bustled past her, carts rattled down halls, and phones rang.

Thankfully, it didn't take long for Kane to come out, his hat pushed back on his head, eyes narrowed, mouth pulled down. Had the visit gone badly?"

"How is she?" Faith asked.

"She's beat up bad." Rage flashed across Kane's face. "And she was terrified about the kids, but I let her know they are fine. I'm going to take her back to the ranch, but I need to get her some clothes first. So, let's get out of here," he concluded.

"Wait," Faith said, as he turned to head back the way they'd come. "Can I see her for just a moment?"

Kane looked surprised, but then he shrugged. "Sure. I just thought since you're leaving..."

"Old friend, remember?" Faith said with a forced smile. She wasn't exactly sure why she felt the need to see Tricia so badly. Yes, they had been friends growing up, but they hadn't seen one another in over two years. Maybe it was the connection she'd made with Tricia's kids. Or just putting closure on the whole missing person thing—like she needed to see Tricia to truly believe she'd been found. All Faith knew was she couldn't walk away without checking in with Tricia.

"Okay," Kane said, still sounding reluctant. "But it's not a pretty sight."

"I understand," Faith said, steeling herself for the worst. She pushed against the door, leaving Kane in the hallway. But in spite of the warning, she still couldn't stop her sudden intake of breath when she saw Tricia. Her friend's once beautiful face was bruised, her lip stitched up and swollen.

Tricia turned at the sound of the door opening, and her eyes went wide with shock.

"Faith. What are you doing here? How did you—" And then her questions stopped as Faith sat down beside her, slipping her arm around Tricia's shoulders, careful to avoid the arm caught up in a sling.

Tricia clung to her, burying her head on Faith's shoulder, crying. Faith closed her eyes and felt her own past and heartache swell upward in unison with Tricia's.

Two old friends clung together, sorrow joining them.

"Oh, honey," Faith whispered. "I'm so sorry."

It was all she could say.

Finally, Faith drew back, they both wiped their eyes and noses with the tissues on the bedside table, and Tricia raised an eyebrow at her. "So, you're here with Kane?" she asked. "You guys back together?"

"No." Faith shook her head. "Absolutely not. It's a long story, but I've been at the ranch for a few days taking care of your kiddos, actually."

"Oh?" Tricia leaned forward. "How are they? Does Cash still suck his thumb? Is Hope having nightmares?"

"Um, I haven't seen him do it. And yes, Hope does have nightmares, poor thing."

"She's such a sensitive soul," Tricia said. Her lip trembled, but she was obviously making an effort to hold it together. "Kane said Lucinda brought them to the ranch. How did my dad react to that?" Tricia looked ashamed and, at the same time, defiant.

"He was surprised," Faith said, stopping there. The last thing she wanted to do was get sucked into whatever issue lay between Zach and Tricia. "But he and the kids warmed up to each other right away."

"Well, I'm so glad you've been helping take care of them," Tricia said with a sigh of relief. "Could you imagine Zach and Kane with two little ones by themselves? Or worse, some stranger? Whatever the circumstance, I'm so glad you're back at the ranch. It will be wonderful to have you around while I recover."

So, Kane hadn't explained any of this to his sister? Great. And now the poor girl assumed Faith was coming back to the ranch and watching her kids.

Won't. Happen.

And yet...

Stick to your own plans. Don't get caught up in the Tye family drama.

But as Faith looked her friend over, she felt more torn than ever. Obviously, Tricia had been through something horrible— something that neither Kane nor Zach would ever be able to relate to the way Faith could. Tricia would need someone, not just for physical help because of her injuries, but for emotional support as well. Then there was the issue of Cash and Hope. If Faith knew Tricia, she'd not be happy about Irma Tunney. In fact, Tricia would probably insist she was ready to care for the kids way before she truly was, and Zach and Kane would go along with it because it would be easier. For everyone except Tricia, that is.

Faith's thoughts spun in on themselves, circling, diving and weaving. Could she walk away from her friend right now? Maybe, but the guilt just might kill her. Besides, the job in Calgary didn't start for days yet. She had time to kill, and that would give Tricia more time to recover. Stacy might be mad about the loss of rent, but she'd get over it.

But no more kissing Kane. That had to be a rule if she was going to stay.

Tricia reached out and clasped Faith's hand, squeezing it gently. "You being here is such a blessing, Faith."

How long had it been since anyone had thought of her as a blessing? A very long time.

Indecision nipped at her like a dog chasing a cow. But what could she do? Tricia wasn't able to take care of her children on her own, and Zach and Kane had too much going on to do it.

It will only be for a while.

"I'm glad I can help," Faith said softly, the decision made. She couldn't abandon Tricia. "Kane said you needed some clothes. I think you're about my size. I'll help him get something decent."

"Oh, thank goodness," Tricia said, leaning back and covering a yawn. "I don't trust Kane's taste."

"No." Faith laughed, standing up. "We'll get you something nice. But it looks like you need to rest. We'll be back soon. Get some sleep."

"Thank you," Tricia said, her eyes welling up with gratitude.

"Bye now," Faith said, pushing out the door.

Kane was leaning against the same wall she'd used, and Faith suddenly realized she had to tell him, somehow, that she was staying. Well, best to just get it out.

"I'm coming back to the ranch," she said, keeping her voice low and moving away from the door. "Tricia assumed I was, to help her and the kids, and I couldn't tell her I wasn't."

"Faith," Kane said, shock in his eyes, "you don't have to do that."

"Yes, I do. I don't know what happened to her, but Tricia is broken. And I'm not talking about her injuries. Do you really think you and Zach have the time, while getting the ranch ready to sell, to help her the way she needs to be helped? And she's not going to let Cash and Hope stay at Irma's. She'll insist on having them at the ranch with her. You know she will."

"Even if all that is true," Kane said as they headed toward the hospital exit. "Is it really your problem?"

"Are you trying to talk me out of it?" Faith shot him a puzzled glance. "Tricia is my friend. And if I'd had a friend when—" She stopped herself before she revealed too much. "I don't abandon my friends in time of need. Isn't that the Tye family motto?"

"Okay." Kane shoved his hands in his pockets as he walked, his eyes straight ahead. "It sounds like you've made up your mind. And I'm not going to lie, I sure appreciate it but—"

Faith knew he was thinking of how easy it had been to talk to each other when they thought it was their final hour together.

And now? She had to be careful. They had to be careful. She couldn't let him nudge open that box of memories again. It was just too painful to deal with.

"It's only until Tricia gets back on her feet," Faith assured him. "I'm still leaving."

"Yeah. I understand." Kane's voice held a curious tone, but he didn't look at her as they exited the hospital and crossed the parking lot toward the truck. His face was a mask. Did he think she was staying because of him—because her feelings toward him were slowly changing back to love?

Well she wasn't. And they weren't.

Except she knew that last one was a lie.

She was falling for Kane Tye again.

And that was not good.

⁓◯⁓

An hour later, after making a quick stop in Okotoks to pick up a few clothes for Tricia and to fill the prescription the doctor had left for painkillers and antibiotics, they had picked up Tricia and were headed back to Rockyview.

Kane still couldn't believe Faith had offered to stick around when he knew she was eager to leave. He wasn't sure how he felt about it himself. Would he have told her everything he did if he knew she was sticking around?

Tricia wanted to sit in the back. Probably to avoid her brother. So they had moved the car seats and Faith's suitcases to the box of the truck so Faith could sit by Tricia. But not her guitar. That sat between her and Tricia as the two of them spoke quietly. Kane tried not to eavesdrop, so he turned on the radio. But despite the distraction, he caught a few comments. Tricia seemed to be apologizing for her behavior, and Faith was assuring her she was still welcome at the ranch.

It should be him saying that, it should be him reassuring his sister. Not his ex-fiancée.

Kane pulled into the ranch, thankful to see his father's truck parked there. He was back from picking up the kids from Irma.

Zach came out of the house holding his grandchildrens' hands when Kane turned off the truck engine. As soon as Tricia got out of the truck, Cash and Hope pulled free from Zach and ran toward her.

"Mommy, Mommy," they called, their voices filled with joy.

Kane caught Hope and Faith caught Cash before they could bowl their mother over. Tricia was unsteady on her feet, and while they still weren't aware of the extent of her injuries, it wasn't too hard to see she wouldn't be able to handle the kids throwing themselves at her.

"Mommy is hurt," Faith was saying. "Be very careful with her."

"Oh my babies," Tricia said, gingerly reaching out for them.

Cash walked closer, then frowned at her. "You face is funny."

"Only for a little while," Tricia assured him. "It will go away." She wrapped her good arm around her children, pulling them close, wincing as she did so. Her eyes drifted shut, and once again tears slid down her cheeks.

Kane's heart broke at the sight of the reunion of mother and children.

But he could see that Tricia was in pain and gently drew Cash and Hope back. "Like Faith said, we have to be careful with Mommy." He hoisted Hope onto his hip and reached out for Cash.

Thankfully the little boy slipped his hand in Kane's and together they walked up to the house.

Tricia and Zach approached each other slowly as if unsure of the reception.

Then Zach opened his arms, mimicking the gesture Tricia had for her children, and drew her into a warm embrace.

"Welcome home, little girl," he said.

"Thanks, Daddy," she replied. She sniffed and dug into her pocket for a tissue, then wiped her eyes. "I seem to be doing a lot of this today," she said, sniffing again.

"That's what coming home is all about," Zach said with a smile. "Now, why don't we have a cup of tea. We bought cookies on our way home that the kids are excited to eat."

"Lady had little dogs," Cash was saying, referring to Irma. He rubbed his arm and made a face. "Doggie bite."

Kane looked in shock at his father, who shrugged. Obviously he hadn't been told about this.

"Show me," Kane said. Maybe it wasn't as bad as he thought.

But sure enough, there was a round little circle on Cash's arm with one small puncture mark. It probably wasn't real bad, but that Irma didn't mention it to Zach did not bode well.

"I guess they won't be going back there," Kane said.

"Obviously not," Faith said, an angry note in her voice. "I can't believe she said nothing to you about this."

"She told me the kids were good," Zach said, patting Tricia's shoulder, letting his hand rest there. "That's all I wanted to know. I was in a hurry to come home and see my girl."

Kane was surprised at how easily Zach brought Tricia back into his love and his home. She had caused so much sorrow and grief, had kept herself aloof from her father and brothers. And yet, Zach easily took her back with no hint of recrimination.

He wished he could be as forgiving and caring as his father was.

"I'm so sorry, Dad," Tricia was saying, looking up at him, her eyes glistening with tears again. "I should have let you know about the kids. It's just…I was so ashamed. I messed up so bad."

"Yes. You should have told me about my grandchildren, but we can talk about that later. For now you're here and you're safe and your children are here and we have to concentrate on you getting better."

"I'll make it up to you," Tricia promised.

Kane suppressed his frustration. How many times had she made the same promises? Except now she had not only had to live up to the promises she made to Zach. She had to live up to the ones she made to her children.

Faith was making tea, setting out mugs, milk, and sugar, and had already poured juice for the kids.

"Wow, Faith, look at you all efficient in my dad's kitchen," Tricia said with a trace of her old snappy humor.

Faith blushed.

"She's been around for a few days," Zach explained, sitting down beside Tricia, his hand still resting on her shoulder. "We found her on the side of the road."

"Literally found me on the side of the road," Faith said, her tone breezy as she set everything on the table.

"This sounds like a story I'd like to hear more about," Tricia said, giving Kane a coy look.

"I think there are other stories we need to hear first." Kane kept his tone even but hoped Tricia got the message. His sister could be oh, so contrite when she got caught but could always, always tease, flirt and cajole her way out of any consequences to her actions.

But this was more than a joyride in the country while driving underage. This was far more than getting caught sneaking in two hours past curfew.

Tricia seemed to catch the hint. When she took the cup of tea Faith had poured for her, she averted her gaze, her flush enhancing the bruises on her face.

"You'll hear them," she said, her tone quiet and, to Kane's surprise, humble.

"But for now, let's have some cookies and tea," Faith said. "Zach, are there any more calves coming?"

"I think we've got a couple of cows due in the next couple of days."

"The calves are so cute."

Faith looked Kane's way, but he couldn't think of anything to contribute. Zach was selling the ranch. Faith was leaving as soon as she could. And so was he. What was there to possibly talk about that covered none of these major circumstances?

Despite Faith's attempt at light-hearted conversation, too many shadows hung over the group. Too many unanswered questions on all sides. Kane knew they would get answered in time, but for now the halted conversation seemed superficial and unimportant.

Once his tea was done, Kane pushed himself away from the table. "I should go give Joe a hand," he said. "We need to get started on that shed."

"I can haul a few things away," Zach said. "I also got a call from Floyd confirming the visit. It's still on for Monday."

"Floyd? The real estate agent?" Tricia looked up from the cookie she was breaking into pieces for Hope, frowning at her father, then looking at Kane. "Why are you dealing with Floyd?"

Kane shrugged as he stood. "Ask Dad. I've got work to do."

He knew he sounded short with her, but he had dealt with too many emotions the past few days. He needed to focus on some physical work that didn't require second-guessing or watching what he said.

As he walked out he heard Trish asking her father again what was going on, but he closed the door and walked away. Tonight he could catch up properly with Tricia. Right now he needed a break from the ever-changing drama that seemed to be his family.

And his life.

$$\backsim\!\bigcap\!\sim$$

The door closed behind Kane, leaving a silence so heavy it echoed.

Faith wondered what was going through his mind. He seemed upset by Tricia's questions about selling the ranch. "So Dad is really selling the place?" Tricia asked. She sat back in her chair, confusion, sorrow, and pain flitting over her face.

"We can talk about this later," Faith said. "I should take the kids outside, and you should lay down for a nap."

Tricia waved her off, then winced at the movement. "I can't believe this is happening," she said looking directly at her father. "Why would you sell the ranch? Why don't Kane or Elliot take it over? That was the plan."

Zach rested his elbows on the table, folding his hands. He tapped his thumbs together as he seemed to measure what he was about to say.

"Have you heard anything from Elliott?" he asked, deflecting Tricia's questions.

"Just a text now and then," she said. She looked down, pressing her fingers on the stray crumbs that had fallen off of Hope's plate. She seemed ashamed.

"Which is a little more than we've gotten from you," Zach said. He kept his tone gentle as he tried to hold her gaze.

"I know. I'm sorry." She stroked Hope's hair away from her face. "And I know those words are too small to cover how I really feel. I made some big mistakes. Made some bad choices." Her lip trembled, and Faith caught the shimmer of tears in her eyes.

Then Zach got up, walked to her side, and placed his arm

around her shoulder, brushing a kiss over her temple. "That's hard to hear," he said, quietly, stroking her hair with one hand much as he would have when she was younger.

"I so wanted to come back here with a career. A plan. A stable life." Tricia's voice faded as tears spilled down her discolored cheeks.

"Shh, you don't need to talk about it now," Zach said, continuing to stroke her hair, looking down at her with a father's love.

Faith's heart pinched at the sight of the love Zach poured out on his daughter. The easy forgiveness. The bruises on her face were such a clear reminder of how her life had veered off course.

Tricia looked up at her father, tears sliding down her face. "I don't deserve this."

Zach gave her a sad smile. "No. But then, none of us do."

"Why is Mommy sad?" Cash piped up, concern wrinkling his face.

"It's okay, honey," Tricia said. "Mommy's okay."

Tricia drew in a shuddering breath, then gingerly started to get up from the table. "I think I'll take that nap now."

Faith hurried to her side to help her up. "I put your stuff in the half-bath off the kids' bedroom," she said.

"Which one is the kids' bedroom?" Tricia asked.

"Elliott's old room." Faith got up to give her a hand. "I put the kids in there, and I've been sleeping with them. Though you might not want to, now that I think about it. They tend to thrash about."

"Believe me, I know," Tricia said. "But I...I really miss them. I don't want to be apart from them again."

Her comment raised even more questions, but Faith knew now was not the time to delve into what she meant.

"I'll help you to the bedroom," Faith said. She turned to Zach. "Do you mind watching the kids for a few moments while I help Tricia?"

"I think we'll be okay for a while," Zach said. He sounded and looked tired. And Faith could well sympathize. Too many things were going on already today, too many changes, and too many adjustments. Too much emotion. She hesitated, but Zach flapped his hand at her. "You go ahead. Me and the kids might watch television."

Faith gave Tricia her arm and together they walked to the bedroom. Tricia leaned heavily on her, showing Faith how weak and in pain she still was.

"I had a shower this morning at the hospital," Tricia said as she sank down on the bed. "I just want to lie down."

"I should change the sheets," Faith said.

"Please. Don't bother. I'll just lie on top of the quilt for now." Faith bent over to help take her shoes off. They were the ones she had worn when admitted to the hospital, the only personal item that had been kept. Faith shuddered when saw a few spatters of blood on the toes. She set them aside then helped Tricia lie down.

Tricia closed her eyes. "Thanks for your help," she said in a strained voice. "I'm so sorry—"

"Don't be," Faith assured her, shaking out a blanket and draping it over Tricia, pulling it up around her shoulders. She was about to straighten when Tricia caught her by the hand, holding Faith's eyes, her gaze intent.

"How did you end up here? I can't believe you're back."

"It doesn't matter. I'm here to help, and that's all you need to know."

But Tricia's intent gaze showed Faith that she would not let it be.

Faith sat down on the side of the bed.

"You're not the only one who made a few wrong turns on this road of life," Faith said, twisting her hair around her finger, looking away from Tricia.

"I wasn't around when you and Kane broke up, but Elliot told me. I couldn't believe it. What happened?"

"I met a band at a rodeo. Prairie Wanderers. Elliot knew the leader, Gavin. They were looking for someone to play. He liked what I did and offered me a chance to join them. I thought it was my breakout moment. My chance."

"But you were going to school. Kane was so proud of the fact that you would be a lawyer."

"I know. So was my grandfather. But it was a huge mistake." Faith glanced over at Tricia. While she had never been physically hurt as badly as Tricia was, her wounds and her guilt ran very deep also. "I ended up in a relationship with the bass player, Keith. It...it was bad." She paused, memories and guilt flooding through her. She managed to push them down but knew they wouldn't stay hidden.

Some day...

"We fought and, well, I broke up with him," she continued after regaining her self-composure. "But that created a lot of tension in the band. I knew I wasn't as important as Keith. I saw the writing on the wall, so I quit. We were in Lethbridge. I phoned a friend in Calgary who said I could stay with her. She said she would get me a job. I got a ride from a guy who took a detour through the Porcupine Hills. But he tried to make a pass, so I told him to drop me off. I was sick as a dog with food poisoning, and your dad and Kane just so happened to come by."

"Of course they picked you up."

Faith nodded. "I was figuring on only staying overnight, but the next day Lucinda dropped the kids off. Your dad and Kane were busy getting things ready on the ranch, so when Zach asked if I could help, I knew I couldn't say no."

Tricia flushed, looking suddenly ashamed. "I'm sorry about that. I had no idea what was going on. My poor kids. I made so many mistakes. I didn't know—"

Faith laid a hand on Tricia's shoulder, stopping her torrent of self-recrimination. "Thankfully, you're back here now. It's over."

Tricia laid her arm over her eyes. "I hope so. When I think what could have happened if I had stayed with Perry..."

"Is he the one who did this to you?"

Tricia nodded. "I broke up with him after he beat me the second time. I thought that would put him out of my life and my kid's. They were scared of him." Her voice faltered, and Faith laid her hand on Tricia's shoulder again.

"You don't have to tell me."

"But I do. I feel like I've been dragging around this huge burden. I haven't been able to talk to anyone about it." She sniffed, closing her eyes as a tear drifted down her discolored cheek. "I dated him because I thought he was the one. He had money and a great job and a beautiful house. And a terrible temper." Her voice faltered, and she drew in a shuddering breath. "I was so hoping to come back to Rockyview married to a successful guy. Respectable. Especially after Drew." Tricia stopped, and Faith fought the urge to tell her it was okay, that she didn't need to tell her anymore. She sensed, as Tricia said, that she needed to unload.

So she simply took Tricia's hand in hers, giving it an encouraging squeeze.

"When I told Dad I was pregnant, he was so upset. He and Mom had always warned me to be careful. Not to give myself away so cheaply." She released a light laugh. "Them and Abby."

Her best friend, Faith remembered.

"Looking back, I think Dad was still grieving Mom's death. After all, it had only been six months before that. I think we all were grieving."

Faith understood. When Grace died, so young and so unexpectedly, it was a blow not only to the Tye family, but the community.

"It was a dark time," Faith agreed.

"So after Drew died, I was lost. When I met Perry I thought it was my chance for respectability. I was so wrong. After I broke up with him, he wouldn't leave me alone. I moved a couple of times. Then I didn't hear from him for a while, and I thought I was okay. I was working in a consulting firm and I had a chance to go to a seminar for a couple of days. Suzanne, Lucinda's mom, was taking care of the kids. Well, Perry found me. And that's when this happened." Tricia gestured to her face. "The last thing I remember is him slamming me against the wall of the hotel. Then I woke up in the hospital, and it was a few days later. I was frantic about the kids, and the nurses told me they would do what they could. Then, the next day, you and Kane showed up." Her sorrow flowed, her sobs increased, and it broke Faith's heart.

Faith gave Tricia a gentle hug, hoping her touch could give her some consolation. She wasn't sure what to say so she stayed silent.

Then Tricia's tears slowed as she drew in a steadying breath. "I'm sorry," she muttered, swiping at her eyes, giving Faith an apologetic smile. "I'm feeling so stranded. So lost right now. I don't deserve to come back here. I don't deserve all that Kane and Dad are doing for me."

"I understand. You thought you were headed to a good place. Thought you were doing a good thing for your children. I'm sure you trusted this guy at one time. It's not your fault he was so obsessed with you."

"I know this isn't easy for you to hear," Tricia continued. "Even telling you makes me ashamed of my choices. Of how close I came to putting my children in harm's way. You were always such a good person. I remember Kane always talking about you with such reverence. He used to believe you were too good for him. That he didn't deserve you. When Elliot told me you broke up, I couldn't believe it."

Faith didn't doubt Tricia's sincerity, which made her words all the harder to hear.

"Your dad sure enjoys having the kids around," she said, changing the subject. "And I know he's glad you came back here."

"It's still home." Tricia was quite a moment. Then she reached out and took Faith's hand. "I've been so wrong, I've made so many mistakes. I need to fix things with my family. And I also need to fix things with God. I know I haven't been living the life I should.

I want to change. I want to go back to church, but I can't go by myself."

"Kane and your dad will be with you," Faith said, not sure she would like the direction this conversation was going.

"I know they will be, but they're supposed to be. Would you come with me?"

Faith had to think this through. Going to church meant probably meeting her grandfather. She hadn't talked to him since she'd been back. She hadn't dared call him. Didn't want to be rejected again.

"Let me think about it," she said. It was only Friday today. She had a day to contemplate this.

"I know it seems crazy asking you to come along with me, but you've always been well respected in the community. And it may sound like high school all over again, but if you're with me, I feel like I won't be judged as harshly."

Her words were like shards of ice in Faith's chest.

"We'll talk about it later. I think you should rest right now."

Tricia nodded, her eyelids flickered, and Faith guessed the medication was kicking in.

"I hope the kids will be okay," Tricia mumbled.

"Close your eyes and have a rest," Faith said. "We'll take care of the kids."

"Like you already have been." Her eyes drifted closed and sleep overtook her.

Faith waited a moment to make sure she was fast asleep, then got up and left the room. She leaned against the door, dropping her head back, closing her eyes as she gathered her composure.

You were always such a good person.

The words rang through her head, and she wished she could shake them off.

If only Tricia knew.

CHAPTER 16

*A*s Kane trudged up to the house in the dark, he stifled a yawn.

He and Joe had been up with a couple of cows who were calving, which meant he missed supper. Now it was late evening, and he was tired. Ready for bed.

But he paused as he heard the soft tones of Faith's guitar. He listened, letting it wash over him, appreciating her talent.

He should go, but he was weary in his soul as well, and the music seemed to fill something in him. He walked toward where she sat on the porch, bent over her guitar, her voice quiet as she sang along to an unfamiliar tune.

"All along this open road, your love has lingered on my soul."

He didn't recognize the words either. But it was her vulnerable, completely open expression that lingered in his own soul. Was she singing about them? Did he dare presume that? Did she miss him as much as he missed her?

He realized he had stumbled upon her in a private moment, but before he could leave she turned, startled, pressing a hand to her chest. "Kane. You scared me."

"I'm sorry. I heard you singing."

"I was just fooling around. A song I've been trying out." Her fingers idly fingered the strings, plucking out a tune even as she stared at him. "You look troubled."

"Sorry. Stuff on my mind." He knew he should leave, but she was smiling, happy in his presence for a change and, quite frankly, he wasn't ready to walk away from this. He had caught a glimpse of the Faith he remembered, and now he wanted to give himself a memory to store once they went their separate ways. He walked up the veranda then leaned back on the rail, watching her.

"Do you want to talk about it?" She set her guitar aside, laying it in the case, standing up to join him.

"I remember when you bought that," he said, pointing to her guitar and ignoring her question. "I thought it was cute that you were so determined to learn to play it. I never realized—" He stopped himself, not sure he wanted to navigate that minefield.

"How much it meant?" Faith released a light laugh, but it held little humor.

"No. I didn't. I apologize for that. I know every time you talked about it, I shut you down."

She folded her arms, resting them on the railing, looking over the ranch below them. The setting sun haloed her hair, creating an answering lift in his heart.

"We were both in a different place, I'm thinking," Faith said, her voice soft and gentle. "We both had a different vision for where we should be."

She was quiet a moment. Kane couldn't keep his eyes off her. She was as beautiful to him as she ever was. As appealing and attractive. And yet, the past two years had changed her. Put hollows in her cheeks and a wariness in her expression.

Where had that come from?

"So where do you think you should be now?" he asked, the question slipping out past the barriers he had erected against her. Barriers of self-protection and caution. "Did you find what you were looking for?"

She adjusted her posture, a faint lift of her chin, a narrowing of her eyes. She looked as if she was casting something off or trying to find an easier way to carry it. "I found a lot. I learned a lot, and experienced even more." She eased out a sigh, then slowly turned to face him. "But no. I didn't find what I was looking for. I found things I hope to never repeat and a few things I wish I could strike from my memory. From my life."

Kane held her defensive gaze, wishing he could plumb her thoughts, her memories. Discover what she held back.

"What about you?" she asked, deflecting any further questions from him. "How has your life's journey been so far?"

"Lonely." The word burst out of him before he could stop it.

Her eyes widened, her lips parted, and then she dragged her gaze away from his, swallowing hard.

He should have kept his thoughts to himself. Like she did. But he was tired of pretending life was great when, in fact, it was anything but. The foundations of his life had been shifted and shaken and now, with the ranch going, he felt as if he would be even more lost.

He turned away from her, mimicking her pose, resting his elbows on the rough wood of the railing, letting the quiet of the evening slip over him. Doves cooed, and the trill of a nighthawk shivered through the darkness. The sounds of settling in for the evening.

"I'm sorry."

He shrugged her apology away. No way was he letting more out. He hated sounding so pathetic.

She was quiet, as if sensing his withdrawal. He should go, but despite the moment of anger, he wasn't ready to go back in the house.

"We had some good times here, didn't we?" she said. "Checking cows on horseback, trips up into the hills?"

He wrapped his hands around the top rail of the deck, the wood biting into his palms. Why was she doing this? Bringing up the very things he had been shoving back into the recesses of his mind.

"We did," was all he would give her.

"It's a good place. I can't believe someday it might...well... might all be gone."

"It will never go away. Someone else will take it over." He spoke the words easily, as if it didn't matter that the closer the sales date got, the more confusion he felt.

She caught her sweater and pulled it around herself, hugging her waist.

"But it won't belong to a Tye." She sent him a sideways glance, her eyes holding a sorrow that pierced his own guilt. "Why won't you buy it?"

The question of the year.

"I can't."

She frowned. "Why not? You were going to when—"

"When you and I were engaged." No matter how careful they spoke they would always bump into their past. Might as well bring it out into the open. "My dad and I had a plan, that's true, but that was then. I walked away from that offer. I have no right to ask for it back. Besides—" He stopped himself before he admitted that he had no desire to be reminded every day of all he had lost, working a ranch they were supposed to be living on together. It was one thing to bring up the events of the past, but there was no sense in pulling out all the stops and dragging in the emotions as well.

"What were you going to say?" Faith pressed.

"Dad wants to sell it," he said, staying with the facts. "He wants out, and I don't blame him. Neither me nor Elliot are around. What's the point? Besides, Dad will need every penny he gets from this place to set himself up somewhere else."

"And you really don't want to buy it? Because if you don't, someone else will own it. Someone who's not a Tye."

He pushed aside the burden her sadness put on his shoulders

and with it, his own. "This land didn't always belong to a Tye. And even if I stay, like you seem to think I should, it still won't belong to a Tye."

Her eyes narrowed, and she sucked in a quick breath. "How can you say that? Your father wouldn't be happy to hear you talk like that."

"I know, but it's the truth. I have a father. He's out there somewhere, at least according to my mom."

Faith tilted her head sideways as if to see him from another angle. "Do you ever think you want to go looking for him?"

"No. He's not a part of my life."

"But Zach is."

"Yes."

"He's your father. The only one you've ever known. Don't you think he would want to help you buy the ranch? Make it easy for you to do so?"

Kane realized how self-pitying he sounded, but he couldn't allow himself to think he held any claim to the Tye ranch. Not anymore. But he couldn't think of anything else to say that wouldn't make him look ungrateful.

Then she stepped closer to him, her eyes holding his. "There's something else happening, isn't there?" she asked, her voice low, quiet. "You can't tell me you really want to be a rig hand or whatever else you seem to think you should do once this is gone? I see what you're like when you're with the animals. How at home you look on a horse. That smile you have when you look out over the pastures to the hills and the mountains beyond. You belong here as much as the grass and the sky and the mountains and any biological child of Zach and Grace."

Kane wanted to step back. Keep his distance from her. But then he made the mistake of looking into her eyes, and caught a flicker of an older emotion.

"So what do you think I should do?" he asked, his voice hoarse as he struggled to keep older, unwelcome emotions pushed back.

"Stay here. Take over the ranch. Stick to the plans you were making when—"

"When you and I were engaged." He cut her off, taking refuge in anger. "And that's kind of a problem, ain't it? We're not engaged anymore, and sticking around here doesn't have the same appeal it once did."

She pressed her lips together and her eyes slid away from his. "I'm so sorry," she whispered. "I wish I could go back…" Her voice faded away, and for a moment Kane wondered where she wanted to go back to.

Then he decided it didn't matter. They couldn't go back. But could they go forward?

"Wishing has never done anyone any good. Has never done me any good. I'm more of an action kind of guy," he snapped, pulling back the protective shell he'd worked so hard on the past couple of years. "I've spent too much of my life wishing and hoping for things to change. Learned the hard way that sometimes the best thing to do is just move on."

"That's enviable," Faith said. Something in her voice caught his attention. "I've spent a lot of time wondering what I could have done differently."

"And what's your conclusion?" he asked, wishing he had the strength to look away from her eyes. This would not change anything, he was certain. And it shouldn't. But there was something going on behind those brown eyes. Something he felt was a key to why she seemed to keep herself distant from him despite their moments of connection.

"That I'm sorry. I…I was wrong. Like I said, I made a huge mistake."

He sucked in a hard breath, knowing he had to be careful. Fool me once…

He should leave, but something in her expression made him want to stay. Made him want to struggle to find a better way to ease the awkwardness that had jumped up between them.

Then, to his surprise, she caught his arm, her fingers warm on his skin. It was just a gentle touch, but too easily it swept away the barriers he was struggling to re-create.

"I know you move on," she said, her hand tightening a little. "You told me enough times you weren't one to dwell in the past. I envy you that, but I think you might spend more time there if you let your father go through with selling the ranch. I think you'll regret this to your dying day."

Her words slipped past the objections Kane had raised to himself repeatedly.

"You saw yourself how happy your father was to have Tricia back despite what she did," Faith continued. "He loves his children, and I know he wants what's best for every one of them. He knows you love this ranch, and I know you imagined us together on it, but I think you need to let go of that. Think about yourself. Put me out of the equation. What do you really want to do?"

What he really wanted to do right now was kiss her.

But her words resurrected at least part of his old dream.

"I don't think taking over the ranch is moving backwards," she continued. "I think it's moving on. It's a way for your father to pass on to his son something that his own father built up. Create a future."

Kane shifted his posture, settling his hip against the rail, his eyes holding hers as he considered what she was saying. In one way she was right. He didn't really want to go back to the rigs. And yet…

"Talk to Zach," Faith said. "See how he feels about you taking over. Have you even asked him?"

Kane sighed. "I don't feel like I have the right. I abandoned him. Then he broke his leg while I was gone."

"You left because of me," Faith said. "That was the only reason you walked away from here. And you didn't break Zach's leg. He did that himself with the choices he made. I know him well enough. He would have climbed on that horse whether you were here or not."

He couldn't say anything to that. It was the truth.

He turned to look as the last light of the setting sun faded into indigo. "I could talk to him, but I think his heart has gone out of ranching. I don't know if he has it in him anymore to keep going."

"I think his heart went out of it when you left. And don't forget, Elliot left too."

Kane released a harsh laugh. "Yeah. I suppose." He was quiet a moment, his mind shifting to the other dream he had. "I had always imagined me and Elliott working here together."

"Do you think he would come back?"

"I don't know. We haven't talked for a while."

"Because of me?"

He nodded.

"But I told you that nothing happened between us."

"I know that now."

"You should call him. Talk to him. I know he misses you."

"I've texted him. I sent a note to tell him we were selling the ranch, and nothing."

"Last time I checked, texting wasn't talking."

Kane held her earnest gaze, silently acknowledging her point. "Why does this matter so much to you?"

"I never had a brother or sister," Faith said. "The closest I came to that was with your family. That's why it bothers me so much to see this family so torn apart. If there's any way I can bring you guys together—"

"And what about us? You and me?" And there it was. The question they'd been edging around for days.

Her eyes widened, and he could see her throat work as she swallowed. "What do you mean?"

He wondered why she looked so surprised. They had worked together. Had shared with each other.

"Us. You and me. Does it bother you that we are apart?"

She blinked, then took a step back. For a moment he thought she was leaving, but she turned back to the railing, resting her tightly folded hands on it.

"It always did." She spoke so quietly, he wondered if he had heard her correctly.

"That song you were singing…"

"It's about you."

Her admission was like an arrow to his soul. Hard, piercing, and life-changing.

Kane couldn't stand the distance between them. He drew her into his arms and turned her head up to him. Her arms slipped around his waist, and he laid his head on hers, holding her close, letting them have this moment.

Your love has lingered on my soul.

"I never stopped caring about you," he said. "Never."

She clung to him, then drew back enough so their gazes locked.

He wasn't sure what to expect, but the pain deep in her eyes concerned him. "I never stopped caring either," she said. "And because of that I made some bad mistakes." She stopped, her voice choking.

He didn't want to talk anymore. He brushed a gentle kiss over her lips. Then another one, and then he kissed her in earnest, his mouth moving over hers, drawing a willing response. Her arms wove around his neck, holding him against her, deepening the kiss.

This was right. This was true.

Each time they were together, each time he kissed her, he felt as if they were moving back to a place he'd been yearning for ever since she left.

"I'm so sorry," she said quietly, finally ending the kiss, laying her head on his shoulder. "Not for the kiss, but for, well, everything else."

He didn't want to say anything more to add to the guilt she

seemed to carry. For now, it was enough that they were together. Holding her close made him dare think of a future beyond the moment.

Maybe, just maybe, things would come together for them.

You have to tell him.

Faith sat down on her bed, her lips still warm from Kane's kisses, her heart pounding from their moment of togetherness. She felt as if they had moved to a place of no return, and she wasn't sure what to do in this new territory.

Tricia's words rang through her head, braided through with Kane's admission that he had never forgotten about her.

You're not the girl you used to be, you're not the girl he remembers.

Faith wrung her hands, her knuckles white, then lowered her head as she prayed.

"Dear Lord, I haven't spent a lot of time with You lately, but I don't know where else to go. I don't know what else to do. I don't deserve what's been happening. Kane doesn't deserve it either. What do I do?"

She waited a moment, as if to give the Lord time to recognize who she was.

What should she feel now? Some answer? Divine guidance?

She walked over to her suitcase. Now that Tricia was back, Faith had moved into the room beside Tricia's. It was smaller but was also connected to the bathroom. She knew this was Lucas's old room. But unlike Elliott's, there was no evidence of its previous occupant.

Faith squatted down, unzipping one compartment of the suitcase. She dug to the bottom of a pile of blue jeans, pulled her Bible out, and walked to her bed. Her grandfather had given her this Bible when she graduated high school. He had her name engraved on it. She opened it up and once again read the inscription inside.

"To my dear granddaughter, with hopes for a bright and successful

future. Trust in the Lord always and lean not on your own understanding. In all your ways acknowledge Him and He will direct your paths."

Faith knew which paths her grandfather wanted her to walk on. Definitely not the one she had chosen.

She flipped through the Bible, feeling tiny jolts of shame as she saw notes she had made in margins. Most of these happened in the Bible study she attended in college. She had been so lonely for Kane and for home that she leaned on her faith and read her Bible regularly. When she wasn't doing homework, she was taking part in one of the two Bible studies she was involved in. Her faith in God helped mitigate the loneliness she felt. Not only the loneliness, but an underlying and unspoken fear that Kane's push for her to go to college was a way to get rid of her. At the time it was the only way she could understand and explain the pressure he put on her. The same pressure her grandfather did.

She knew better now, but as she saw the comments jotted down in the margins, she felt as if time had slipped back, and once again she was that lonely, uncertain, and frightened young girl.

A corner of a page was folded over. She turned to it and saw a highlighted passage from Psalm 103.

He does not treat us as our sins deserve or repay us according to our iniquities. For as high as the heavens are above the earth, so great is His love for those who fear Him; as far as the east is from the west, so far has He removed our transgressions from us.

Faith traced her fingers over the words, remembering herself as an earnest student, a sincere Christian girl struggling with forgiveness for—what? Not studying hard enough? Not getting top grades like her grandfather always insisted she do?

Oh girl, what little you knew of sin, Faith thought, speaking to her younger self. She leaned back against the headboard of the bed, pulling her knees up, the Bible resting against them.

She reread the passage, wondering what her optimistic and innocent younger self would say to her now.

Could God really forgive what she had done? What she had thought? What she had hoped for?

And what had actually happened?

Unconsciously she laid her hand on her stomach, feeling once again the confusion of emotions that had spun through her when she first saw those lines on the pregnancy test. Positive.

Her first emotion had been panic, and right behind that fear of how he would react.

She hadn't always feared Keith.

When she first met him, he was full of compliments over her music. Encouraged her to try writing songs. He'd been the one to convince Gavin to try some of her songs.

That was the ultimate rush for Faith. Singing her songs with the band as the audience clapped along, and cheering when a set went well. The drums, guitars, electric piano blending with their voices in perfect harmony, belting out tunes they spent hours practicing in small, rented halls. Her tunes.

It made up for the lousy wages and the crappy motels they stayed in when they were touring.

And every time a performance went especially well, Keith would grab her and swing her around, tell her how amazing she was. They spent more time together, staying up after a performance, jamming, trying out new songs. Keith would look her way, grinning his encouragement. She was caught up in the excitement, the thrill of it all. Then glances turned to touches, which turned to kisses. She tried to keep it at that, but he kept pushing and pushing. The nights were long and lonely, and she finally gave in. Eight weeks later she was pregnant. She kept it quiet, not sure what to tell him. Not sure what to think.

Keith became more demanding. More possessive. He was angry whenever someone in the audience paid her a compliment, or, worse, tried to buy her a drink after their set if they played in a bar.

She wanted to break up with him, but if she did it would cause such incredible tension for the band, and they were starting to go places. And she was carrying his baby.

She wondered how much longer she could keep her pregnancy a secret from not only Gavin but Keith. Because this was his child too, she knew she had to tell him eventually.

Then, after a horrible performance at a rodeo, things went downhill. Gavin berated them all for not being in the zone. For letting distractions infiltrate the music. The most important thing was the music, he kept saying, zeroing in on Faith, as if it was all her fault.

She thought he would kick her out. Thought he had found out about the baby. Fear had gripped her and that night, she wished the baby was out of her life. She had nowhere to go. Her grandfather wouldn't take her back, and she couldn't live on the road with a baby. She felt cornered and lost.

And then, two days later, she had a miscarriage and lost the baby. She was inconsolable. She blamed herself. The erratic lifestyle.

Her horrible wish.

When Keith found out, he didn't comfort her. Didn't give her any sympathy.

Probably for the best, he had said. A baby would mess up what they had going. Would mess up the music and the band.

She had been crushed by his indifference and weighed down with a burden of sorrow and guilt.

Their relationship went downhill from there. Professionally, the time between gigs grew larger. Gavin kept promising that he had a line on a great tour they could open for.

However, Keith grew distant. Angry. Sullen. He drank more.

Then, one day, as Faith was ignoring the heckling from the crowd in a particularly sleazy bar, the sadness that had haunted her since she lost the child overcame her like a dark, heavy blanket. She couldn't do this anymore.

That night, Keith got drunk and belligerent. He accused her of flirting with someone in the crowd. Told her she wasn't playing like she should. That she'd lost her touch. The more he drank, the louder and more cruel he got. Finally, she'd had enough. She told him she was leaving. Leaving him, the band, this life that was nothing like she'd imagined.

His slap across her face sealed the deal. She wasn't sticking around to find out what would happen next time. After contacting Stacy and discovering she might have a line on a decent job for her, Faith packed her backpack, grabbed her guitar and, in the middle of the tour that was supposed to be the band's big break, she walked away.

But as she did she felt as if she was moving backwards, returning to the life she had left behind.

And now she was here. Back at the ranch. She'd come full circle. Her emotions for Kane resurfacing, shifting. Her choices for her life going in a direction she couldn't see the end result of.

If Kane had been enraged over an innocent kiss with Elliot, how would he react to her relationship with Keith? With her pregnancy and the loss of her child? If she told him would she lose him again?

But in spite of her doubts, she owed Kane the truth.

Maybe, possibly, he could forgive her.

That would take some kind of miracle.

All she could do was pray.

CHAPTER 17

"*H*old still, munchkin," Faith muttered as she twisted Hope's hair into the second pigtail, setting the brush down on the bathroom counter.

"Owwie," Hope shrieked, pressing her hands to her head.

"Oh, honey. It doesn't hurt that much." Faith chuckled at the dramatics.

"Sounds like another Sunday torture session," Zach called out from the kitchen.

"Hope sure seems to think so." Tricia stood in the doorway of the bathroom, leaning against the doorjamb, smiling as she watched Faith work. Tricia's face still held remnants of bruising despite a liberal application of foundation. Her eyes still held a haunted look, and Faith knew she was still in a lot of pain.

"Are you sure you want to go to church?" Faith asked, smoothing the little girl's hair, still hoping that Tricia would say no.

Not only did Faith want an out, Tricia had really struggled yesterday. Her arm had ached, she had excruciating pain in her ribs when she breathed, her legs kept cramping, and she'd slept most of the afternoon.

Saturday hadn't been a great day for Faith either. All Friday night her mind relived the kisses she and Kane had shared. Again. The kisses that held hope, promise, and potential.

Things were moving in a direction she never thought possible, and because of that she knew Kane deserved the truth. She couldn't put it off any longer.

However, when she dragged herself out of bed Saturday morning, hoping to catch Kane at breakfast, she'd discovered that he had left early to take the tractor into town for repairs.

Kane didn't come back until later that night, and then he had to deal with a cow calving. He only had time to give her a discreet smile and touch her hand as he came through the kitchen to get a cup of coffee. She had hoped to go out and sit with him, but the twins were rambunctious and Tricia wasn't feeling well, so she'd stayed with them. Finally, exhausted, she had crawled into bed herself.

This morning, Kane wasn't at breakfast either. She didn't know if he was sleeping in, prepping the ranch for the showing, or getting ready for church like they were.

Every time she missed him it was as if the burden of the story she was carrying grew heavier.

Maybe she should just leave it? Maybe it wouldn't matter?

Tricia pushed herself away from the doorjamb and limped into the bathroom. "To tell you the truth, part of me wants to stay home. But I need to go to church. It's been ages, and I need spiritual nourishment. People will find out I'm back. They always do in Rockyview. Might as well face people now, rather than later."

Faith wished she had Tricia's confidence. She wasn't too eager to head to church and face a God she'd disobeyed and ignored.

She turned back to Hope, who was squirming on her chair, and tied a curly ribbon on each pigtail. "There you go, missy. All done."

Hope pulled her hands away from her face and scowled in the mirror. Her dark look brightened as soon as she saw her reflection. She patted her pigtails, grinning now. "Pretties," she said. "Show Grampa."

"Do I look okay?" Tricia asked Faith, tweaking her own blonde curls, pulling them closer around her face.

"You look almost as beautiful as you usually do," Faith said with a smile, brushing her own hair. She wore it loose today, dark against the white shift she had chosen. She didn't have a lot of choices, and she hoped it would be okay.

"Well, you're looking especially gorgeous," Tricia returned. "I hope Kane is impressed."

Faith couldn't stop the faint blush at Tricia's comment. "I don't know if he'll be coming to church today. He's been busy."

"He'll be there. He knows how important it is to Dad to show up. Plus, I think Kane will want to be with you."

Her words were a gentle comfort, and she held them close as she caught Cash and Hope by the hand and headed out of the room.

❧❀❧

She looked amazing.

As Faith walked into the kitchen, leading Cash and Hope all dressed up in their Sunday best, his heart lifted. She wore a simple white dress that set off her perfect complexion and contrasted with the dark curls falling over her shoulders.

He wanted to get up and walk over to her, pull her close, and kiss her again.

Yesterday had been one long train wreck of busyness and running around. He got up early, hoping to get the cows fed on time so he could spend part of the day with Faith, Tricia, and the kids. But then the tractor broke down, and he had to take it into town. Things went downhill from there.

The whole time he had been gone, he kept thinking about what Faith had said. The fact that she had encouraged him to talk to his father about taking over the ranch made him wonder if her plans were changing.

When he had kissed her, and she had responded so eagerly, hope had once again bloomed in his chest.

"Good morning," he said, looking up at her.

"Good morning to you too," she said, sounding formal. But the smile she gave him was anything but. Her eyes held a glimmer of affection, and he knew he hadn't imagined her response the other day.

As she settled the kids in their chairs, Tricia limped into the kitchen. She wore her hair loose, curling around her face, hiding the bruises. He recognized the pink dress as one they bought for her when he and Faith brought her home from the hospital.

"You look nice, Tricia," Zach said to his daughter. "You coming to church too?"

"I really want to," Tricia said. "Is that okay?" She sat down beside Zach, and he took her hand in his, holding it close.

"Of course it is. Church is the place we go when we need each other and God." He leaned closer to her and gently brushed a kiss over her cheek. "I'll be very proud to have my two kids with me in church." Then he looked up at Faith. "Are you coming as well?"

Faith nodded. Her response made Kane sweep in a deep breath of thanks. Each moment they spent together solidified the faint hope that grew with each kiss.

"Kane made breakfast," Zach said, pushing a platter with a large stack of pancakes on it toward them.

"Aren't you getting to be the domestic," Tricia said with a teasing note in her voice.

"I can hold my own with the flipper," Kane returned.

Kane was glad to see his sister smiling, but part of him felt she was a little too flip. A little too comfortable. She seemed to act as if nothing had happened. As if he and Faith hadn't picked her up from the hospital battered and bruised. As if they hadn't taken care of the children they knew nothing about while she was there. Had she learned anything from her situation?

He pushed the questions aside as he helped Faith get the kids' pancakes ready. It didn't matter what he thought. Tricia had to figure things out for herself. He didn't feel like getting pulled into the drama of her life. He had other priorities.

He looked over at Faith, the largest part of his other priorities, just as she glanced at him. Their eyes held, and Kane felt as if the possibility could become a reality. Did he dare make plans yet?

"Yummy pancakes," Cash said. "Want another."

"What do you say?"

Tricia and Faith spoke at exactly the same time.

Faith held her hand up to Tricia in a gesture of apology. "I'm sorry," she said.

"Please don't apologize," Tricia said. "You are taking care of my children, and you have every right."

The note of contrition in her voice made Kane feel a little better.

"You guys better hurry up," Zach said, wiping his mouth and slowly getting to his feet. "We have to leave for church in about fifteen minutes."

This created an immediate hustle as food was eaten, plates were cleaned, brought to the dishwasher, and loaded up.

Kane still had put the car seats back in the truck, so he took Tricia and the children, and Faith rode with Zach.

"So you and Faith seem to be getting reacquainted," Tricia said to Kane as they backed out of the driveway.

Kane wasn't sure what to say, so he shrugged as he followed Zach out to the highway.

"I think she's delighted about that," Tricia said.

"You think so?" As soon as he asked, Kane felt like smacking himself. Junior high all over again. Him quizzing his sister about how Faith felt about him, looking for affirmation to pursue a relationship.

"She's had her own difficulties," Tricia said. "I don't think life on the road was everything she thought it would be."

"She said the same to me."

"So what is she doing now?"

"Apparently she has a friend in Calgary who might have a job lined up for her." He didn't want to think about that too much, and Faith hadn't mentioned it again.

"Well I'm glad she's back." She reached over and gave him a gentle poke. "And I'm sure all you have to do is turn on the charm, and that friend in Calgary won't matter anymore."

Kane was quiet a moment, looking at his dad's truck. Through the back window, he saw Faith's head silhouetted against the sky.

"You still love her, don't you?"

Kane's heart jolted at the question. He let her question hang a moment, weighing the repercussions of telling his sister.

"I don't think my feelings for her have changed much, sorry to say." He felt foolish admitting it. Like he was some lost puppy unable to forget a master who'd treated him badly.

"Have you told her?"

Kane's only reply was a quick shake of his head.

"I think you should."

"There are too many other things going on. Too many questions right now." He glanced over at Tricia. "And there's a bunch of questions we need to answer between the two of us too. Plus, I have the feeling she's holding something back, and it scares me."

Tricia nodded her acknowledgement of his comments, looking back at her children sitting quietly in the back seat. "And you have every right to ask those questions." She turned to face him. "And you and Dad have been pretty circumspect about asking me those questions. I'm not scared to answer them, you know."

Kane glanced over at her, his heart aching at the sadness on her face. "I'm glad you're acknowledging that. And we'll be talking, I'm sure, but not right now. Right now we are headed to church. Dad is over the moon that two of his kids will be sitting with him again."

"And you are happy Faith is."

Kane let a slow smile slip over his lips. "I am."

The church parking lot was half full when they pulled in. Kane was glad for Trish's sake. He knew this would be a difficult time for her, but he was proud of her for not staying home, licking her wounds.

They pulled up beside Zach. Faith was already out of the truck waiting for them. Kane touched her shoulder as she walked past him, and she gave him a shy smile.

Faith pulled Hope out of her car seat and Kane got Cash. As Tricia got out, both children ran to her, grabbing her hands.

Kane was surprised at the disappointment he felt.

He walked around to the other side of the truck and joined Faith.

"How quickly we get replaced," he said, dropping his hands on his hips and shaking his head.

"Right? Ungrateful little creatures forgot how much we've done for them." But she was smiling.

Tricia peeked over her shoulder, "Sorry, not sorry. I'm just glad they didn't forget about me."

Zach joined Tricia while Faith and Kane followed the four of them. Without thinking, Kane reached out and slipped his hand into Faith's. He hadn't even realized he done it until he heard Faith's faint gasp.

His first instinct was to pull away, dismayed at how automatic the gesture had been and how easily he slipped into old patterns with her.

But then her fingers clung to his, and as he looked her way, he felt as if the world was turning in small quiet circles, with them in the middle. They had come back to the beginning.

His heart was overflowing as they walked into church. He let go of her hand for a moment to open the door for her, but as soon as they stepped inside he caught it again.

Zack and Tricia took the kids to Sunday school while Kane and Faith waited for them in the large open foyer.

People milled about, chatting and laughing. Strains of music flowed out through the doors of the sanctuary to Kane's right.

Then, suddenly, Faith's fingers became like a vise as she gripped his hand harder.

Puzzled, he turned to see what had caused this.

Her grandfather was glaring at her.

Mick turned away, then paused, as if changing his mind. He strode their way, his eyes narrowed, his eyebrows pulled together in a harsh frown. Faith's fingers clung even harder, and he squeezed back, reassuring her.

"I heard you were back," Mick said, coming directly to the point as he stopped in front of them.

Faith was quiet, her eyes downcast.

"Good morning, Mick," Kane said, his tone deliberate, a faint lash of warning in it, remembering how this man had turned Faith away at the hospital when she came to see him.

Mick looked annoyed as his eyes flicked from him to their joined hands.

"So you two are back together again?" he asked. "You're on her side now?"

"I didn't think there were sides," Kane said. He released her hand and draped his arm over her shoulders, drawing her closer.

Mick turned back to Faith, who was now looking directly at him. "So how long are you here for?"

"I'm not sure," she said, her voice quiet, her expression pained.

"Of course you aren't. You really are just like your mother." Mick shook his head, his eyes narrowing. "When I think of all the sacrifices I made for you. Everything I've done. And you repay me by doing exactly what your mother did." He spoke quietly, but

Kane could see from the way his hand clenched at his side that he was holding his anger in.

"I don't think this is the time or place to have this discussion," Kane said, trying to diffuse the growing tension.

But Mick ignored him, his voice growing more tense. "I can't believe you wasted your time and talents on that stupid guitar. And where did it get you?"

Faith bit her lip, and Kane thought of the look on her face whenever she played her guitar. The joy she had. But juxtaposed against that was the sight of her standing by the side of the road, wet and bedraggled, hitching a ride.

"I love playing my guitar," she said, looking up now and holding her grandfather's gaze. "I enjoy making music."

"So much that you had to come back here?" Mick turned to Kane, his tone pleading now. "Can you talk sense into her? You used to. You understood what I wanted for her."

Kane looked into Mick's eyes and saw, behind the bluster, a confused and lost man. A man who wasn't sure where he stood anymore.

And for a small moment he felt sorry for Mick.

"Faith can make her own choices," Kane said with more conviction than he felt.

Mick's expression grew confused, as if he had lost an able ally.

Then, without another look at Faith, he turned and strode through the doors, into the sanctuary.

Faith leaned against Kane, her head resting on his shoulder. Kane held her close, ignoring the curious onlookers. "I'm sorry he did that," he said.

For a moment Faith said nothing, then she drew away from him, her head bent as she carefully wiped her eyes.

"I am too," was all she said.

He wanted to say more, but there were too many people around, and it wasn't the time. Though he felt bad for Mick, he felt he had seen a different side of him he hadn't seen before. A side, he suspected, Faith had seen all too often.

Then Tricia and Zach joined them and together they walked into church.

◦ↄᚑↄ ◦

Faith's eyes drifted to her grandfather sitting ramrod straight, his immaculately tailored suit coat sitting perfectly aligned on his shoulders. He looked the way he lived. By the book. Follow the rules.

Trouble was, her own emotions were such a tangled push and pull. She couldn't divorce her shame from his unmet expectations, her regret from his demands. Her love for him from his rejection of her.

She couldn't deny who she was compared to who he wanted her to be. She would never be a lawyer. Never work with him in his firm. Never live up to what he wanted.

And can you be a musician? After you've seen what life on the road is like?

But if she couldn't be either of those, who was she really?

Kane, as if sensing her swirling emotions, put his arm around her, pulling her close. She gave him a tentative smile, feeling as if he was her safe harbor. Her port.

The musicians played, and Faith felt a rush at the sound of the drums, the bass guitar, the piano, and the singers. She couldn't help tapping her fingers along to the music, getting pulled in.

Kane leaned over. "I think this is a new group. I don't remember them from before."

"They're good," Faith said.

"Could use a good guitarist," he said with a lift of one eyebrow.

Faith was wondering if he was serious. Wondered what he meant by that, but took it at face value. A throwaway comment, a sideways compliment to her.

But, even better, an acknowledgement of something she loved doing.

The singing was over much too quickly for her. A few of the songs were known to her, some new. She caught herself thinking of how she would have written them. What she might have done. As she sat down a tendril of promise wove through her soul. Could she stay? Find a place here? With this group?

Then her grandfather glanced backward, his scowl telegraphing his disappointment with her. Just like that, condemnation and the old guilt tamped down the hope she'd allowed herself. No matter what she did, she could never live up to his expectations.

The pastor took his place at the podium, looked around the gathering, a smile on his face.

"Our last song really means a lot to me. It helped me through a time when I thought God seemed far away. When I didn't think I had the right to approach Him. I had fallen so far from grace I didn't think God could find me anymore."

Faith felt a jolt at his words. It was as if the pastor had been reading her mind.

"Then a friend of mine, who knew what I was dealing with, gave me this passage from Ephesians." He opened his Bible, giving the congregation a few moments to follow along if they wished. He started reading, "'But because of his great love for us, God, who is rich in mercy, made us alive with Christ even when we were dead in transgressions—it is by grace you have been saved. And God raised us up with Christ and seated us with Him in the heavenly realms in Christ Jesus.'"

He paused a moment as if to let the passage sink in, then he looked up. "Grace. It's such a simple word, and yet, holds so much. Grace is a gift. It's a word that hasn't lost its beauty, it simplicity, and its power. Grace is a gift. There's nothing you have to do to get it. It comes to us freely from a God who longs to be a part of our life."

Faith heard the words on one level and struggled with them on another. If the man who told her he loved her, who had done so much for her, couldn't forgive her, how could God, who was more perfect? More powerful?

You're just like your mother.

Faith closed her eyes, her grandfather's words battling what the minister was saying.

"But because grace is a gift," the minister continued, "we have to reach out and take it. Let go of the burdens we carry and let God take them for us. His grace is sufficient."

Sufficient.

The word resonated through Faith's mind. God's grace was enough. Something she had known her whole life but never seemed to need. Until now.

She felt the unwelcome prick of tears at the same time she felt as if a wave was washing over her, then retreating, taking all she had done away, leaving her clean.

Pulling in a deep breath, she glanced over at Kane. He was smiling down on her, and the connection that was growing between them seemed to solidify.

She had to tell him. She knew that much.

She just hoped that God's grace, sufficient for her, would be sufficient for him as well.

CHAPTER 18

"Will you and the kids be okay for a while?" Kane asked Tricia as he helped clear off the lunch dishes. Faith was putting the kids down for their nap and Zach was already sleeping in his recliner. He and Tricia were alone.

Tricia looked exhausted, but curiously happy. After church Kane thought she would want to leave as soon as possible. As soon as they sang the last song, she was heading out the door until Melinda Bogal stopped her.

Melinda had been friendly and welcoming. As they talked, others joined them.

Faith, however, made a quick getaway. She got the kids from Sunday school, and when Tricia was ready to leave, they found her playing with them on the small playground by the church parking lot.

Kane didn't blame her. Her grandfather's reception had made things doubly difficult for her. And she seemed to struggle with something during the sermon.

"Yeah. We'll be okay," Tricia said. I imagine you want to go out riding? And I'm guessing you want to take someone else along?"

She gave him a conspiratorial smile and added a flick of the dish towel.

"I was hoping to ask Faith."

Tricia leaned back against the counter, the dish towel now slung over her shoulder. "I'm guessing things are moving into a good place with her?"

"I'm not sure what makes up a good place," Kane said, "but I feel like we're getting to a better place than we were when she first came here."

Tricia's smile diminished as she looked through the arched doorway leading to the family room where Zach was now sleeping in his recliner. "And what comes after that? For you? For her?"

"I'm not sure."

Tricia folded her arms over her chest, her expression serious. "You going back to the rigs?"

"Again, I'm not sure."

"Dad told me Floyd found a buyer."

"That's happened before," Kane said, fighting down a jolt of fear. Just before Kane came to the ranch, in fact, but the prospective buyer hadn't been able to get financing.

"Apparently this guy has deep pockets. Money isn't an issue."

Kane couldn't say anything to this.

"Are you going to do something about it?" Tricia asked.

"What?" Kane asked, his frustration spilling over into his question. "You put a place up for sale, you expect to get buyers."

"There shouldn't be buyers. There should only be you. And Elliott."

"Well, guess what, Elliott isn't here." He yanked open the dishwasher and shoved the plates in.

"But you are."

Kane paused, looking over at Tricia who was holding his gaze, her expression intent. He wished he knew what to say. So many things hung in a delicate balance right now. Push too hard in one direction, and he was afraid it would all fall down. He and Faith were getting closer, and she too had urged him to talk to his father.

But if she wasn't sticking around…

"I don't know what to do," he admitted, a sigh easing out of him as he finished loading the dishwasher. He glanced over his shoulder to make sure Faith wasn't around. "I had my chance with Dad but I walked out. It wouldn't be fair to ask for another chance."

"Dad loves you, and I know he would much rather have you run the ranch than some stranger."

"Well, that may be, but I can't afford it. He needs a certain amount to live on, and the only way that will happen is if he gets his asking price for the place."

"I can't see Dad living in town no matter what kind of positive spin he puts on it. He was willing to help you out before."

She made it sound so easy.

"I can't really talk about it now. I've got too many other things going on." He gave her a warning glance, and she nodded, acknowledging that he wasn't talking about this anymore.

The sound of Faith's footsteps coming down the hall ended the conversation.

When she came into the kitchen she glanced from him to Tricia, as if she sensed the gravity of their conversation.

"I was just asking Tricia if it was okay with her if I went out on a ride," Kane said. "And I was wondering if you wanted to come along?"

Her huge smile was his answer.

"I'd love to," she said. "I haven't been riding in ages."

"Perfect. Let's get the horses ready," Kane said.

"Before you go, Faith, could you drive me and the kids into town on Wednesday?" Tricia asked. "Melinda Bogal was telling me about a Bible study they run. I'd like to go."

"Of course," Faith said. "I'll gladly take you."

"You can come too," Tricia replied.

"I'll think about it," was all she said, clearly avoiding the issue. "So, Kane, did you want to leave right now?"

"If the kids are sleeping, I think it would be the best time." Kane turned back to Tricia. "You make sure you get some rest now too. We won't be gone long."

He stood aside for Faith to precede him, then together they walked out to the horse corrals.

Twenty minutes later they were mounted up and headed across the pasture to the hills beyond. Tatters of clouds floated across a sharp blue sky. The sun shone benevolently down, and a faint breeze kept the bugs away. It was a perfect day.

"Stirrups okay?" he asked Faith. She was using Tricia's old riding saddle, and it seemed to fit her pretty well.

"They feel perfect."

"Saddle sitting okay, cinch tight enough?"

"Everything is just fine," she said with a chuckle. "This isn't my first rodeo." She had helped him saddle and bridle the horses, her movements quick and efficient. It was like she had never been away from the ranch.

"Actually, it would be. You've never ridden in a rodeo in your life," he said smiling at her good humor.

"And you would know," Faith said, angling him a coy glance. "Do you miss it? Competing?"

Kane thought about this a moment, then shook his head. "I don't miss the injuries, the stress, and all the running around from town to town."

"Traveling sure can wear a person down," Faith agreed.

"I'm sure you did your share of it too," Kane said. "When you were touring."

Faith shifted in the saddle, looking suddenly troubled. "We did enough of it."

"You guys stay in motels too?"

She nodded. Kane sensed her sudden retreat, wondering what

had triggered it. He had hoped this ride would give them a chance to get closer. To test the emotions he knew were growing between them. To find out what she wanted and where she saw herself headed. He didn't know if he dared make any plans, but he held out hope.

"I know some of the motels we stayed in on the circuit were less than optimal," Kane said, trying to keep the conversation going.

Again silence from her. He had hoped she would open up more, but he sensed he needed to back off that line for a while.

The only sound after that was a muffled plod of the horses' hooves on the packed dirt of the trail as they wound their way up through the trees. The rustling leaves and the call of birds created a gentle counterpoint to the squeak of leather and the clink of the bridles. After half an hour of riding, Kane pulled his horse up and Faith drew up beside him.

"I always like coming here," Kane said, dismounting and tying his horse to a tree with the halter rope. Faith got off as well and tied her horse to a tree beside his.

He sat down on the edge of the opening in the trees, resting his elbows on his knees, pushing his hat back on his head to see better.

"You've brought me here before," Faith said, dropping gracefully onto the ground beside him.

Kane nodded, his eyes following the fence lines to the river that spilled from the mountains beyond, rushing over rocks and sending sparkles of light back to them. The grass was the bright new green of late spring. A color that had always created a wave of optimism and hope in him.

"Whenever my soul got restless, I would come up here and just sit," he said.

"I don't imagine Elliott came along," Faith said. Then caught herself, waving her hand as if in apology. "Sorry. I...I...didn't mean..."

"It's okay," Kane assured her. "He's my brother. Of course he came along. We spent a lot of time together once. Though I'm glad you told me that nothing was going on between you."

"No. Definitely not with him." Her voice held an odd tone and Kane looked sideways at her. But she was staring ahead, a curious expression on her face.

He let it go. Right now she was here, and he was feeling more content than he had in a long time.

"Coming here feeds my soul," he said.

"Do you come back to the ranch often? While you're working rigs?"

"Not as often as I should have. I stayed away the first…the first while."

"Bad memories?"

"No. Good ones."

"Just ones you didn't want to pull out?" Faith turned to look at him. "I'm sorry. I don't know how else to say it, but I'm sorry for how things went between us."

Her words should have made him feel better, but they created an answering guilt in him. "You're not the only one who has something to apologize for. If I hadn't gotten so angry, if I hadn't jumped to such a stupid conclusion…"

Faith covered his hand with hers, squeezing lightly. "It was a bad situation all the way around."

He turned to her, gripping her hand. "I also need to apologize for how I pushed you to go to school. To get your degree. I never realized what you experienced with your grandfather until I saw him in action this morning."

"He was rather in full form," Faith said with a nervous laugh. She pulled in a deep breath. "I wish I knew how to explain to him why I did what I did so he would understand."

"Do you want to?"

"He's my grandfather," she mumbled. "He's the only family I have."

"I understand that. But if that's what he has to say to you after all this time, I'm wondering how you would get through to him."

"I don't know either. I can't be what he wants me to be, but at the same time…"

"At the same time what?" Kane prompted.

Faith pulled her hand away from his, fingering a strand of hair. "Much as I hate to admit it, he was right. The life I chose wasn't a good one. I wish, now, I had at least finished my college degree."

Kane frowned at that. "You never completed your degree?"

"Two courses short. I had crammed too much in the first couple of years, trying to be everything Grandpa wanted me to. I was never the scholar he was, though he didn't seem to want to admit that."

"I never knew that." Kane was rather shocked to hear it.

"Wasn't something I was proud of. That was also another reason I didn't apply for law school like I was supposed to. I didn't want to let you both know all your sacrifices were in vain."

"I never made any sacrifices," Kane protested.

She turned to him with a melancholy smile. "You did. I know how hard it was to see me leave every Monday, back to the city. Back to school. I hated it too."

The sadness in her voice sent him back to those years. "It was hard to let you go," he agreed. "But I figured it was worth it if you would finish."

"Well, I didn't. I'd like to complete it now, but, well, courses cost money."

And he guessed she didn't have much.

He let an idea linger, let it take shape. Wondered how she would take it.

"I could help you," he said, speaking before second thoughts stopped him. "I've got money saved up."

Faith shot him a puzzled look. "What are you saying?"

"That I could help pay for your courses. You could finish your degree." It would give her other options. Other career choices. A way to pay her grandfather back if she so desired.

She brushed her forehead with her fingertips, as if letting the idea settle. "You would do that?"

"Yes. Of course." He knew he would do anything for her. "Unless you're not interested anymore or you think I'm overstepping. I don't want you to think it's charity. I want to help you. If you want." A flash of nervousness made him spill out extra words as she hesitated.

"No. That's not it. I'm just..." She released a gentle smile. "I'm really touched. That's kind of you. And I am interested. In fact, I was trying to do correspondence courses, but life on the road wasn't too conducive to that."

"I imagine you were busy."

"Too busy." She sighed as if remembering. "There was never any quiet time."

"But there must have been things you liked about it." Or she wouldn't have done it for so long.

She plucked a blade of dried grass and twirled it in her fingers, her expression shifting. "Yeah. I loved making music, loved singing, loved writing songs."

"When you play, I see how much you love it."

Her genuine smile warmed his heart. "I'm so glad you understand."

"So where does that leave you?" He was afraid to ask, because that meant looking ahead. He wasn't sure he was ready to go too far in that direction without knowing if Faith would be alongside him.

"Conflicted," she said, twirling the grass one way, then another. "I want to make music. I don't want it to be just a hobby, but I know I can't make a living with it. And if I can't make music, who am I? I feel like I would lose an important part of myself."

He understood what she was saying, but it still created a

feeling of unease. If she stayed here in Rockyview how could she fulfill who she thought she should be?

"So you think you would go back to the band?" He hated to ask, but he felt he had to put it out there. Had to know.

"So much would have to change before I could."

"Like what?" Her answer didn't help his unease much, but she was here, and he had to be content with that.

"I don't know if I'm ready to talk about it yet," she said.

"Will there be a time?"

"I hope so."

He didn't like the direction of the conversation so he did the first thing that came to him. He slipped his hand around her neck and drew her close for a kiss.

She slipped her arms around his neck, her ardent response warming his soul.

Yet, as he drew back, slipping his fingers through her silky hair, he knew they were getting closer to a place where decisions had to be made. Where choices had to be discussed.

But not now, he thought, raining light kisses on her forehead, her cheeks and then again, her mouth.

Not now.

⌒◯⌒

"Are you sure you don't mind doing this?" Tricia asked yet again as Faith helped Hope out of her car seat. Cash was already free, running circles around the truck in the church parking lot. "I know it's been a busy week for you."

Busy didn't really describe it.

On Monday Zach got sick and Faith was busy tending him and Tricia, who was still in a lot of pain and sleeping a lot. The kids had been fractious and, on top of it all, Kane was as busy as she was. Because Zach couldn't help, Kane and Joe were working overtime, calving out cows and working on fences in the far pastures. He'd stumbled in late Monday night then again last night. They only had time for a quick hello, a shared look, a brush of their hands, and then Kane trudged off to bed. Every morning he was gone before she got up. She felt as if they were losing touch with each other at a critical juncture in their growing relationship. But she also didn't know what to do about it.

"No. I don't mind at all," Faith said as she took Hope's hand and closed the truck door. She'd been uncomfortable driving Kane's truck but, thankfully, the church was closer to the edge of town. Kane had offered to take Tricia to church, but Faith knew he and Joe needed to head out to the far pastures to work on the fences there and would be tied up all day.

So she said she would take Tricia and the twins.

"And you're also sure you don't want to come to the Bible study either?"

Faith shook her head. "No. I'm sure."

Tricia looked troubled, so Faith gave her a reassuring smile.

"Look. I'm not ready to share my deepest feelings and my struggles with my faith yet," Faith said. "Besides, I need to get groceries." Nothing like delving into the practical to switch the tone of the conversation.

She wasn't ready to face the mess of her past, which she knew would come out if she sat in on a Bible study. She'd been to enough Bible studies years ago to know when women got together and talked about their faith life, it was also an opportunity to open up and talk about what they were dealing with.

Not yet. Not near yet. Not before she told Kane.

Trouble was, she wasn't sure if she was ready for that either.

"Dad was telling me that Carmen Marie finally opened her deli and lunch place," Tricia said, dropping her line of questioning as she slowly got out of the truck. She winced but waved off Faith's offer of help. "You could go check it out after you're done with your grocery shopping."

"Really? She's been talking about doing that as long as I can remember," Faith said, thankful that Tricia was willing to go along with her change in topic.

"Dad told me it's been doing great. Of course, he's spent most of his lunch time there the past few days. Not that I blame him. He's spent so much time by himself the last couple of years." She sounded troubled, and Faith gave her shoulder a gentle squeeze.

"You're here now. So is Kane."

Tricia gave Faith a sideways grin. "You two must have had quite the 'talk' when you were riding up in the hills on Sunday."

An unwelcome flush warmed Faith's cheeks. "We talked."

"About your relationship?"

Faith wasn't sure what to say. She felt as if she were walking along the edge of a cliff. Not sure which step to take next. Things were moving toward the point of no return with Kane. Was she ready for that?

If not now, when?

"Not really, though we edged toward it."

"Sounds intriguing," Tricia said with a frown. She walked toward the church, her steps slow. Faith was glad to see her on her feet again, but knew her ribs were still bothering her.

"Not so much intriguing as complicated," Faith said, walking alongside, holding Cash's hand. Hope clung to Tricia.

Tricia said nothing to that. Faith guessed Tricia knew enough about complicated. While she had apologized repeatedly for not telling Zach about the twins, Faith sensed it would be a while before Zach's trust in Tricia was fully restored.

The muted sound of a band playing greeted them when they came into the church foyer. The doors to the sanctuary ahead of them were closed, and Faith guessed the band was inside.

"Do you know where you're supposed to go?" Faith asked Tricia as they stopped to look around.

"Not really."

Right then a young woman marched toward them, her pink sweater flowing behind her, dark hair held up in a messy topknot. "Welcome, welcome," she said, opening her arms wide. "I'm Angela." She laughed and pointed to her name tag. "Which you would know if I gave you the chance to read. You must be Tricia." She turned to Faith. "I'm sorry, I didn't catch your name."

"I'm Faith, but—"

"Beautiful name. Welcome to you too," Angela said, cutting her off. "Why don't you come with me, and I can show you where the nursery is for the littles." She spun around and walked away as quickly as she came.

Faith looked over at Tricia, who just shrugged. Oh well, may as well help get the kids settled before she left.

Angela was a whirlwind of information and energy. In no time she had the kids registered in the nursery and all the while she was explaining the basic tenets of the Coffee Break program to Faith and Tricia.

But when it came time to enter the large room where women were milling about, chatting, laughing, and drinking coffee, Faith held back.

"I need to go," she said, edging away from the doorway.

Angela looked puzzled but thankfully seemed to accept her weak excuse. "Of course. No problem."

"What time do you want me to come for you?" Faith asked Tricia.

"We'll be done in an hour and a half," Angela told her. "If that's okay with you?"

Faith held up her hands in a gesture of acceptance. "Absolutely fine. I'll be here."

Angela nodded, then with a gentle hand on Tricia's back, escorted her into the room. Faith moved back before anyone else saw her, then walked down the long carpeted hall, back to the main entrance.

One door of the sanctuary was open a crack, and the music flowed out, enticing and beguiling. Faith's steps slowed and then she pushed open the door, standing in the entrance, listening. Watching.

The group stopped playing, and the person who looked like the leader was talking. "There's something missing," he was saying. "Something that doesn't seem to work."

"I know what's missing," the guy on the drums said. "A decent guitar player."

Faith felt her heart jump at his words. This was too coincidental.

A sign?

She dismissed that as quickly as it came. She doubted God was that involved in her life.

Then the woman on the piano looked up and saw Faith. She jumped up, clapping her hands. "And just like that our prayers are answered."

What was going on?

Faith frowned as she looked closer at the woman behind the piano, then recognized a friend from high school, Marianne DenEngelson.

"You're such a joker, Marianne," the leader said. He waved his hand at Faith. "Ignore her. She's trying to be funny and spectacularly not succeeding."

"No. I'm serious. That's Faith Howard. She plays guitar for real," Marianne said, waving to Faith. "Come on up here and prove it to this doubting Thomas. He's new to the community so he has yet to learn our ways."

Faith rubbed her now damp palms on the legs of her blue jeans. This conversation was almost surreal.

"I don't know…"

Then Marianne was rushing down the aisle toward her. She caught Faith's hands in hers, her expression pleading. "You've got to help us out. Our other guitarist up and quit and we've been feeling the loss. Like badly."

Marianne added a bright smile, lifting her shoulders in a self-deprecating shrug. "Pretty please? For all the times I helped you with your homework and all the times I covered for you in Chem class."

This was so not fair. Marianne was right. She had helped Faith out. Endlessly. Too easily Faith remembered her intense frustration with Chemistry, a class she didn't understand.

"I'll always be grateful for that, but I'm not...going to be... won't be around..."

Stacy had called last night to tell Faith she couldn't hold the job much longer and to say she was looking for a new roommate if Faith didn't show up soon. Once again Faith felt rootless and unsure of her future.

But...she had never been the answer to anyone's prayers before, and it seemed like a nice situation to be in. Even if just for awhile.

"Okay. I'll jam with you guys."

Marianne beamed her joy. She dragged Faith up the aisle. "She's helping us out, oh ye of little faith," she crowed as she released Faith. She walked up the stairs at the front and then disappeared into a side room.

"Sorry about the railroading," the band leader said, resting his hands on the frame of his bass guitar. "Marianne can be quite the force of nature. I'm Nestor, the guy on drums is Ian. And Marianne you already know."

"And look what I found." Marianne reappeared, brandishing a guitar. "So glad that Brendan left this behind when he took off on us."

Faith took the guitar, surprised to see her hands trembling. *It's just for fun,* she told herself.

"So, not sure you know all our songs, but here's a binder," Marianne said. "Chords and notes, but I don't need to tell you that."

"Here's a stand." Nestor supplied her with that. He turned to Ian. "You want to set up the sound while I plug the guitar in?"

Ian was off like a shot. Faith looped the strap around her neck and took a deep breath, surprised at how nervous she felt. Singing praise songs? With the church band?

If only Keith could see her now. He'd be mocking her like crazy.

Well, he's not here and he's not an issue and his opinion means less than dirt.

Faith brushed aside the hovering voices then jumped as the amp she was plugged into squeaked.

"Sorry," Ian said from the back of the church, where, Faith suspected, the sound board was located.

Faith strummed a few notes, pleased to note the guitar was just about in tune. She adjusted some of the strings, plucked out a few notes, and then was ready to go.

"Okay. We're doing number twenty-three," Ian told Faith. "From the top."

She nodded, turning the binder to the appropriate number. Two pages. Key of C major. Not too complicated.

"You can follow?" Nestor asked.

"Let's get started and we'll see."

Ian beat out a rhythm, Marianne played the first few bars, and Faith and Nestor jumped right in. She fumbled a few chords, unfamiliar with the tune, but soon she picked it up, reading the music on the fly. By the second verse she was leading better and by the third, improvising.

Fourth verse she dared sing along.

Marianne finished the song with a flourish. Nestor followed behind and then pumped his fist.

"That was awesome. Thank You, Lord," he shouted.

Faith jumped, startled by his enthusiasm.

"That really was tight," Ian called out. "Can't believe you jumped in like that," he called out to Faith.

"We found the missing link," Marianne called out. "Faith, you are the bomb. Can we try number seventeen next?" Marianne suggested.

"That'd be great. Haven't played that one since Brendan left." Ian beat out another rhythm, and they were away. This time Faith sang along, slowly gaining confidence, her alto weaving through Marianne's soprano, enhancing Nestor's tenor. The song echoed through the church, growing louder as they all gained more confidence.

Faith played with her whole heart, letting the music nourish the part of her that still yearned for the thrill of singing and performing with a group. The richness of the various instruments playing off each other, enriching each other, all held together by the beat of the drums.

One song led into another, and Faith let the lyrics soak into a soul that, she realized, had missed this more than she knew. Songs that had meaning, depth. Songs that praised God, celebrated life and grace. Songs that called out for mercy and forgiveness.

Songs she had sung as a young girl, innocent and believing there was nothing beyond God's love.

Did she believe that now?

❧◦❧

"I'll call you if Faith and Tricia aren't finished," Kane said to Joe as they pulled up beside his truck in the church parking lot. "Tricia figured the Bible study would go until eleven-thirty."

It was eleven-twenty now.

"And what about lunch?" Joe asked with a hopeful note.

Kane knew Joe was angling to head over to Carmen Marie's new deli and restaurant. Ever since she had opened it up, he'd been eating there as often as possible. Kane suspected Joe was developing a small crush on the owner. Not that he blamed him. Carmen was beautiful and adorably smart and efficient.

And her baked goods were indescribable.

"Depends on how the kids are," Kane said. He would have preferred to head back home. They finally got caught up, but they still had old wire to roll up and dispose of and four more cows were calving today.

But he'd been working Joe hard the past couple of days and, if he were honest, he was tired himself. Joe nodded, but the light of hope shone from his eyes.

Kane shook his head, then strode up the walk to the church, wondering if that same hope beamed from his own face. After their ride on Sunday, he and Faith spent the rest of the afternoon at the ranch, playing games with the kids. Faith played some songs for them and, at Kane and Tricia's urging, played a few of her own compositions. That night the moon was full, and they went for a 'walk.'

But the last couple of days work had piled up, and he and Faith had had no time together. It bothered him, but there wasn't much he could do.

This trip to town wasn't done willingly. If it wasn't for the fact that they couldn't keep working until they got more fence posts and wire, he would have stayed home. And now Joe was angling for lunch at the deli.

But maybe he could see Faith. Maybe he had to stop working so hard. Trying to get everything done before he had to head back.

This morning he got a call from his boss telling him they would start up in a couple of weeks. When would Kane be back?

Kane hadn't answered or responded to the message his boss had left. He hadn't wanted reality to intrude in this time out of time he'd been living in.

But yet, how long could he carry on in this limbo? He had to make a decision.

With a sigh, he stepped into the church, not sure where to go when he heard music coming from the sanctuary. It stopped and then he heard people talking. He paused, listening.

Was that Faith's voice?

Then the music started up again, and his heart flipped over in his chest. It was Faith. And she was singing.

Intrigued, he opened one of the double doors and slipped inside, hoping he wouldn't be noticed. He didn't have to worry. The pianist and the bass player from Sunday were looking at Faith, who was looking from them to the drummer. It was as if something electric was flowing between the four of them.

He didn't recognize the music they played, then realized it wasn't a praise song.

It sounded very similar to the song Faith had been playing the other evening.

He couldn't keep his eyes off her. She looked more alive than he'd seen her in a while. She was smiling, her eyes bright, shining with an inner light. She swayed with the music, tapping her toe, moving her shoulders as she played. Notes spilled from her fingers, chords that harmonized with the piano.

It was raucous and fun and mesmerizing.

And Kane, suddenly, felt as if he was seeing the side of Faith that he had caught only glimpses of before.

Faith fully alive. Doing what she loved best.

It made him smile, and it frightened him.

He watched for a few more moments realizing he hadn't even been noticed, then slipped out of the auditorium.

Stunned, and still trying to absorb what he just saw, he leaned back against the door.

Dear Lord, now what?

The sound of excited children punctuated by women's laughter broke into his scattered and half-formed prayer. Sounded like the Bible study was over. He sucked in a deep and calming breath, then pushed himself away from the door and walked down the hall toward the voices.

He saw his sister standing with another woman, talking seriously. The twins were sitting on the floor beside her, playing with some blocks. Kane recognized Angela Rigo, the owner of a fabric store downtown.

Angela gave Tricia a careful hug, followed by an encouraging smile.

"I'll be praying for you," she said.

"Thanks for that," Tricia said. "I know I don't deserve it."

"None of us do," Angela said with a chuckle. Then she looked past Tricia and waved at Kane. "Looks like your ride is here."

Tricia looked back and frowned when she saw Kane.

"I thought Faith was driving me and the kids home with Dad's truck."

Kane walked toward her, then bent over and picked up Cash and swung him onto his hip. "I needed a truck to pick up some fence posts and stuff."

"But where's Faith?" Tricia repeated.

"Apparently she's playing with the praise band from Sunday," Kane said, hoping he sounded more casual than he felt.

"That's amazing," Tricia exclaimed, her hand on her chest. "Wouldn't that be cool if she played with them all the time? I know she misses playing with the band. She would love this."

Kane wished he could share her enthusiasm. While he saw it as a positive on one hand, on the other it raised questions about how staying in Rockyview would fill the need he had heard her speak so eloquently about.

"Yeah, it's pretty cool," he said.

"I'm hungry," Cash said.

"You're always hungry," Kane teased him.

"What do you say to going to Carmen's new deli?" Tricia said. "I'm hungry too, and I'd love to try it."

"Have you and Joe been talking to each other?" Kane teased. "He's always campaigning to eat lunch there too."

Tricia shrugged. "I know the kids are hungry, and I think it would be a nice break for Faith if she didn't have to make lunch for us."

"You're not too tired?"

"I'm tired, but I'm not ready to go back to the ranch."

Kane knew she and Zach still had some issues, and he didn't think running away was the way to solve them. But he understood that it was nice for her to be out and about. Especially if she had someone to help her take care of the kids.

"Unless you're in a rush to head back," Tricia quickly added. "I know you and Joe have been busy getting things ready for the potential sale."

Kane didn't want to talk about the sale right now. He had a few other things on his mind. After his conversation with Tricia and Faith's comments the other day, he was thinking he wanted to talk to his dad first.

"We're getting on top of stuff," Kane said, shading the truth a hair. "So if Faith is okay with meeting us there, I think we could probably have some lunch in town."

"That would be awesome," Tricia said. "Let's go find out."

As they walked down the hall Faith stepped out of the sanctuary. Her cheeks were flushed, her eyes bright.

"So how did it go playing with the group?" Tricia asked.

Faith jumped. "You scared me," she said, her hand pressed to her chest.

"And where were you?" Tricia teased.

Faith ignored her, catching Kane's gaze. Her smile was wide and welcoming, and Kane's unease settled down. A bit.

"You looked like you were having fun," he said. "I snuck in to have a listen. You all sounded good together."

"They are a tight group," Faith said. "And yes, I really enjoyed playing with them. They asked if I would play with them on Sunday."

"And…" Tricia encouraged.

"I'm…I'm not sure…" Faith let the sentence drift off. Kane wondered what was holding her back.

"Are you willing to go to Carmen's deli for lunch?" Tricia asked. "I thought it might be a nice break for you."

"You're not too tired?" Faith asked, looking concerned.

"I'll probably be ready for a nap when we get home," Tricia said. "But I'm not ready to head back. It's been nice being out and about. And the kids are still really good, so I thought we could do this."

"Then I'm game." Faith bestowed another smile on Kane, then picked up Hope, giving her a quick kiss.

It was just a simple gesture, but it settled into Kane's heart. And as they walked out of the building together, he allowed himself to think of a potential future for him and Faith.

CHAPTER 19

"*K*ane. Just the fellow I needed to talk to."

The hearty voice behind them startled Faith. She almost dropped her soup spoon onto the table, but caught it in time.

She turned to see a short, portly man, with a fringe of red hair framing a balding head. He wore a golf shirt and plaid Bermuda shorts and a smile that made her uneasy.

"Hey, Floyd," Kane said, turning. "What can I do for you?"

The man named Floyd bit his lip, looking around the group. Joe had just finished his second muffin and was helping Hope finish her fries.

Tricia was picking at her sandwich, looking more tired than she let on.

The deli was busy when they came in so Carmen put them at a table tucked away in a corner. But somehow, Floyd had found them.

"I came to give you some good news," he was saying. "I was wondering if you want to come by my office and talk there. You're looking kinda busy right now."

"I don't have time to come afterwards," Kane said. "Why don't you talk now?"

Floyd fidgeted with the cell phone he was holding. "Well, I was hoping to do it more privately."

"That's okay," Tricia said, pushing her sandwich away. "You stay here and talk to Floyd. I want to go back home. I'm feeling kind of beat."

"I can take you," Faith said.

"No, it's okay," Tricia said. "Joe can take me."

Joe looked pained. "I was going to get another piece of Carmen's astounding cheesecake."

"Really, Joe? Astounding?" Tricia shook her head, then looked directly at him as if she was trying to say something more. "Regardless of how astounding the cheesecake is, I'd like to go, remember?"

Joe sighed and licked his fork, cast one more longing look at the dessert case, then pushed his chair back. "Right. Of course. We need to go. I should get back to the ranch. Done with my lunch anyway."

"Perfect," Tricia said. "And Faith needs to get groceries yet, so she may as well stay behind. We can move the car seats to Joe's truck."

Faith nodded, feeling a tad guilty that she hadn't done that yet. She should have been shopping instead of playing with the band. However, she had enjoyed it more than she thought she would. Singing the songs of forgiveness and love spoke to her in a way she knew a Bible study couldn't.

"Maybe I'll do that while you're talking," Faith said, getting up as well.

"No. Give me the keys to Dad's truck. I can move them," Tricia protested. "Stay. Enjoy your lunch." She turned to Floyd. "Surely you don't need to talk to Kane right now? I mean, he's kind of occupied already."

Now Faith was really confused, but then she caught Joe's grin, and everything clicked into place.

Tricia and Joe were trying to get her and Kane to spend time together. Alone.

While she appreciated the sentiment, she would have preferred this happened somewhere else than downtown Rockyview.

"I can help you shift the car seats around."

Tricia just rolled her eyes signalling her acquiescence, and then they all walked out of the cafe. Faith helped Tricia and Joe get the kids move the seats and get the kids in the truck.

"You guys aren't obvious at all," Faith said, giving Tricia a grin as she leaned on the open window of the truck, looking from Joe to Tricia.

"Joe and I thought it would be nice for you and Kane to be together away from the ranch. That was all. But then Mr. Floyd Picthall had to come and wreck it all." Tricia pouted, looking so much like the young girl she used to be that Faith had to laugh.

"Don't worry about me and Kane," Faith said. "We'll get our time together. We don't need meddling matchmakers' help."

Joe's grin and Tricia's wink made her realize how that sounded.

Suddenly she didn't care anymore what people thought about her and Kane. She was tired of the indecision and the wondering. Singing with the band this morning showed her other possibilities. Other opportunities. Sure, it wasn't touring. Sure, it wasn't glamorous. But it was a way to express herself.

And maybe, just maybe, the music was a way to find her way back to a God she had also turned her back on.

"That's good to know," Tricia said. "I'm so glad to see you and Kane together again. It makes my heart so happy. I feel like the accident…well…it had such far-reaching repercussions."

"What happened all those years ago had nothing to do with that," Faith said, pushing herself away from the truck. "Now you better get the kids back to the ranch and make sure you lay down, yourself. You look beat."

Tricia gave her a grateful smile. Then the window slid closed and Faith stepped away, watching them leave. She had to smile at their machinations and somehow felt self-conscious about it. But it was a good feeling to know people saw them as a couple.

She was about to get into Zach's truck when she realized that in the fuss of getting the kids and Tricia to Joe's vehicle, she had forgotten her purse.

The deli was even quieter now, and Carmen waved at her as she came in. "Coming back for seconds?" she asked.

"No. Just forgot my purse."

"Well good thing Kane and Floyd are still at the table," Carmen said.

Faith just grinned and walked toward the nook where Floyd and Kane still sat. They both had their backs to her, and she hesitated as she heard them talking, voices low.

Then something Floyd said caught her up short.

"The buyer, Stan Withers, wants to come tomorrow. I'll bring him in the afternoon if that works for you."

Faith felt a jolt of pure fear. Was Kane still considering selling the ranch? And if he did, what would happen to the two of them?

"Okay. I guess we'll see you then," Kane said.

Faith swallowed, wishing she could turn around and leave. But they still needed groceries, and for that she needed her purse.

So, holding her head up, she walked over, excused herself, grabbed her purse. Without looking at Kane she walked out of the deli, her heart pounding in time to her hurried footsteps.

What did you think would change, she asked herself as she walked to the grocery store. Even if you and Kane are getting close, why would you think he would put his life on hold for you again?

But she couldn't follow through on this line of thinking.

They had talked. Come to an understanding.

You still haven't told him everything, and he knows you're holding back. Maybe that's why he's moving on.

She thought of the song she sang with the band. How it spoke of God working His way in our lives on His own time and His own plan, which is more perfect than ours.

So what is Your plan for me, she wondered as she pulled open the door to the grocery store. *Where do I fit in Kane's life, and where does he fit in mine?*

Because one thing she knew for sure. The more time she spent with him, the more she knew she wanted to be with him. Which meant she had to tell him everything. About Keith and, even harder, about her pregnancy.

"This is really prime real estate," Stan Withers was saying, standing in the yard, looking around. "Not too far from town. It's perfect."

"Didn't I tell you, Stan?" Floyd's forced grin sent a shiver of annoyance down Kane's back. He sounded positively gleeful and, no wonder. If Stan bought the ranch, Floyd stood to gain a hefty commission.

Stan looked over at Kane. "So you've got most of this fenced and cross-fenced, Floyd was telling me?"

"Yeah. We spent the last couple of weeks fixing it up. They're all solid."

Stan strolled toward the barns with Kane, Zach and Floyd trailing him like lost puppies. "And how many cows can this place run?" he asked when they came to the wooden fence blocking off the spring pasture.

Zach rested his arms on the top rail of the fence, squinting against the morning sun.

"Right now we've got about one hundred purebred cows. One quarter of them have calved already. We can run, when we're at full capacity, about six hundred head. That's taking hay land into account as well."

Stan whistled his appreciation. "That's amazing." He was quiet a moment, then he turned to Floyd. "So, tell me about bylaws in this county. How hard is it to subdivide?"

"What do you mean?" Kane asked, unable to keep the edge out of his voice. "What would you want to subdivide?"

Stan waved his hand over the yard and the land beyond. "You've got some primo views of the mountains. I know there's people in Calgary who would pay top dollar for a place out here. You could easily break this down into twenty parcels. Sell them for a premium price. You could then take the rest of the land and flip it. Or run a dude ranch."

Kane released a harsh laugh. "I'm sure you could."

Floyd glanced over at Kane, as if sensing his displeasure.

Stan seemed oblivious to Kane's mood, grinning as he looked around. "It would take a big chunk of change to bring in power and all the services, but it would be worth it in the long run."

"I can see that," his father said, nodding as if in agreement with Stan's ideas. "You certainly have a vision."

What? Vision? His father couldn't seriously be considering this nonsense?

Floyd joined Stan and together they walked towards the barns, talking about the logistics of how this could be done.

Kane caught his father by the arm before he went to join them. "You can't sell the ranch to this guy, Dad."

Zach sent Kane an aggrieved look. "He's the first serious buyer we've had since I put the place up for sale."

"But...subdividing...flipping...this guy won't run it as a ranch."

"I knew that would happen," Zach said, looking away from Kane. "It's a valuable piece of property. I can't expect that any new buyer could simply take it over and pay me out what it's worth."

Kane wanted to protest, but what could he say? It was his father's ranch.

Zach held his frustrated gaze but said nothing, as if waiting for some response from Kane.

Take it over. Swallow your pride and ask him to help you out. Then you can stay here with Faith.

If she's willing.

Kane felt conflicted, still not sure what to do. Then Floyd and Stan returned to where they stood.

"So, I need to make a few calls," Stan was saying. "But I think we can come to a mutual agreement."

Fear slithered through Kane as he looked over the yard again, the thought of acreages filling this ranch twisting his stomach.

"That's good," Zach said. "You know what I need out of this place, so I'll let you and Floyd come up with a number and we'll talk."

Floyd looked so pleased and Stan looked so smug, Kane couldn't be here anymore.

He spun around and walked toward the house. He needed to get his hat and jacket and head out.

The house was quiet when he stepped inside. Tricia and the kids were probably lying down. Then he heard the strains of Faith's guitar coming from the deck.

His heart clenched at the sound, thinking about her playing the other day in church. Part of him wanted to walk away, but a larger part wanted to connect with her. To find out where they were now.

"You look grumpy," Faith said as he dropped in the chair across from her.

"The buyer is here."

Faith said nothing, understanding what that meant.

"He's talking about subdividing the property."

"What? That's terrible. What does Zach say to that?" Her horror aptly reflected how he felt about it all.

"Nothing. Nothing at all." Kane shoved his hand through his hair in a gesture of disgust. "He doesn't seem to care."

"I can't believe that. Can't believe he wouldn't want this to stay a working ranch." Faith reached over and took his hand. "You need to talk to Zach. Ask him if he'll work with you to take over the ranch."

Kane curled his fingers around hers, thankful for the connection. Thankful for her encouragement.

"Like I said, you belong here, Kane. This place is as much your legacy as it is your father's. You can't let it break apart. Be run over by people who would never, ever, appreciate it for what it truly is."

Kane let her passion resurrect a tiny smile. "You sound pretty emphatic about this."

"I am."

He held her gaze, growing serious. "This matters to you, doesn't it?"

Faith nodded. "It does. A lot." She stopped there but Kane allowed himself a small dream. The two of them here, together.

"Please, talk to him," Faith said.

"Okay. I will."

"Tonight. Before he goes to bed."

"Or, I could follow him to his bedroom and sit on his bed like I used to. Talk to him there." Kane's smile grew, remembering four kids, crowded onto Grace and Zach's bed, early in the morning, drinking tea together. Planning the day.

Now he and Tricia were the only ones left here.

"Or you could just ask him to talk in his study," Faith said with a light laugh. "Make it more official."

Kane got up and pulled Faith to her feet, then drew her into his arms. "Thanks for the pep talk," he said. "I think I needed that."

"We all do from time to time." She reached up, pulled his head down, and brushed a kiss over his lips.

"You want to come with me?" he asked.

She shook her head. "Nope. You need to do this on your own."

Kane agreed, but it would have been nice if she agreed to

come. Would have been nice if she saw this decision as something they would make together. Follow through on.

Together.

Faith stood on the veranda, watching Kane walk back across the yard. He didn't look back, his stride determined.

She shared his frustration, his puzzlement at his father's willingness to sell the ranch without seeing it taken over by another rancher. Someone who would appreciate what he was buying.

Not someone who only saw it as an opportunity to make more money. Just land, without the legacy.

Please, Lord, give Kane the courage to face his father.

Her prayer was automatic, and even as she prayed it, she had to think of her own grandfather. She hadn't tried to contact him since Sunday. What would be the point?

If you're not leaving here...

The words drifted through her mind, ethereal as smoke. She tried to catch them, study them.

Where else would you go? Can you really walk away from Kane again?

But she wasn't the girl she was before. So much in her life had changed.

Then tell him.

She thought of his comments about Tricia. Would he understand her situation? Would he judge her?

Her stomach turned at the thought of Kane turning away from her again. Rejecting her.

She set her guitar aside, tired of the back and forth of her thoughts. *Do the next thing. Face up to your past and forge your own future.*

Though she was struggling with forgiveness deep in her soul, she knew God's love was greater than she could imagine. When she sang the songs with the group on Wednesday, it was as if she had felt all the parts of her life on the road getting sloughed off. All her sins shifted, sent away.

So, for now, her growing relationship with God would have to be enough.

And all she could do was pray that Kane would understand.

Before she talked to Kane, however, she had someone else she needed to connect with. Pulling in a steadying breath, she picked up her cell phone and dialed her grandfather's number. *One reconciliation at a time,* she told herself.

She prayed as the phone rang. Asking God to help her through this conversation. To soften her grandfather's heart.

He picked it up on the fourth ring. "Yeah," he said, his tone abrupt. His voice holding the impatient note it often did when he was working.

"Hey, Grandpa, it's Faith. Are you busy?"

"Why are you calling?"

"I was hoping we could meet for lunch or supper sometime."

A deep pause followed her suggestion. The longer it went on the harder Faith gripped her phone. This was a mistake. She should never have called. Her grandfather was clear on Sunday what he thought of her.

"What could we possibly have to talk about?"

Faith walked to the edge of the veranda and leaned forward against the railing, looking out over the fields that flowed to the hills edging the distant craggy peaks of the Rocky Mountains.

"I lift up my eyes to the hills. Where does my help come from?"

The Bible passage quieted her troubled soul, stilled her fears. She may not have been faithful to God, but He had been faithful to her and would help her through this.

"Choices I made. Mistakes I made."

This netted her another moment of silence. "I'm glad you realize that," he said, his tone gruff.

"I also want to say thank you for all you've done for me. I

know I didn't become what you wanted, but you need to know that I hope to pay you back for every course you've paid for." At one time it was about being free from him. Releasing herself from his expectations, but now, after spending time here at the ranch and being enfolded back into a place where she had one time been so happy, she knew there was another reason. "I want you to know how much I appreciate and respect what you've done."

"You want to pay me back?" His voice held an angry tone that made Faith close her eyes, draw in another deep breath, send out yet another prayer.

She hadn't spoken to God this much since she'd left Rockyview.

"Why would you do that?" he continued, his voice still holding a tense edge.

Faith was glad she had called instead of dealing with him face to face. She would cave or cry, and that would never do. Her grandfather didn't appreciate weakness.

"Like I said, to show you that I respect what you did for me and that I take it seriously."

"You want me out of your life."

You started it, she wanted to say, the hurt still sharp from the time he turned her away at the hospital.

"No. I just want to acknowledge the sacrifices you made for me." More silence.

"I wanted so much more for you," he said finally. "I didn't want you to end up like your mother."

And they were back to that. Faith turned away from the view. She could see Tricia with her children in the family room. Cash and Hope were sitting beside her while she read them a story. A mother with her children.

As she watched, something else came to her in a way she had never considered before. Yes, her mother felt pushed, and yes, there had been pressure.

But she left Faith. Abandoned her, so to speak. She said she was coming back for her but what had been her plan? How did her mother see their future?

And didn't you abandon your child? Sort of?

Faith pressed her fist against her mouth, fighting the usual regret that surged through her whenever she thought of the loss of her baby.

And with it, the guilt at her relief when it happened.

What kind of a mother wants to lose her child?

"Maybe I did after all," she said, her voice quiet.

He said nothing to that. Their silence stretched out, heavy, weighted with past pain, feeding on itself as it grew.

She either had to end this call or find something else to talk about. "How are you feeling after your heart attack?" she blurted out.

"Good. I'm good. Thanks for asking."

"I wish I could have seen you in the hospital," she said, deciding to go right to her next point.

And, once again, she was treated to a pregnant pause.

"I...I was angry...and...well...my doctor told me that sometimes, after a heart attack, your personality changes. I knew I couldn't see you. I was still too upset."

"You were still upset on Sunday," she said, trying to keep the recrimination out of her own voice.

"I heard you were in town. I had to hear it from someone else. My own granddaughter couldn't let me know she was around." His voice grew progressively louder, harsher.

"Because I thought you didn't want to see me. After I tried to visit you in the hospital."

Another pause.

"I see."

She hoped he did. She hoped that, somehow, they could find their way back to each other. She knew all he had done for her, but she wished it hadn't come with such a web of obligations and expectations attached.

"Well, I…I made a mistake then. And on Sunday. But you made mistakes too."

Faith ignored the last words of his reply. She knew how difficult it was for her grandfather to eke out the first words. While it wasn't exactly what she had hoped to hear, for now, it was enough. Their conversation had built a fragile bridge over the chasm that had yawned between them for the past few years.

"I have, for sure," she admitted. "And that's why I want to pay you back. To pay for those mistakes."

"I don't think we need to talk about that right now," he said with a heavy sigh. "We can discuss how you can pay me back another time."

"Okay. Another time." That was good enough for her.

"I have to go now. Client's waiting." He cleared his throat and then added, "Thanks for calling."

Faith smiled, then whispered, "You're welcome."

He ended the call, and Faith held onto her phone a few moments longer, the old anxiety she felt whenever she thought of Mick Howard gently loosening its tenacious grip on her life.

She turned to look back at the view in front of her, feeling cleansed and relieved.

A gentle hush settled on the ranch as Faith blew out a hard breath, releasing her concerns.

Thanks for that, Lord, she prayed, pushing herself away from the railing. Thanks for the small step of reconciliation between me and my grandfather. It wasn't far. It wasn't dramatic. But she was now closer to him than she had been since she'd left.

She wanted to tell Kane about it. Wanted to share it with him. She knew how much he respected her grandfather. It would make him happy to know they were making steps toward reconciling again.

And right now she wanted nothing more than to make Kane happy.

Now, and in the future.

Before she made too many plans, however, she knew she would have to have another difficult conversation.

But as she walked back into the house to make supper, her step was light and her heart full. God had guided her through her discussion with her grandfather. She knew He would help her with the next one.

CHAPTER 20

"*A*re you really selling the ranch to this guy?" Tricia was asking their father as she wiped Cash's mouth. Every day she seemed to get more mobile, but Kane could see she was still in a lot of pain. What he wouldn't give to get hold of the guy who did this to her.

"He's the only serious buyer we got," Zach was saying.

"But he wants to subdivide the property," Tricia said. "Surely you can't think that's a good thing."

"Once I sell it, it doesn't matter what I think. It will belong to a new owner, and he can do what he wants."

Kane glanced at Faith, who gave him an encouraging smile. He hadn't eaten any dinner, he was so nervous. He had to talk to his father tonight. Before Zach signed any papers with Floyd and Stan.

The thought made his own unease shift up another gear.

It had to be tonight. If his father said no…

He couldn't bear to think of that. Slowly, each day, he'd been allowing himself a few dreams. Of thinking maybe he and Faith could make a home here. Though he sensed hesitation on her part, he had been heartened by her urging him to talk to Zach. The ranch was important to her too.

"Where's Joe tonight?" Faith asked as she got up to clear the dishes off the table.

"He's out on the town. Said he had a date," Kane said.

"Did he say with whom?"

"Nope. Just kept it to himself."

"Can't blame him for playing his cards close to his chest," Zach said.

Which was what his father had been doing after Floyd and Stan left. Tricia had quizzed him when they sat down for dinner, but he just shrugged. Said nothing.

Kane took a small sliver of hope from that.

As his dad got up from the table, Kane drew in a deep breath and raised a prayer for strength.

"Can I talk to you, Dad? Alone?" he asked. Zach gave him a searching look, which made Kane even more nervous. Then his father nodded. "Yeah. Sounds good. Let's go to the office."

Kane looked over at Faith again, and she gave him another encouraging smile. He caught a thumbs up from Tricia. *Well, here goes nothing,* he thought, following his father out of the kitchen, through the family room, and to the office adjoining it.

He closed the door as his father eased himself into a chair. Kane stayed standing, trying not to fidget.

Kane tried to catch his father's gaze, but Zach was massaging his leg, wincing. He hadn't been out on the ranch for a couple of days and had mentioned that he was feeling punk lately.

"You okay, Dad?" he asked. "Leg bothering you more than usual?"

"I think I overdid it the other day when I was helping you and Joe."

"That's not good."

"Nope."

His father wasn't helping him at all.

Then he folded his hands over his stomach and looked up at Kane. "Sit down, Son. Tell me what's on your mind."

Kane dropped into the chair across from him.

"So what do you think of Stan's ideas?" Zach asked. This was it. His chance. Yet Kane hesitated.

"You didn't seem too enthused," Zach continued.

"I wasn't. I'm not. Subdivide this place? Really?"

"So I'm guessing you don't want me to sell it to him," Zach said, as if it was a foregone conclusion.

Kane looked down at his hands, twiddling his fingers, not sure what to say. Not sure what he should say. "It's your place, Dad. I have no right to tell you what to do with it."

Zach leaned forward, his gaze intent, his eyes narrowed. "You are my son. You have every right."

The ferocity in his voice startled Kane.

"I'm hurt that you don't see yourself as part of my legacy," his dad continued.

"I'm not... I don't..." Kane wasn't sure what Zach expected him to say.

"You and Tricia were talking the other day," Zach said, changing the subject, taking control of the conversation. He leaned back in his chair, holding Kane's gaze, not looking away. "About the ranch."

"I'm sorry. I thought you were sleeping," Kane said.

"Just resting. Shouldn't have been eavesdropping, but I wanted to hear what you had to say." Zach was quite a moment, biting his lip. "I have to confess, I'm hurt you didn't think to come to me. I didn't think you wanted to run the ranch."

"At one time I didn't," Kane said.

"At one time? That sounds like you're changing your mind."

"Do you want me to?"

Zach released an exasperated sigh. "Like I said, you're my son. You have as much right to this place as I do. You've worked it since you first came into this house. You've worked alongside me for years. Once you wanted to take this over. At one time we made plans," Zach continued.

"I left. I walked away from what you offered."

"So you don't think you have the right to ask again."

Kane closed his eyes, trying to marshal his words. To find the right ones.

He stuck with simple.

"No. I don't."

"So, your pride will force me to sell Tall Timber to a guy who wants to dismantle this legacy."

Pride? Is that how Zach saw this?

As he held his father's gaze, Kane realized that maybe his father was right.

"Don't let your pride hold you back from taking what I want to offer you. This place is as much yours as anyone's."

Kane swallowed, hardly daring to believe what his father was saying.

"You're still hesitating?"

"There's something else."

"Faith."

Kane nodded. "Our relationship has changed. I think we're coming to an understanding."

"Understanding?" Zach released a short laugh. "I've seen how you two look at each other. There's more than an 'understanding' going on. You really care for her. Don't you?"

"I always have," Kane confessed.

"So what's the problem now?"

"Her music."

"How is that a problem?"

"I know it's what she wants to do, and I don't want to hold her back from it. I see how she looks when she's playing her music, and it cuts me to the bone. I don't feel like I can take that away from her."

"How would you be taking that away from her?" Zach asked.

"What kind of chance is there for her here? To play music like she always has?"

"I know this may sound cliché, and maybe a little flip, but don't you think the Lord will provide?"

"It sounds a little flip," Kane said. "And a little convenient."

"I really believe if God wants her to play music, he will make it work."

Kane wished he had his father's confidence. At the same time, he thought of what Faith had told him about her life on the road. How that was not the life she wanted to lead. He saw her again standing in front of the church, her smile a glorious thing to behold as she sang. But was playing in the band in church enough for her? Would she come to resent staying here after a while?

"You're overthinking this," Zach said.

"I have to this time. I messed it up the last time," Kane said. "I can't afford that risk again. She's too much a part of my life now, even more than before. I can't lose her again."

"Have you talked to her about this?" Zach asked.

"We skirted the issue," Kane said. "It's like this awkward dance. Neither of us dares make the first move."

"The longer you wait, the harder it will be," Zach said.

"You're right." Kane pressed his fingers to his temples. "Life was so much simpler a few years ago. It's gotten so complicated now."

"Life never really gets more complicated, there's just more factors to consider." Zach tapped his fingers on his arm. "So now I want to talk to you about the ranch. Would you be interested in taking over?"

Kane considered this a moment, then nodded slowly. "Of course I would. But I don't feel like I have the right—"

"Why don't you let me decide if you have the right or not. You're my son. I want to do everything I can to help you."

"I don't deserve this. Besides, I can't afford to buy you out."

"You wouldn't have to buy me out. We would keep working

the ranch, and I would keep taking an income. We can put the income I take against buying out the ranch."

"But what about Tricia? I want to make it fair for her too," Kane said. "It's not right for you to help me out this way, and not Tricia or Elliott or Lucas."

"Tricia can stay here as long as she needs to," Zach said. "And if she wants, we can work her into the ranch too. There's room for her. Even Elliott and Lucas, if they want to return. You know how much land I have rented out, land we could use ourselves. There's lots of room to expand. Room for all."

Kane hardly dared let what his father say register. Hardly dared think the dream he thought he had thrown away was still available to him.

Zach leaned forward and rested his hand on Kane's knee. "I know you think you don't deserve this, but do you think I did? I took this over from my father, who took it over from his. It was passed on down, gifts to each of us. I want to give you that same gift. I don't want this land to be taken over and run by someone we don't know. I want it to stay in the family."

Family. That word wound around his heart and created a surprising ache.

"I know you never really felt like a true son." Zach gave him a rueful smile.

Kane looked over at him in shock.

"You don't need to look so surprised," Zach said. "I know you've always seen yourself as second best, but you couldn't be more my son than if you were born from me and Grace. We took you in, and we gave you a home. And it's your home. I'm not lending it to you, you are a part of this place. It's in your blood. Even if that blood isn't Tye blood. We chose you. We wanted you in this family. We brought you in for a reason. I love you so much, and I wish you would take this. Accept this gift I want to give to you. A gift from a father to a son."

Kane felt his throat thicken as his father spoke, and he swallowed and swallowed to keep his emotions in check. But he couldn't stop the tears rising, from spilling over.

Suddenly he was in Zach's arms, being held close, a father holding his son.

"I love you too, Dad," Kane said. "I always have. I just never felt I deserved—"

"Please don't say that anymore. Like I told you, none of us deserves what we get. It's all a gift, a blessing, but it's also a trust. This land was entrusted to me, and I want to entrust it to you. Because I trust you."

Kane closed his eyes, letting his father's love wash over him. It was more than he expected, and it was an answer to a prayer he never dared articulate.

They stood together a moment, then drew away. Kane swiped a hand over his eyes, trying not to feel embarrassed at his display. His father smiled at him and patted him on the shoulder.

"I guess we'll have to make a trip into town tomorrow. We need to talk to Floyd. I feel bad for Stan, but that's the nature of buying and selling. You win some, you lose some."

"I need to talk to Faith," Kane said.

Zach looked suddenly serious again. "Do you think she'll stay?"

His father asked his question softly, but the words held an ominous tone.

Kane nodded. "I think she will. She was the one who encouraged me to come talk to you."

Zach looked like he was about to say more when the door of the study flew open. Joe stood there, panting. "Kane. You gotta come now. Misty is foaling, but it's not looking good."

Kane shot out of his chair, grabbing his hat. Misty had been his mother's horse.

"Should I call the vet?" Zach asked.

"Let me look first." Kane stopped at the door and gave his father a reassuring smile. "We'll do what we can, Dad."

"Misty first, okay? Colt second."

Kane nodded, then left. His conversation with Faith would have to be put off for now. But he felt like a huge stone had been lifted off his chest. Like he had released a burden and could now walk. Heck, he could almost fly.

Faith scribbled a few notations on the song she was working on, then stuck the pencil in her mouth as she played it again. Yes. Much better.

The setting sun cast shadows over the ranch and a hint of chill crept into the air. She should go inside, but she wasn't ready. A light still shone from the window of the study, and she wondered if Kane and Zach were still in there. Still talking.

They had been there a long time. Was that good? Bad?

She missed a note and stretched her trembling hands out, trying to quiet her nerves. Things were coming to a head, and she had to decide. She had to tell Kane everything and pray he understood.

Finally, the door to the porch opened, and Faith spun, trying to suppress the unwelcome pounding of her heart.

But it was Zach, backlit by the glow of the family room, not Kane.

"Hey there," she said, setting her guitar in its case and standing up.

Zach patted the air between them, stopping her. "Sit down. I've come to join you a moment."

Any other time the thought would have given her pleasure. But now? After knowing he and Kane discussed the potential sale of the ranch?

Her heart fluttered with nerves and she perched on the edge of her chair, her fingers twisted around each other.

"Don't worry. I'm harmless." Zach sat back in his chair, stretching his leg out, but he was smiling.

"Kane hoped to come out here and talk to you first, but Misty, Grace's horse, is foaling and having trouble, so he went out there." Another beat of silence that didn't help Faith's struggling heartbeat. "Anyhow, you may as well know Kane and I have come to an agreement. He's taking over the ranch from me."

Her breath whooshed out in a huge sigh of relief. "I'm so glad to hear that. When Kane told me how Stan wanted to subdivide the main place, I was just sick."

"Me too," Zach admitted, folding his hands above the large rodeo buckle he always wore. "Though part of me was glad the guy had such extreme plans for the ranch. It gave Kane the push I was hoping for. Saved me from thinking I would have to manhandle the boy to get him to take it over."

Faith frowned. "Wait, you mean you didn't want to sell the ranch?"

"Naw. Not really. I admit I was faced with the reality of running this place on my own after I got dumped off the horse and I broke my leg. I knew I couldn't carry on. I guess I kept hoping my boys would come to their senses and come back before that. Thankfully, Kane felt the responsibility. Now, he's working with me to take over." Zach patted his injured leg and grinned. "The Lord moves in mysterious ways, and I guess this was one of them."

Faith relaxed against her chair, thankful and relieved. "He certainly does," she said, flexing her fingers.

"So now, that leaves you."

"What do you mean?" Anxiety flushed through her at his serious tone.

"I'm coming straight out and asking, what are your intentions?"

"Intentions?"

"As in, what do you intend to do? Are you staying here? Kane seemed concerned that you wouldn't find an outlet for your talents. That you would feel stifled here."

She held that thought a moment, knowing she had to give it the consideration it deserved. Zach was genuinely worried, and she needed to find the right way to let him know what was happening in her life.

"I care so much for Kane. He's always been the best thing that's happened to me," she said, feeling she needed to preface her comments with that statement. "I'm thrilled that he'll be partners with you. And I…I want to be at his side…beside him…" She lost the fragile thread of her thoughts. "There's something Kane needs to know before we decide about us. And while I'd like to tell you, I can't. It's something between Kane and me."

His frown clearly showed he wasn't thrilled with her answer, but then he nodded, as if accepting it.

"Okay. We'll leave it at that then." He painstakingly got up and chucked his chin at her guitar. "You play nice," he said.

She felt as if she had been given a small blessing. "Thanks. I'm hoping to play with the praise band on Sunday in church."

His smile grew. "I like that. I think that's amazing."

Faith picked up her guitar and settled it on her lap, its curves familiar and comfortable. "I'm thankful for my music. I believe it will be what ultimately brings me back to a proper relationship with God."

Zach patted her shoulder. "I don't think you were ever that far away from Him," he said. "You were always such a good girl."

She knew he intended his words to comfort her. The same words Tricia had given her. Instead, she felt a chill feather up her spine. The sooner she could relieve herself of this secret, the sooner she and Kane could deal with it. *And, hopefully, please, Lord, move on.*

⚬⁓◯⁓⚬

Kane scrubbed his hands over his face, fighting the sleep that threatened. The morning sun slanted into the barn, glistening on the straw spread out over the pen. Misty still hadn't stood up long enough that Kane felt comfortable leaving her.

The horse lay in the pen in front of him, her neck stretched out. She'd been up and down a few times, but mostly down.

"Hey, girl, I sure hope you're gonna be okay," Kane said, stifling a yawn. He should get some coffee. Try to keep himself awake.

Last night he and Joe had a struggle to get Misty loaded on the stock trailer. Usually pregnant mares moved slowly, always protecting their baby. But Misty sensed something more serious was going on and had been restless and balky, throwing her head around and pawing at the ground. It had taken time and patience, but thankfully she had loaded with no injuries.

But when they got to the vet, it was too late for the foal. It had broken Kane's heart to see his mother's horse in such pain and all for nothing.

Delivering the dead foal had been a long, hard operation. And now Misty was exhausted and had been lying down too long.

"You should get up, girl," he said, kneeling at her head. She had been on this side for a couple of hours, and she needed to either get up or move to the other side. He stroked her head, talking to her, encouraging her, his voice pitched low, quiet.

Since coming back from the vet at one o'clock that morning, he'd sat up with her, watching her, determined to help her pull through. He knew how much Misty meant to his father. He'd trained her for Grace. Misty was his mother's horse as long as Kane could remember. She was too old to be foaling. The pregnancy had been a risk, and though it bothered him that she lost her foal, it wasn't a surprise.

But Kane didn't want to lose her too.

Joe had offered to stay and even Zach had come, but Kane had waved them both off. He needed to see this through. This, his first job as co-owner of the ranch. He almost felt that if he could do this, all would be well.

Misty struggled, and then, thankfully got laboriously to her feet, only to lie down again. At least this time it was on the other side.

Kane pushed down his concern and straightened, arching his back to get the crick out of.

A faint knock on one of the stall uprights caught his attention. Then he smiled.

Faith stood there, the rising sun silhouetting her slim figure, setting a halo of light over her dark hair. She moved a bit closer, and he could see she was carrying a travel mug in one hand, a muffin in the other.

"I brought you some coffee. I made muffins and brought one of those along too. Joe had said you've been here all night."

"I have been."

"You must be exhausted."

"Yeah. Pretty beat, but better now that I see you."

"And coffee," she said, holding up the travel mug as she came closer.

"That's just icing on the cake, or the muffin as it seems." Kane dropped onto a square straw bale pushed up against the side of the stall and patted the space beside him. "And there's lots of room for you here."

He was never so glad to see her as now. Despite the evening's tragedy, they had much to talk about.

And, for once, they were all alone.

She returned his smile, then sat beside him. Kane took the coffee and muffin and stole a kiss.

"Sorry I'm so scruffy," he said. He took a sip of the coffee.

"I think you look rugged," she teased, running the back of her hand over his scruffy face. Then she turned back to Misty.

"Has she been laying down long?" she asked.

"She just got up and switched sides, so she'll be okay for a while, though I won't relax until she's standing up more."

Faith rubbed his back. "Your dad told us about the foal. I'm so sorry to hear that."

"Yeah. She seems to be pretty upset, in her own horse way."

Faith was quiet, her expression serious. Then, to Kane's surprise, a few tears slipped out of her eyes, creating silver tracks on her cheeks.

"Hey, it's okay," Kane said, setting his mug on the ground and slipping his arm around her shoulders. "It's hard to see, but it's part of the circle of life."

"She carried it so long. She probably really wanted that baby."

Her comment surprised him. "Well, she probably did."

"And now she has empty arms."

"Arms?"

Faith choked down another sob, her hand pressed to her chest as if holding something in.

"What's wrong, Fiddy?"

She lifted her hand to wave him off but then another sob slipped out of her.

He tossed his half-eaten muffin aside and gently drew her into his arms. "Honey, what's happening?"

She pressed her head into his neck, her hands grabbing at his shirt, her knuckles white. He was puzzled, but sensed he needed to give her time. She was overcome, her body shaking. Something huge was going on, and she couldn't talk.

Finally she drew away, swiping her palms over her damp cheeks, sniffing. She folded her hands on her lap, her eyes fixed on Misty.

"I'm glad you're buying the ranch," she said.

Kane was taken aback. Really? This was what she wanted to talk about? This is what made her so upset?

"Yes. Stan was supposed to meet us in town today to sign the Agreement for Sale," he said, deciding to play along. See where things went. "But instead Dad's calling Floyd later to tell him it's not a go."

His words sounded so prosaic compared to the emotion she was grappling with.

This netted him a nod, but her hands, twisted on her lap, constantly moved.

"I'm thrilled about that. This is where you belong."

He gently stroked her hair away from her face so he could see her better. "And what about you? Where do you belong? Is being around your grandfather going to be a problem?"

She shook her head. "I called him last night. We had a little talk. It will take time, but I think we have the beginnings of an understanding."

He rested his hand on the back of her neck, his fingers stroking, trying to maintain a connection with her. That was good, but they still hadn't come to the heart of her anguish.

"I'm happy about that," he said. "I knew that was a hurdle you had to get past."

Faith's hands twisted again, and she pressed her lips together. She swallowed again, then turned to face him. Her desolate expression dove into his heart, creating an unwelcome chill.

"What's going on, Faith? What's happening?"

"I need to tell you something. Something important."

The chill spread from his heart to his extremities at the harsh tone in her voice. But after dropping that, she went silent, staring at Misty, tears tracking down her cheeks.

He wanted to shake her, force the words out of her, but he knew he had to take his time. He sensed whatever she had to say would have a long-term effect on their future. If there was one.

He pushed that last thought aside. He knew what was happening between him and Faith. He refused to believe she didn't care for him as much as he cared for her.

"So what do you need to tell me?" he prompted, unable to keep his silence.

"While we were on the road, I was lonely. Especially after Elliott left. There was a guy..." She caught her lower lip between her teeth, and Kane sensed what was coming next. He didn't want to hear it, but he knew they had to get it out of the way. "We were intimate, and I need to tell you…" She paused, her cheeks flaming now. She looked down at her hands, her fingers twined around each other, working. "I got pregnant…but…I lost the baby…"

Though he understood her shame and his heart broke for her pain, a surge of torment so strong it almost blinded him pushed him to his feet. He stood there, facing away from her, fighting it down. He clenched his fists and forced his anger down. It wasn't fair to her. They had broken up. They weren't together. Of course someone as beautiful and amazing as Faith would find someone else.

But to have had a baby together…

Help me help her, Lord, he prayed, clenching his fists, understanding now why she had been so desolate.

He gave himself a moment to make his expression neutral and nonjudgmental. He knew he had to be careful. If she sensed he was upset, it would come between them, and he didn't want that to happen again. Inhaling a deep breath, he gathered his thoughts to think of something to encourage her. Something positive to say.

Then a hard knock on the stall's frame broke into the emotions of the moment.

"Faith, there you are." Tricia hung over the half door of the stall, looking at Faith, who was now standing with her back to Kane.

"Kinda busy here, Tricia," Kane said, shooting her a warning glance over Faith's hunched shoulder.

"I know. Sorry, but… There's someone here who says he really needs to talk to Faith." Tricia pushed herself upright, wincing as she did so. Kane knew how much work it was for her to walk from the house to the barn, so it must be something serious.

"Did he say who he was?" Faith asked. From behind, Kane could see she had her arms wrapped around her waist. A defensive gesture. He didn't blame her. He wished his reaction hadn't been so strong, but it was difficult to hear what she'd said. He wanted to reach out to comfort her. To find a way through this, but Tricia was speaking again.

"He said his name was Gavin Wiles. And he's driving a big white van, one of those sprinter vans, with the words Prairie Wanderers on the side."

Faith sucked in a quick breath at that, her back still to Kane, so he couldn't see her reaction.

He remembered that name. It was of the group she used to play with. Was this the father of the child she'd lost?

"Okay. I'll be right there." Then, without a backward glance, Faith scurried out of the stall, as if in a rush to be reunited with Gavin. As if in a rush to get away from him.

"Well, she sure seems to be in a hurry," Tricia said, not helping Kane's alarm one bit. Then Tricia stepped inside the stall and sat on the straw bale, drawing in a slow breath. "Oh Misty, you poor thing," she murmured.

Kane stayed where he was, watching Faith stride across the yard. He saw one corner of the van Tricia had talked about, and then a tall man bounded down the veranda, his arms open wide.

Faith went directly to him, and they hugged. Tightly.

He felt as if he had been punched in the gut.

He spun around and dropped onto the straw bale beside Tricia. He couldn't watch anymore.

"Will she be okay?" Tricia asked.

"I don't know. It depends on what that guy wants."

Tricia gave him a melancholy smile. "I meant Misty."

He pulled his attention back to the horse, shaking off his reaction to Faith's sudden departure. To this man from her past showing up unexpectedly.

To their tight hug.

He tried to shake off his feelings. Tried to push them down. All he wanted to do right now was run after Faith. Pull her back. Tell her he loved her. That he cared for her. That he…

That he…

He stopped himself right there. He couldn't think further than the moment.

"I sure hope so," he said, leaning forward to watch the horse more closely. "Though she lost her foal."

"I heard." Tricia leaned against him, slipping her arm through his, and they sat there together, brother and sister, watching their beloved mother's horse as it lingered between life and death.

Kane squeezed Tricia's hand, thankful she was here. She was family, and he knew how important that was. They needed each other. He knew he shouldn't depend on Faith to give him happiness. He had so hoped for a secure future for both of them, but he knew he had to let go of that dream. He had to focus on why he wanted what he did for himself. Not for some imagined future with Faith.

CHAPTER 21

*F*aith's boyfriend was still here?

Kane stepped out of the barn, easing a crick out of his back. Tricia had offered to stay with Misty. Zach was watching the kids.

And the Sprinter van Tricia was talking about was still parked in front of the house.

He knew he should turn around and go back to the farmyard. Joe was working on equipment, getting the hay binder and baler ready for the haying season. Now that Kane was staying and working his way into taking over the ranch, they could make plans further ahead than simply making the ranch look good.

His poor reaction to Faith's tearful confession lingered like a bitter taste. He needed to let her know he was stunned. Plain and simple. That he felt bad for her. That was why he reacted the way he had.

But Faith and that Gavin guy weren't outside on the veranda. He stepped up his pace, fighting down his second thoughts. It was his house, or would be soon. He had every right to get a drink of water, he told himself.

But even so, he paused by the garden doors leading to the

kitchen. No one sat at the table in the kitchen. He stepped inside and heard voices coming from the family room.

Just go, his rational mind told himself. *You don't need to hear this.*

But he did. This was the woman he loved, talking to someone from her past. A past that held shadows and pain and grief probably connected to this man. A past he knew still called to her musical soul.

"It's a great opportunity," the male voice, Gavin, was saying, sounding earnest and excited. "It won't be anything like the previous tour. We're talking high quality busses, upscale hotels and motels. A decent living allowance. And a chance to split the profits. We'll be able to sell our own CDs and showcase our own music. We need you aboard. Want you aboard. You have a unique talent that shouldn't be squandered here."

"I don't know…" Faith sounded hesitant, which ignited a hope.

"We really could use you," Gavin said. "The band hasn't been the same since you left."

"It sure sounds amazing."

"And, even better, we've got someone else on bass. Keith is gone. I kicked him out of the band." A moment of silence followed this declaration. "It's a fresh start," he continued. "It's a chance to let your talent really shine. You can't be satisfied playing in a church band or maybe teaching kids lessons like you said you might do. You were made for bigger things than that."

More silence, heavy and dark.

Kane heard his own doubts and concerns about Faith's music being spoken aloud through this guy's words. He was afraid that the old boyfriend was right. Maybe for now, Faith was content playing music in church, and apparently, teaching music lessons. But that was no outlet for her true talent. He saw her face when she sang, when she was playing her guitar. He heard the songs she wrote. He sensed a completeness he doubted would come from staying here in Rockyview.

He grabbed the back of a kitchen chair, clutching it hard, as his fears and doubts fought each other. He loved Faith, of that much he was sure. Did he love her enough to let her go with the father of her child?

He'd done it once before and hadn't thought he could get over it.

But that was different. She said herself that her choice was more of a reaction than a decision. She wasn't the same person she was then. By any stretch.

He dropped his head, struggling as he heard this guy laying out all the positives, trying to convince her to come with him. It sounded so good. So much more than anything Rockyview could offer her.

"Dear Lord, show me what to do." Kane sucked in a deep breath, then another.

"Let me take you out for lunch," Gavin said. "I can tell you what we've been doing and a bit more of our plans."

Kane's heart lurched at that.

He turned and walked quietly out of the house, carefully closing the door behind him. It wouldn't look good for Faith to find out he'd been eavesdropping.

As he walked along the corrals, he heard the van starting up. As it drove away, Kane felt as if every connection he had to Faith was being stretched thinner and thinner.

He walked through a copse of trees, following a trail that led up a hill that overlooked the ranch. He and Elliot used to come here and build forts in the bushes. If he looked hard enough he could find remnants of those forts. Such an innocent time. When the biggest problem he had was trying to finagle more nails out of his father. Hoping his dad wouldn't notice the missing lumber.

As he sat looking out over the ranch, his father's truck pulled up beside his. The doors opened, and Zach walked around to let the kids out. Even from up here, Kane could hear them laughing and whooping as they ran toward the play center.

It was good to have kids around. The ranch needed that.

Kane had dreamed many times that his and Faith's children would run around in the yard. Would come up to these hills to build forts as he and his brothers had.

And now? They had made plans, but did he dare assume that she would still want them?

He dragged his hands over his face, his dreams fighting with Faith's reality. He got up and walked down to the house.

His father was calling for the kids to come with him. They were walking to the barn where Misty and Tricia were.

"What's the matter, Son? You look upset." Zach frowned as Kane joined them. "Everything still okay?"

"Yeah. It's fine."

"Good. I want to check on Misty."

Kane shoved his hands in his pockets as they walked toward the barn, forcing himself to look around the ranch, to think of the positives. No more living in camps, working stupid long hours with foul-mouthed crews and guys who drank too much after work because they were as lonely as he had been.

And Faith?

He almost stumbled at the thought of her, now with the man she had once been intimate with. A man she'd gotten pregnant with. Her past melding into their present.

Would she choose him? Would their joint grief bring them together again?

His heart was heavy when they stepped into the barn, but then, over the edge of the stall, they saw Misty. She was standing, watching them.

"Hey, girl," Zach said, walking toward her, stretching out his hand to touch her. He petted her head, ran his hands over her face, her neck, comforting her the only way he could.

By connecting. By touching. By simply being there.

Kane held the twins back as he watched the happy reunion, so thankful that Misty had turned a corner. Thankful that, on this horrible day, God had given their family one positive sign.

"Where's Faith?" Tricia asked, shooting Kane a concerned look.

Kane held firmly onto Cash's hand as he leaned away from him, wanting to go to his mother. "She went out with the guy that came."

"What? Why?"

"I didn't ask," Kane said. "Not my business."

"But you have to go after her." Zach's phone beeped, signaling an incoming text message, and with an annoyed look he pulled it out of his shirt pocket, frowning at the screen. "It's Floyd. He says we need to come in and sign some papers if we're not going through with the sale."

"Okay. I guess we may as well get that over and done with," Kane said.

"And while you're there, you can try to find Faith. Convince her to stay," Tricia put in.

"No. I'm letting her do what she wants to do. Giving her space to make her own decision."

"But what if she...what if she wants to go?" Tricia protested. "You can't let her."

"Tricia, honey, you're not making things easier for Kane, you know," Zach said quietly.

His sister nodded. "I'm sorry. I guess you're right."

"Wow. I wish Elliot was here to hear this," Kane said with a chuckle.

"Yeah, I wish he was too."

"Once he stops chasing his dreams, he'll probably be back."

Kane nodded, thinking again about Faith and her dreams. About her loss and the man she had shared it with.

"I need to do something before we go to town," Kane said. He released Cash's and Hope's hands, and they immediately ran to the door of the stall, climbing up and leaning over the top. He made sure they were okay, then he turned and walked to the house. He went directly to his father's study, sat at the desk, and pulled out a piece of paper.

He found a pen, clicked it, and then stared at the blank paper. Was this over the top? Too much?

He thought of how he had turned away from Faith when she told him about her baby. He should have run toward her, pulled her close, held her tight, promised she would be okay. Just like he hoped Misty would be okay.

Instead, he had turned his back on her. Let her think who knows what as he fought down his own petty jealousy.

He claimed to love her but when the true test came, he'd abandoned her. He wished he could do it over, but at least he could do this one thing for her.

He clicked the pen again and wrote.

Faith stood on the driveway, waving as Gavin drove away in a cloud of dust.

She stood there a moment, watching him leave, her head buzzing with too much information. Too many thoughts.

Though what he had promised sounded appealing, she knew better. She knew that no matter how fancy the bus, how nice the hotels, it was still a transient life. It was still exhausting, and she wondered how much applause, how much money, could make up for the jagged loneliness of life on the road. No community other than a band who got on each other's nerves. No sense of place or permanence.

Even though she had balked at her grandfather's restrictions and Kane's support of them, at the same time she recognized that deep down, she wasn't cut out for such a fugitive life. Her faith life and her trust had been badly battered by life on the road. The loss she had experienced had cut her deeply and had left her lonely and yearning for someone she could share the pain with. Someone who would understand. The past weeks on the ranch and going to church had fed the part of her that had yearned deeply for spiritual nourishment, for community and permanence.

And more than all of that was Kane.

He turned his back on you when you tried to tell him everything.

She held that thought a moment, then switched her point of view. Tried to see it through his eyes.

This was a lot to deal with. She could hardly blame him for reacting the way he did. His view of her had to deal with a drastic switch. A huge change.

And yet, his rejection of her had cut her to the core. When Tricia had arrived, announcing Gavin's presence, Faith saw it as a small gift from God. A chance for her to catch her breath and try to figure out how to regain Kane's trust and love. To explain to him what had happened.

She heard voices coming from the house. She walked over to the French doors and stepped inside the kitchen.

Tricia sat at the table with Hope and Cash, cutting up a hot dog for them.

"Is Kane still sitting with Misty?" Faith asked, looking around.

"No, she's doing well." Tricia gave her a careful smile. Faith wondered if Kane had told her what she had told him. "Dad was happy about that. And so were we all."

Faith looked around the kitchen, listening. "Is Kane in the house then?"

"No, he and Dad had to go to town. They had to talk to Floyd. Something about signing the sales papers."

Were they selling the ranch after all? Was Kane that upset with her?

"Kane also told me before he left town he wrote you a letter. I think it's in Dad's study on the desk."

"A note? As in a letter?" That sounded forbidding.

Tricia shrugged. "Who knows? He seemed kinda distracted.

Like he had lots on his mind. I know he talked to Dad about the ranch."

Faith's heart skipped a beat at that. "Yes, your dad told me they talked last night."

"Well, they were talking about it again this morning. I'm not sure what's going on, but Kane didn't look too happy."

Faith fought down a troubled reaction. Was everything falling apart? Had her news been that hard on Kane?

She had to read that letter. Then she had to call him.

"Excuse me, I should go," she said to Tricia, then scooted to the study and shut the door behind her. Sure enough, an envelope leaned against a picture of the Tye family. Zach and Grace with Elliot, Tricia, Kane, and Lucas.

She grabbed the envelope, her fingers shaking as she ripped it open. She yanked the paper out and unfolded it, her eyes flying over the neatly penned words.

"…Love you… Should have been more supportive… So sorry for your loss… Wish you the best… Thankful you can use your talents… Will pray for you… Hope God will bless you… Watch over you… Then her eyes slowed, and she read the next sentence more slowly.

"I love listening to you play, and I want you to use your talents to the best of your ability. I hope that this tour will bring you more happiness than the last one did. And I hope and pray it will bring you success. I have my own decisions to make, and I don't want them to interfere with yours. I don't want to hold you back, and I only wish the best for you."

Her heart flipped over at that last sentence. His own decisions to make?

He and Zach were at Floyd's office. Had he changed his mind about taking over the ranch? He seemed to think she was going on tour with the band. Did that mean he no longer wanted to work on the ranch?

She didn't know what to think, her mind twisting and turning, stumbling over every thought that jumped into it.

She had to go find Kane and talk to him properly. Not worry about his reactions and let him know exactly how she felt about him. She realized he must have heard them talking and how it must've sounded to him He seemed to think that Gavin was the one who had been her boyfriend.

It would've been funny if she wasn't feeling so upset right now.

At the bottom of the letter were four words that fell like water into her parched soul.

"All my love, Kane."

She folded the letter and shoved it into her pocket. She pulled her phone out to text him, to ask where he was, to tell him to wait until she got there.

Then groaned when she saw the battery was dead. She ran out of the study. Tricia was still at the table.

"Are you good to be on your own?" Faith asked.

"Yeah, I'm going to lay the kids down and have a nap myself." Tricia looked puzzled. "Why? What's up?"

"I need to go to town right now. Where does your dad keep the keys to his truck?"

"Where he always does, in a cubby in the truck."

"I'll see you later then," Faith said and, without another word, ran out of the house.

CHAPTER 22

*W*here were the keys? Where would Zach keep the keys?

Faith scrabbled through the console between the seats, but nothing. Then she yanked open a small cubby below the stereo. There they were.

She fitted the keys into the ignition, and a few heart-stopping moments later she had the truck backed up and was headed down the highway. She felt tiny in the huge truck, but she sat as straight as she could, fighting a need to step on the gas. She realized with a sinking heart that she had left her backpack at the ranch. Which meant she didn't have her driver's license with her or anything. The last thing she needed was to be stopped by the cops.

Twenty minutes later she slowed as she turned onto Main Street and was greeted by a line-up of vehicles. She felt doubly nervous now driving this huge beast of a vehicle as she passed small cars and slowed for jay-walking pedestrians. She tried not to rush, fighting down her inclination to panic.

"Please, Lord, don't let him sell the ranch. Don't let him sign those papers before I get there."

Finally she found a spot she thought was wide enough for the truck. Thankfully, all the parking on Main Street was angle parking. It was just a matter of pointing the nose in the right direction and turning it in.

But she underestimated the size of the beast and ended up taking up two parking spots. No matter. She jumped out of the truck, ignored the guy behind her honking his horn as she slammed the door and then ran down the street.

Kane's truck was still parked outside the Realtor's office. She yanked open the door and stepped inside. A woman at the front desk looked up with a broad smile, "Can I help you?"

"I need to see Kane Tye right now. Please."

"They're with Mr. Picthall, right now," the woman said.

"Which room?"

"Well, they are rather busy," she said primly.

Faith ignored her, listening for voices. Thankfully, she heard Kane talking.

Ignoring the woman's protests, she hurried down the carpeted hallway, looking through the doors to each office and then, there he was, scrawling his signature on a piece of paper.

Without stopping to knock she burst into the room. "Don't sign any more papers. Don't sell the ranch," she said. She held her hand up as if that would make all the difference.

Floyd's, Kane's, and Zach's heads all spun around, and they looked at her with amazement. Kane got up, looking puzzled. "What's the matter? Is everything okay?"

"No, everything's not okay. You can't sell the ranch. You and I have to move onto it. We have to live there and raise our kids there. We have to have our happy ever after there." The words spilled out of her in one long rush. "I'm not going on some stupid tour, but thanks for giving me your permission." She stopped herself there, realizing how bad that sounded. Her thoughts were such a jumble.

"You're not going on the tour?" Kane asked, latching onto one thing she had babbled out.

"No." She paused, catching her breath, her eyes pleading with him to understand. "I don't want to live that life. I want to be on the ranch with you. And I don't want you to sell it."

"So you're staying here," Kane said, as if he couldn't believe it. "But your music—"

"I can play music here. Teach music. Finish my degree. Teach music in school. Write songs. Play with the worship band, maybe start a band of my own." She lifted her hands and let them drop. "I don't care. I'll find an outlet. But it will not be on the road, and it won't be touring. I want to live here, in Rockyview, with you. On the ranch." She stopped there, catching her breath, holding Kane's puzzled but curious gaze. "Just don't sell it. Please."

"But we're not selling it," Kane said.

Faith blinked as his words registered. She looked from him to Zach to Floyd sitting at his desk. Floyd looked annoyed, and Faith didn't blame him. Having some irrational woman bursting into his office was probably not how he expected this meeting to go.

"Well then, what are you guys doing here?" she asked, pulling in her breath, flushing with embarrassment now.

"We're signing off on the papers we had set up. But not to sell the ranch. To cancel the whole deal," Kane said.

Relief prickled through Faith, like blood rushing through a dead limb.

"Cancelling? You're cancelling the whole deal?"

Kane nodded, taking a step toward her, laying his hand on her shoulder, making the tenuous connection. "Yes. I want to make my life on the ranch. Dad is working me in slowly."

Faith felt like her bones had turned to rubber. And behind that came a sense of foolishness. She had rushed all this way, made an idiot of herself, for nothing?

"Well, that's good to know. I'm glad. So, I guess I can go back then." She flashed them an awkward smile and took a stumbling step backward. She really had to get out of here. But then Kane stopped her, curving his hands around her shoulders. "I guess you can, but why don't you go back with me?"

"How did you get here?" Zach asked.

"I took your truck," Faith said, blushing. "I hope that was okay."

"Sure." Zach gave her a pained look but, thankfully, said nothing more. "So why don't you give me the keys, and I can go back to the ranch, and you and Kane can go somewhere, just the two of you, and sort a few things out."

"Excellent idea," Kane said, smiling gently at Faith, his fingers stroking the side of her neck.

As their eyes locked and held, Faith thought of the last words of his letter.

All my love, Kane.

"So, are we done here?" Zach asked Floyd.

"Yes. Everything is completed. If I need anything more, I'll let you know." Floyd shuffled the papers on his desk, tapping them once and giving them all a polite but forced smile.

Faith almost felt sorry for him, so she mustered up a returning smile.

Then Kane said goodbye to his father, shook hands with Floyd, and ushered Faith out of the office.

"My truck is right outside the door," he said.

Zach was right behind them. Faith dug into the pockets of her blue jeans and handed Zach the keys. "I didn't speed with it," she said.

Zach smiled at her. "I'm sure you were careful." He turned to Kane. "So we'll see you sometime later on?"

Kane nodded, draped his arm over Faith's shoulder, and escorted her to the truck.

Minutes later they were headed out of town, down the highway.

"Where are we going?" Faith asked, fidgeting with her seat belt.

"To the lookout point over the river."

They were on the highway now, and the turnoff was a few

kilometers ahead. Faith loosened her seat belt and, ignoring the warning dinger, shifted to the side and clipped it up again so it would stop.

Then she moved closer to Kane, tucked her arm in his, and laid her head on his shoulder.

"That's not very safe," he murmured, brushing his cheek over her head.

"We're almost there, and I couldn't stand being away from you one second longer."

She clung to his arm, inhaling the clean scent of his shirt, the underlying smell of his aftershave and soap.

True Kane.

He turned off the highway, the truck bouncing through the ruts leading to the opening in the trees ahead.

Then he stopped the truck at the guardrail, switched the engine off, and turned to her.

He pulled her close, and as their lips met, she leaned closer, her arms twisting around his neck, pulling him as close as she could. His hand cradled her head, his fingers stroking her hair, his other arm wrapped around her waist.

Their kiss deepened, lengthened, then to her dismay, he pulled slowly away. He dropped gentle kisses on her cheek, her forehead, and then one last light one on her parted lips.

Then he leaned back against the door of the truck, curling his hand around her head, pressing it to his shoulder. She lay against him, her hand on his chest. His heart thumped below her ear, a steady reassuring rhythm. Kane's heart that gave her all his love. She pulled in a long, slow breath, then another, a sense of peace that had eluded her the past many years settling over her.

"I'm glad you're not selling the ranch," she said.

"I'm glad you're not going on tour," Kane replied, his voice a deep rumble beneath her ear.

She lifted her head, pulling back from him, her hand still

resting on his chest. "I want to thank you. For giving me the space to do that. To head out."

His expression grew serious as he fingered a strand of hair away from her face, letting it drift through his fingers. "I wanted you to realize that I understood how important your music was. I stood in the way before. I didn't want to do that again."

She laid her head back down on his chest, closing her eyes. "Thanks. That means so much to me. I know how hard that was for you to do."

"I was terrified." His chest rose as he drew in a deep breath. "But I wanted to give you space to make your own decision knowing that no matter what you decided, I was behind you." Then his arms tightened. "But I'm so thankful you're staying."

She smiled, rubbing her cheek against the rough material of his shirt, reveling in this moment of quiet closeness. It felt so right, she never wanted it to end.

But other thoughts crowded into their space. Other events they had to deal with.

"I'm sorry about something else too," he said before she could say anything. "I reacted badly when you told me...when you said what you did about your baby."

She grew still, thankful she was in Kane's arms when he said this, trying to stifle the chill that slithered down her spine.

"It was a surprise...well...a shock, I guess. It wasn't anything I would have...would have..." He stumbled along, and Faith felt bad for him.

"Would have expected from me," she said, finishing the sentence for him.

"Yeah. I guess. Though that's not fair to you."

She toyed with the button on his shirt, twisting it around while she tried to grab a coherent thought. "It wasn't who I was," she admitted. "And my relationship with Keith wasn't a quick thing. But we spent so much time together, and he made no secret of his interest in me. I was lonely, and one thing led to another—"

"So it wasn't Gavin who you were dating?"

"No. Never him. It was a guy named Keith. You see-"

"You don't need to explain," Kane said, breaking into her confession, stroking her head as if to connect with her. "You don't have to act like you've done something horrible. My life on the rigs wasn't something I was proud of either."

"Maybe not," she said, looking past the truck to the river valley below them, her mind slipping backwards. "But I want it out of the way. I don't want you thinking I'm pining for him or anything like that. He really wasn't a good guy. In fact, after I had the miscarriage, he grew verbally abusive."

"And the baby...how do you feel about that?"

She waited before replying, testing her emotions, hoping he understood. "I was sad. It's always hard, but there was a part of me that was relieved. I know that sounds horrible," she hastened to explain, hoping, praying he understood. "I wanted the baby...but not like that. Not living on the road. And not, not with him." She drew in a shuddering sigh, struggling to maintain control. "I knew exactly what he was, and he was not husband, let alone, father material. In fact, when he found out I was pregnant, he told me to get rid of it."

"Oh, Fiddy," Kane breathed, his hand cradling her face, turning her head to look at him. His eyes were brimming with compassion and love. "I'm so sorry you had to deal with all of this on your own."

She held his gaze, thankful for the caring and sympathy she saw there. Not one shred of condemnation.

"Thank you," was all she could say.

He kissed her again, his lips warm, soft and gentle, moving slowly over hers in a long, lingering kiss. Finally he drew back. "I'm so thankful you're back here," he said, his mouth shifting into an easy smile, his eyes crinkling at the corners. "I want to help you deal with this, and I'm hoping that spending time at the ranch will help you."

"I am so thankful for you," she said, returning his smile. "I think being at the ranch with you will definitely help. Now that I know I'll be staying."

"I hope to take you riding up to the hills for picnics," he said. "I hope we can spend so much time together. Of course, you'll be a bit busier in a few months."

"Why is that?"

Kane pushed himself away from the door and sat up, taking her by the shoulders and helping her sit upright. He took her hands in his, and his smile faded away. "I want us to go back to where we were before," he said. "Though I know we can't really go back, I want us to be engaged again. I want us to be making plans for our wedding again."

Her heart plunged, and tears threatened.

"I was hoping to do it proper. I still have the ring you gave back to me. But I don't want us to waste any more time. I want to get married soon. I want us to get started on our life together, soon. If that's okay with you."

Faith got on her knees on the bench seat of the truck and cradled Kane's face in her hands. "I want it too. We've already done the long engagement thing. I think we can use some of that banked time now."

She leaned forward and gently pressed her lips to his in a soft, sweet kiss. She drew away and eased out a gentle smile.

"And here we are. After all this time. Back together." She still couldn't believe how things had come together. How she and Kane had worked their way through all of this. A few tears prickled her eyes.

"What's the matter?" he asked.

"Those lonely nights, toward the end, when I thought I had thrown everything away, blown every chance I had ever been given, I never, ever imagined that my life could have come back to here. Back with you."

"God moves in mysterious ways," Kane said. "Maybe we both

needed to learn a few things. Maybe I needed to learn how much my father really loves me and sees me as his own. I know for a fact I needed to learn to give you space to follow your heart."

Faith smoothed Kane's hair, her eyes following her hands. "I know it was a hard thing for us to deal with, but I think I needed to be with the band. To maybe push myself further away from what people expected of me. It maybe wasn't the best way for it to happen, but I know I value the lessons I discovered on the way. I know I need to be true to who I am and my gifts, but that doesn't mean throwing everything away in the meantime."

She leaned forward and kissed him again. "I love you with all my heart, Kane Tye. And I will spend the rest of my life showing you how much."

He shook his head as if in disbelief. "I don't deserve all that, but I'm taking it. Because I know how much I need you in my life. How much I need your presence. Your light and your music. I love you so much. I'll make you so thankful you came back."

"I already am," she said, settling back on her haunches. "Even though it took a detour and a jerk for that to happen."

"Like I said, mysterious ways." Kane grinned, then kissed her again. "And now, we should head back to the ranch. Let my dad know what's going on. And then, I want to talk to your grandfather. Ask him for his blessing."

"I'm sure he'll give it less reluctantly this time," Faith said.

"And even if he doesn't, we're still getting married," Kane replied. "Now, buckle up, missy. I don't want anything happening to you now, or ever again."

She smiled, her heart so full she thought it would jump out of her chest. She buckled up and sat back, her hand stretched across the seat, wrapped in Kane's large strong one.

Then they drove back down the highway and back to the ranch.

Back home.

EPILOGUE

"*Freedom from guilt is waiting for you,*
Receiving it is easy to do.
Lay down your soul, lay down your pride,
Take your place, at the Father's side."

The words of the song rang through the sanctuary, and Kane couldn't help a burst of pride as he watched Faith singing, her hands dancing over the frets of the guitar, her other hand picking out the notes. Her voice rang out, a rich alto, filling in Marianne's soprano. The last words rang out with a triumphant sound, the tune echoing through the sanctuary.

Kane felt he should clap but didn't.

The service was over and people moved down the aisles, talking with each other.

"They sure sound much better than last Sunday," Kane said turning to Mick Howard who stood beside him, a light frown puckering his forehead. He looked as if he was still trying to figure this all out. Trying to mesh the vision he'd always had for his granddaughter with what he was seeing.

"How do you mean?" Mick asked.

"Well, Faith's singing, her guitar playing. They sure add a lot."

Mick nodded, then turned to Kane. "She's very talented."

"You should let her know you think so," Kane said.

"No. That's okay," Mick said.

Kane took a chance and rested his hand on Mick's shoulder. "I think you should. It would mean a lot to her."

Mick fiddled with the precise knot of his tie, his head shifting to one side as if thinking.

"Please," Kane said.

"You're kind of pushy about this, aren't you?" Mick frowned at him. Several years ago that frown from Mick Howard would have made Kane back down.

But now? Not anymore. Kane knew who he was. Beloved child of God. Dear son of Zach and Grace Tye. He didn't need to prove himself to anyone. He had gone by himself to talk to Mick about marrying Faith. He hadn't so much as asked for Mick's blessing as told him this was happening, and if he wanted a relationship with his only living relative, it would be a good idea to simply smile and nod.

Mick had been shocked, but then he shook Kane's hand and, indeed, did give his blessing.

"Faith is an amazing person with a gift God has blessed her with," Kane continued. "I think that needs to be acknowledged as well."

"I suppose you're right." Mick glanced over at Kane. "Will you come with me?"

Kane was going to say no, but saw a rare glimpse of sorrow in Mick Howard's eyes. He felt a flicker of sympathy for the man.

"Sure. I'll come."

They waited until the aisles were clear, and then together they walked up to the front of the church where the band was winding up cords.

Faith looked up and saw Kane approach, but the wide smile she gave him shifted a little as she looked past him to where her grandfather stood.

She came down to meet them.

Kane caught squeezed her hands. "You sounded amazing. Great job."

"Just using my gifts," she said. She said it in a light tone, but Kane heard the faint edge in her words. As if she was challenging her grandfather. *Good for her,* he thought.

Then Mick walked up, his hands shoved in the pocket of his pants, breaking the tidy line of his suit.

He gave Faith a tight nod. "I really... I enjoyed..." He lifted his hand and held it out at his side, as if he was trying to emphasize a point. "You play well."

Faith held his steady gaze, and a slow smile curved her lips. "Thank you. I enjoy playing."

"I can see that." He cleared his throat, rocking on his feet. He scratched his chin with a forefinger, then gave her a careful smile. "I like listening to you. I think you should share your gift. I think you should become a teacher and teach music." Then he held his hand up. "But, of course, only if you want to. I would be willing to help out."

"Thanks, Grandpa. Kane said he would as well." Faith leaned into Kane, slipping her arm around his waist, looking up at him. "That is, if the offer still stands."

"Of course it does," he said, brushing the top of her head with his chin.

"Well, that may be, but I think if you will be taking over your father's ranch, you'll need all your money for that," Mick said. "I mean, that's what I would recommend." He cleared his throat again. Kane had never seen him this unsure. "I'm trying to be practical. But I would like to pay for it. And I don't want to hear any talk of you paying me back," Mick continued. "I'm your grandfather and I...I want what's best for you."

Faith straightened and then, to Kane's surprise, walked over to Mick, slipped her arms around him, and gave him a hug. He stood a moment, looking surprised, but then, to Kane's relief, dropped his arm around her, the other hand patting her shoulder.

It looked awkward, but Kane realized it was a big step for this undemonstrative man.

Faith pulled back and Mick cupped her face in his hand. "I'm glad you're back," he said. "I'm really glad."

Then, without another word, he gave Kane a tight nod, turned, and strode down the empty church aisle, his head held high.

But Kane was pretty sure his step was a little lighter, his shoulders held a little higher, and his arms swung a little further.

"He looks happy," Kane said.

"As happy as Mick Howard will look in public," Faith agreed, slipping into Kane's embrace.

"I'm happy," Kane said, dropping a kiss on Faith's head.

"So am I," Faith returned, looking up at him. "Happier than I've been in many years. I feel like I've found my way home."

"I like the sound of that," Kane said, holding her as he looked down the aisle. "And just think, in a few months you and your grandfather will be walking up this aisle, though I have to say I wish it was sooner."

"I know," Faith admitted, toying with the button on his shirt. "But I'd like my old roommate to do the wedding and I want time to plan it."

"For you, it's worth the wait."

"I think so too," Faith said.

Kane pulled back to look down at his beloved fiancée. "It took a while to get there, but I'm not one bit sorry for the detours. God brought us to this place, and it's a good place."

Faith kissed him, then smiled. "I'm done here. Let's go home."

And they did.

SWEET HEARTS OF SWEET CREEK

This is new series of mine that is out now. Tap the title to find out more.

#1 HOMECOMING

Will past bitterness blind her to future love?

#2 - HER HEARTS PROMISE

When the man she once loved reveals a hidden truth about the past, Nadine has to choose between justice and love.

#3 - CLOSE TO HIS HEART

Can love triumph over tragedy?

#4 - DIVIDED HEARTS

To embrace a second chance at love, they'll need to discover the truths of the past and the possibilities of the future…

#5 - A HERO AT HEART

If you like rekindled chemistry, family drama, and small, beautiful towns, then you'll love this story of heart and heroism.

#6 - A MOTHER'S HEART

If you like matchmaking daughters, heartfelt stories of mending broken homes, and fixer-upper romance, then this story of second chances is just right for you.

In this series you'll get to know the residents of this town set in the Kootenay mountains and surrounded by ranch land and populated with interesting characters.

Nadine Laidlaw, a newspaper reporter, who can't seem to get rid of her meddling, matchmaking Grandmother and Clint Fletcher, her new boss, who is a reminder of all she wants to forget.

Tess Kruger whose pain has sent her back to her hometown of Sweet Creek trying to find redemption. When her ex-fiancee, Jace Scholte shows up and she's forced to work with him on a fundraiser she struggles with her old feelings for him and the secret she can never tell him.

Cory Luciuk is working her way through life, waitressing at the Riverside Cafe. And then the man who broke her heart and tainted her past shows up again.

Kelsey Swain, a widow with a small boy has seen her share of sorrow when her husband died. She now runs the Riverside Cafe, struggling to get it off the ground. Then his ex-partner comes back to Sweet Creek and with him a reminder of what she lost.

The series is complete and ready to be binge read at your leisure!!!

THE HOLMES CROSSING SERIES

The Only Best Place is the first book in the Holmes Crossing Series.
Click on the title of each book to purchase.

#1 THE ONLY BEST PLACE

One mistake jeopardized their relationship. Will surrendering her
dreams to save their marriage destroy her?

#2 ALL IN ONE PLACE

She has sass, spunk and a haunting secret.

#3 THIS PLACE

Her secret could destroy their second chance at love

#4 A SILENCE IN THE HEART

Can a little boy, an injured kitten and a concerned vet with his own past
pain, break down the walls of Tracy's heart?

#5 ANY MAN OF MINE

Living with three brothers has made Danielle tired of guys and cowboys.
She wants a man. But is she making the right choice?

Made in United States
Orlando, FL
20 April 2024

46004502R00150